I0732481

# GABBY

by

William Bradbury

Copyright © Gabby by Bill
Control Number ISBN
PAPERBACK: 978-1-77419-106-4
Ebook: 978-1-77419-107-1

All rights reserved. No part of this book may be reproduced or transmitted inany form or by any means, electronic or mechanical, including photocopying, recording, or by any information storage and retrieval system, without permission in writing from the copyright owner.

This is a work of fiction. All of the characters, names, incidents, organizations, and dialogue in this novel are either the products of the author's imagination or are used fictitiously.

Print information available on the last page.
Rev. date:
To order additional copies of this book, contact:
Maple Leaf Publishing Inc.
3rd Floor 4915 54 Street Red Deer, Alberta T4N 2G7, Canada
1-(403)-356-0255

# ABOUT THE AUTHOR

In January 1939 William L. Bradbury came into this world as a farm boy. Raised in southeast Kansas, never got to be a child. He became a farm worker at the age of four. He grew up to early, supported himself from age sixteen on. He wanted to be a farmer, but God wanted him to be something else. He never got what else. At nineteen he left the farm to work in the city. He has done about every kind of work thinkable. At twenty-four he moved his family to Indiana for seven years. That work closed up, and he moved his family to Michigan where he spent twenty-five years. Nine years of that time he lived alone with his young son. Then remarried his second wife. He became very sick and he and his wife moved to Arizona where they lived for ten years then they moved back to Michigan. Being bored in Arizona he started writing then took two courses in children literature, which he passed. He has lots of short stories he has written. Most are of his child hood and life all having something to do with Jesus Christ and praying mostly for children, also twenty two books. Some day he will get someone to edit them and they just might be sale able. If they ever do then he wants the proceeds to go to help children in poverty state in all countries through Advancing Native Missions in Charlottesville VA. When not writing and reading he carves birds and fish for fun. He builds a lot of toys for his grand kids.

GABBY

BASIC


This story is about one very withdrawn girl, and one girl who is very out spoken. They met for the first time in school, and start an instant friendship. In a short time, they become separated by a kidnapping and even though separated they still are praying and thinking about the other. After all they go through they find each other again to restart their friendship. Only through prayer does this happen, as they say it is God in their lives.

# CONTENTS

# DEDICATED TO

Parents who believe they are going the right direction and bring up their children the way God has intended for them to do. Children who know that mom's and dad's know the right from the wrong yet try to manipulate for something different to be right with their friends. Those who care, those who know, those who fail, those parents who stand in the test and not let their children raise them or themselves.

# PREFACE

This is coming to each family somewhere and sometime soon. If they are Christians or not or just talk like they are. It will be scary to just let it go. This will be a case of any family who knows what God wants and what God does not care for. It will bring love to a standstill and yet let it grow and blossom for some. There will be kindness and loneliness yet all will come to a different place in life.

# MEMO

It will take at the heart of some. It will put others on a different plain. It will make some not want to go on, but it is about the world we live in, and the culture we have made for our children to live in. it is about trusting in God and His Son Jesus and listening to the Holly Spirit as we grow and go forth into the unknown each day we live.

# PRAYER

Dear Heavenly Father with this over flowing mind please let me and those who read this get something of an understanding. Let us all grow into the vast space that we only see. And that which we dream of to come or we can know more about it then your word lets us go into. Lord this is a time for all to open up and look into the time we have each day, and what we have done to let so much go astray for the children you gave us to raise and care for. Let us all know and have the vision to see what we do today will do to someone in the future and not know what to do with it. Let us be more like you and more like your word and let us know what it means when we read it. And let us grow closer to you and your son Jesus Christ. Jesus we love you and thank you for the kindness and love you showed us so long ago. In your name we pray, a-men.

# SONG

Open my eyes Lord and let me see through the window towards the light where you want us to see and go. Let all the haze and darkness go away each day we look. Let it be much brighter so we can see all you want us to see.

Each night when darkness comes let us remember that tired bodies need recharged from the strains of the days' toils. Let us sleep and have hope and dreams that the day comes again and we will be ready to go forth and do your will.

Pull back the blinds and let me see. Pull back the blinds so the light can come through. Help me Lord so I can see what is on the other side. Let me take what I see and make it something for you.

# PROLOGUE

It is a dry cool day in this small town of Littleton even through it has forty thousand plus people in it. There are four different towns of different size of the main town. The subdivisions are almost a town each with all the stores and other businesses in each. Yet on this day a school is going to start, and Gabby the quite shy one is going to get to meet twenty plus other children in her class of the first grade. She has never met any of these girls or boys before. She and her family Don and Sue and Jan her little sister had moved to town just three weeks ago. This was going to put her to the test to understand about friendships of someone she did not know.

Don and Sue were up at the usual time of six thirty to see Don off to work at seven. She then had time to get Gabby awake and ready so she could, take her the first time to school.

"Gabby time to get up. Today is your first day of school remember so let's get dressed and eat a good breakfast so you will have the energy to get through the day."

Sue went to prepare her children pancakes, that is what they liked most for breakfast.

"Gabby I do not hear anything are you up yet?"

"Mom do I have to go I do not know anybody at this school?"

"I am afraid you do not have a choice it is going to be our choice and you have to go. Now get a move on I will fix your hair after you eat. Come on shake them legs, break some eggs, let's make this a fun day."

"But mom what if they do not like me at this school?"

"Honey come on let's think about all the kids you will have to pick from."

"I don't want to pick from them kids I like it here with you and daddy and my sister."

"Gabby you do not have a choice this is going to happen so before mom has to raise her voice let's get your clothes on that I laid out last night, and come to the table. Bring your hairbrush with you. We are going to be late on your first day."

"Mom what if I do not like any of them kids?"

"Gabby look at the good side what if you like all of them kids. Won't that be something?"

"No they won't they will make fun of me just like the ones did where we moved from."

"Gabby, just eat while I do your hair I have to get your sister ready to go with us. Think of something else all kids have freckles and wear glasses well not all but a lot of them do. You are not a bad girl and you are just as pretty as most of them will be. There now you finish up while I get Jan ready to go with us."

"Jan, up and at 'um. We need to get going your sister has to go to school and you have to go with us today."

"Okay mommy I get to go to school too."

"No just to take your sister and then you will come home with me for the day it will be just us."

"Mommy who do I get to play with?"

"Well we need to get out and see if there are any kids around here. We are all unpacked about and we should have time to go and meet our new neighbors. Then we can check out the kids so you will have someone to play with."

As this house gets ready for the first day of school for their oldest there is another family just five blocks away with their problem of getting their unhappy girl ready to go to school also.

Betty Taylor is very outgoing and she is unhappy

because they moved a long way from her friends and home where they lived because of her dad's job. Joe and Mary Taylor with Betty and her brother Al had moved just last week from Indiana where Betty had to say goodbye to all her friends of which everyone she meet was her friend whither they wanted to be or not. As Joe was eating his breakfast of toast and coffee Betty was eating her cereal and talking a blue streak like she did every morning.

"Dad today I get to go to a new school and mom said there are going to be about twenty kids in my class what do you think of that. Yea neat, by tonight I will have a lot of friends, but I will still miss my old friends back home."

"Well it may be neat but let's go easy the first day. You don't want to scare them all away before you get to know them."

"How can I scare them away I am not that bad am I."

"No you are a very pretty girl who has a lot going for you, but just go easy and get to know all of them and then you can pick your new friends. Remember half of them will probably be boys."

"I know and I can have boyfriends can't I?"

"Yes you can and I hope you do. They will help you when you play games outside."

"Dad do you think I am old enough to have a real boyfriend?"

"Betty it scares me some, and yes you are older than some of us think you are. Think of it like this boys and friendship come later in life now all you need to know is they are not much different than girls are. So yes you can have boyfriends. Now I have to go to work and you need to help your mom get you and your brother ready so she can take you to school. Give me a big hug and you have a great day at school."

"Bye dad see you later."

"Bye sweetheart we have us quite a girl in there and

some day she is going to be running this place and that scares me a little bit."

"Goodbye and you have a great day and make us rich and happy."

"Happy yes rich maybe never."

"Betty come and get into your clothes you cannot go to school in your P. J.'s and hurry so I can get your hair done. Al get out of that bed you are going to make your sister late for school. We have to take her today so get with it."

"Mom you go and I can stay here I am to tired."

"Buddy you get a move on if you don't want to change your clothes then you can wear your P. J.'s and stay in the car."

"Mom can I wear my other clothes?"

"Yes but you need to eat now while I get your sister all spruced up so she will be pretty for her first day at school."

"Mom why does she always have to be pretty?"

"Because I am a girl and that is the way we are. Mom I am ready for my hair."

"Okay come in here I am fixing your brothers breakfast."

"Mom you come in here so I can watch you do my hair."

"Hey young lady you are not a movie star yet so get in here so we can get this day started and then I can set down and rest. Mark my word this is not going to be like this every day."

"Mom you have to do my hair I cannot do it."

"Well maybe we need to cut some of it off so it will not take so long."

"Mom, do not even think of it this is my hair and my dad likes it long and so do I."

"I am not going to cut your hair but it is not going to

be as thirty-minute job every morning or I will cut some of it off."

"Okay mom, I am coming."

"Al you jump down and get into your clothes I put them on your chair. Hurry we have to leave in fifteen minutes or we will be late."

"There now get into the car. Come on Al we need to go."

"Mom do I have to put my shoes on?"

"No jump in the car get, move."

Mary needs another cup of coffee but she want to go and leave before to many others get there. She remembers how it was last year when Betty started kindergarten. She would go to class and not with her to sign her in, and give them all the information she knew that they needed. She had it all on a piece of paper and they could copy it off. The school was only six blocks from their house straight down the street they lived on. She had it timed so she would be twenty minutes early. When they got to the school there were not many cars in the front she would be one of the first ones to sign in her daughter.

The Meede family was hurrying to get to school on time Sue looked at the clock and she had only ten minutes left and she had to drive four blocks.

"Gabby get in the car and take your sister with you it is time we left and I do not want any more back talk it is time we had left. Jan, quite fighting with your sister come, go! Go! Go! Get into the car."

As they arrived at the school she was late and yet there were other cars in front of the building so maybe the first day would not matter.

"Okay Gabby, we are here so let's go see what your class is going to look like."

"Mom this school is so big, why do I have to go here?"

"Because it is where they told us you had to go so

now let's get the lead out and quite stalling. You should be excited about going to school."

"I would be excited if I got to stay home."

"Come on my little shy darling lets go and meet the big monsters and see if we can keep from being eaten up. Gabby sometimes I do not know what to do with you. It is going to be okay nothing is going to happen nobody is going to hurt you, trust me your mom okay."

"Okay but I do not have to like it."

"I know God please help me with this precious gift you gave to us."

"Mom is God going to be here today?"

"I hope so he is usually everywhere we go isn't he."

"Well yes but will he be in this big place."

On the first day of school all the children were put into different rooms as they marched down the long hallway. Each child in line went into a different room there they all took a set around the tables. When they were all seated the teacher took one of the children at a time and asked them to come forward so they could be introduced to the other children. Betty and Gabby were in the same class and seated at the same table their teacher name was Miss. Norcutt as she explained to them as she wrote her name on the black board.

"Good morning children, I am your new teacher and my name is Miss Norcutt."

As she addressed the students for the first time.

"Now if you look on your table each one has a number in the middle from one to four. Remember that number it is your number for the rest of this year. It may not be on the same table each time so you have to go to the table with your number on it. Now I am going to find out who you are and let each of the other children know who you are at the same time. To get started I am going to call the boy at the table with the number one on it will you please come forward and tell me your name and also the class. What is your name?"

"My name is Tim."

"Thank you Tim you may go and set down and will the next child come forward and state your name."

"My mane is Ruth and I want to be in the same class as my sister we are twins."

"Well now let's go and see just where she is. Does anyone else in this room have a twin in this school?"

There was no one raise a hand so Ruth was taken to find her sister. When they returned the teacher asked if anyone in the class wanted to be in a different class then it was time to change. No one raised his or her hand.

"Okay you two girls seat down and Tim you come with me you are going to be in the other class."

This was supposed to work for all the teachers but sometimes things do not go according to the best plans and judgments.

"Now class lets go on with your plans to let all of us know who each of us are because we are going to spend the whole year together in this room."

When it came to Betty's turn she jumped up and was telling her name before she got to the front.

"My name is Betty Taylor and I live at."

"Betty just your name please."

"But my mom said I had to tell you where I lived and my telephone number. Why can I not tell it to the kids?"

"Because all we want is your first name. The school office has all the rest and I have a sheet of paper that has all of that on it. Now Betty will you go back to your seat please. Next."

Gabby got up very slowly and with her head down she went up to the teacher and stood beside her.

"And what is your name young lady?"

Gabby whispered it in her ear.

"No tell them your class mates what your name is."

Very softly she said "Gabby."

"Say it louder if you will so they all can hear."

Gabby put her head down and turned red in the face and the teacher saw her eyes glass over then said.

"Her name is Gabby and that may be wrong but she in time will open up you may take your seat."

When all the kids had come up front the teacher said to them.

"Today is just going to be a fun day. Now I want you all to put your chairs closer and get to know the other kids at your table and keep it quite no loud talking. In twenty minutes we all get to go outside and play it is our first recess time."

Betty was talking a mile a minute to all the kids and Gabby was just looking at the table finally Betty said.

"Gabby why do you set there and not talk we want to know all about you, you are going to be one of our team table. We need to know who you are and what you like."

"My name is Gabby and I like to be my own self."

"Well we need you to be on our team or it will be five against four each time. Don't you want to help us when the time comes?"

"Okay children it is time to go to recess and you have to line up and follow me. Young man you go to your table and line up with your team. It is like this kids you line up like number one then two and then three and four when you are ready then we can go. Good that looks better now follow me, and no noise until we get outside. Then you can yell, scream, or say nothing but only outside."

As they passed outside there were other kids coming back inside on the opposite side of the hallway. When they were all outside they all took off in different directions except Gabby and she stayed by Miss. Norcutt.

"Gabby, don't you like to play with other children?"

"I don't know I only have my little sister to play with at home. All the kids I knew at church stayed there when we moved."

"I see so you need a friend am I right?"

"I don't know what is a friend?"

"It is someone you like very much and want to be with whenever you can."

"Who would I pick?"

"I know let's start with one girl and go from there."

"I guess who would it be?"

"Let's get that girl over there she has the same snickers on as you do. She is also wearing blue jeans like you have on."

"Which one?"

"The little blond girl she sets at your table."

"She talks to much."

"Well maybe she can get you to open your window and talk to her. Let's give it a try, I will be right back. Betty will you come with me I have someone who dresses about like you. She has on the same shoes as you do."

"You mean Gabby that does not gab any?"

"Yes I think you will have something in common let's go and try okay."

"Okay but."

"Just try take her over there all by your selves and talk to her. I think she is very shy and maybe a little home sick and she needs a school friend."

"Okay I will try. Gabby come with me I want to be your school friend if you want me to be."

She then led Gabby over to the corner and set down under a small tree.

"My name is Betty and I have a little brother at home do you have a brother or sister at home."

"Yes I have a little sister her name is Jan."

"My brother's name is Al and he is a big pain. I wish I had a sister instead of him to play with."

"You can have mine she is a blabber mouth she is talking or crying all the time."

"Can we be sisters when we get to know each other better?"

# PART ONE     1965

# CHAPTER ONE

Gabby and Betty started out on very loose gravel and over a period of a few weeks they got to know each other rather well.

"Betty why do you want to be my sister?"

"Because I don't have one and you are very nice and I like you better each day, and I want to know you better."

"Okay we live so far apart if we go around the street."

"That is okay we can ride our bikes it won't take long that way."

"Do you think we can be sisters you are my size but your hair is blond and your eyes are blue? No one in my family has blond hair and blue eyes."

"Well no one in my family has brown hair and green eyes. What does that have to do with anything? We can still be sisters we both have some freckles does that count."

"I guess it could we do have the same shoes so maybe we can try. We can pray about it and see what God wants us to do."

"Pray are we old enough to pray?"

"Yes I do all the time."

"What do you pray about?"

"I pray for my mom and dad and little sister that they will be protected each day. Sometimes my dad lets me pray for our meal."

"So where is this God you talk to by praying?"

"Silly he is up in heaven don't you know."

"He must have good ears if he can hear you that far away."

"No he is up in heaven but his spirit is all around us he knows everything we do and say."

"Well my mom told me there was a God, but she did not tell me where he was at. Does he speak back to you when you pray?"

"No, but he shows us what he wants us to do."

"Can you tell him that I want to talk to him and meet him?"

"You have to do that yourself you can do it at night before you climb into bed."

"There is the bell we need to hurry and get into the line. So do you want to be my sister?"

"If you want to Betty we can ask our mom's and see what they say."

"Here is my phone number have your mom call mine and see if we can stay at each other's house sometime."

"Okay I will ask her and see if she will do it tonight."

The rest of the day was more of the same and Gabby was having some doughty about Betty because of the things she said and not knowing about God. Outside of that she seemed okay and maybe she would be a good sister or friend. When her mom came to pick her up she ran to the car with a wave back at Betty who was talking to Lucy and Sarah they also set at their table. Bill was the only boy at their table.

"I see you have meet someone today is she nice?"

"I guess so she wants to be my sister, but she does not know anything about God, and she talks all the time."

"Gabby a lot of girls talk more than you do."

"Mom she gave me her phone number and she wants you to call her mom tonight and see if we can stay over at each other's house sometime."

"Well your dad and I will discuss that and even then we would like to meet her folks and check out where she lives."

"Okay."

Was all Gabby had to say?

"Gabby do you want her to be your friend or sister where ever that came from."

"Mom I do not know we have just met and I already have a sister. She wants a sister because she has a brother who is rowdy all the time."

"I will talk to dad and then I will call and talk to her mother."

"Do you think I should be her sister since I already have Jan as my sister?"

"I believe that if this is what Gods wants or has in store for the two of you, then I will not stand in your way of thinking that this girl is your sister."

"How can I get her to understand about my God if she is not interested in learning."

"Gabby you know how and if you play your cards right she will follow you and want the same things in her life."

"Mom."

"What do you know you have not talked this much in the last year maybe this girl will be good for you. Why don't you go and see what your little sister is doing while I start dinner? Your dad should be home very soon and first will you set the table for me?"

"Before or after I go and check on my sister."

"Why don't you do it now and then I will not have to remind you again?"

"Plates or bowels mom?"

"Plates tonight we cannot serve your dad soup all the time."

"Why not he says he likes soup."

"I like this I can or am having a conversation with my oldest daughter I am excited wow."

"Mom are you going to call Betty's mom tonight?"

"Soon as I talk to your dad and I think I just heard his car door close."

"I had better go and check on Jan call us when you are ready to eat."

"Okay you little jabber box."

"Hi sweet heart how was your day?"

"My day was great and why are you smiling so big?"

"Our daughter has said more words since she came home from school then she has said in months."

"Is that good or am I not reading something?"

"You will have to wait she has met a girl who wants to be her sister. She wants to know if we will let them stay at each other's house sometime."

"I do not know do you know this girl or the parents of this so called sister of hers."

"No I told her we would talk and then if we agreed I would call her mother to see if we could get to know them. She did say that Betty her name has funny things about God when she asked her about him."

"Nothing to get ashamed about lots of kids their age does not know all they should know about God and the working of his gospel."

"I know what do you think is it early or do we go ahead?"

"Let me ask her one question and if she knows the answer then you go ahead and call the mother."

"Okay dinner is about ready you go and clean up and call the girls."

"Hey girls daddy is home and mom wants us to come to the table."

Gabby and Jan both run to see who can get to dad first with as usual Jan gets pushed to the side and Gabby gets the first hug. Jan winds up crying because she wants to be the first just once. Of course she is the one who gets carried to the table, which puts the smile back on her face.

"Daddy did mom talk to you about my new sister yet?" Yes, but now we have to eat while it is hot. We can talk after we pray."

"Daddy do you think she can come over some time?"

"Shu we have to pray."

"Dear Father we as a family want to thank you for all that you have given us. We thank you for this food you have graciously provided for us. My wife and I thank for these two wonderful girls that you have given to us. We pray that you will keep blessing them and this home for us. We thank you for this new area in our daughter's life that you have brought to her. We pray that it is good and will grow to help her to know about another child her age and the things they do and need help with in knowing you. In these things we praise you and do thank you in Jesus name and we give you all the glory. A-men."

"Okay girls pass your plates so mom can dish up your dinner this dish is very hot. Thank you dad for your wonderful prayer."

"Jan, tell mommy when it is enough."

"Enough for now. Um I like the smell I think I will like this."

"Gabby say when and pass your daddy's plate so I can load it up."

"Here mom and thank you. Dad can we talk about my new friend or sister and can she come over to night?"

"Let's eat first Jan will be done before we get started and then she will want her desert and we will be wanting it also instead of the good food that mommy has blessed us with for dinner tonight. One question for you to think about while you are chewing all that food."

"Mom can I have more pleases?"

"Yes Jan you can have more please pass me your plate."

"Thank you mommy I love you."

"Well I love you too thank you."

"Gabby this new girl that you met today is she in your grade and now if we say yes can you still believe that God or Jesus brought you together and for what reason. Do you think you can be friends and both of you not know Jesus or have him in your hearts and still stay the way you are and believe this day?"

"Daddy."

"Wait I want you to think about this for a minute or two before you give me an answer. Make sure that Jesus wants this as much as the two of you want it."

"Sweetheart do you want me to make a call and talk to Betty's mom and see what is happening with that family, and see if they would like to meet some time."

"Since we have the only phone number it might let us get to know and who knows maybe some new friends."

"Dad."

"Yes Gabby do you need more information to make your decision?"

"No I want to know why Jesus would not want me to be her sister."

"Well you will have to pray about that, and see what transpires from it you do think he will answer you."

"Yes and you and mom can help me you are older than I am, and I want you to help me to make the right decision."

"We can do that after we have met her mom and dad, and see where they live so if this happens you can get back and forth to each other's house."

"Dad I have been thinking I could take her to our church and help her to know our God."

"That is a good answer and if you think she will not try to lead you down the wrong road then just maybe it will be a good idea. Maybe Jesus has put you both together for this same reason so that her and her family will be led to know Jesus."

"Hello Taylor residence, this is Mary."

"Hi Mary this is Sue Meede and I am calling because my daughter brought home your telephone number and she and your daughter after one day have decided to become sisters."

"Yes we have worn out the carpet waiting for this phone to ring. I am very pleased to meet your voice and maybe we can get together and talk about this and other things."

"That would be nice before we decide to give them an open invite to change their lives and ours also. When would you like to get together I am home most all the time."

"Well I work mornings and pick up my son at one-clock and I could meet you at your place or somewhere else for a late lunch."

"While you are out why not come by and we can talk where there is less noise and our two little ones can play for a while. We can have tea or coffee."

"Tea will be fine we do not drink coffee can I bring a snack or something?"

"No I will have all we need we live on Apple street just off main up two blocks on the corner in the blue and white trim house. It is the only one in the neighborhood so you cannot miss it. What day would you like to get together?"

"Well at the rate my daughter is talking it should have been yesterday so how about tomorrow if you are open."

"That will be great I will see you a little after one-o-clock, you have to knock the door bell is not working yet."

"See you then bye now."

"Well Mary seems nice and we are going to meet here at one tomorrow so I guess we have started a new thing in our news life here in this new house in this new town in this new state. And we owe it all to two young girls who think they are supposed to be sisters. They found all this out in just one day of meeting each other."

"Oh mommy! Mommy! You are just going to love Betty she is really nice, and"

"Woe wait a minute I am going to meet her mother and little brother not Betty, and then if I decided then her dad and your dad has to get tighter before anything is going to be happening with the two of you getting together at each other's house. There is more to this then the minds of two six-year-old; little girls who decided they just like each other."

"Oh mommy, thank you, thank you this is the best day in a long time."

"Would you look at this Mr. Meede do you think that we will be able to live with this wound up girl or should we stop it before we get in over our heads. Can we stand that quick of a change in Gabby or just let it go wide open?"

"Let her have her day we will get ours later."

"That is what I am afraid of."

"What is that?"

"Can you imagine this change and one more together I have to be here all day you get to go to work."

"That's is what dad's do."

"Well I am not sure this is what mom's do all alone."

"Sweetheart we have talked about Gabby's shyness for all her life and in one day she opens up let her see what is outside of that window she has been hiding behind. Let her out into the light even if it is for just a short time or for the rest of her life. I think it's what she needs even though I do not know if I can stand three women talking all the time."

"Well you have said yes to this and you had better not say anything down the road or I am going to be all over you."

"Sounds like a night of fun and I am ready."

"Oh you and your night fun I am dead serious about this."

"Well do not die on me tonight I may be to weak to roll you off of me."

"Don, oh never mind. You are on your one-track mind and I have dishes to do. It is time for you to get the girls ready for bed."

"Yes dear you know we are supposed to be on the same page. Remember you are to pay attention to my affection Don's Bible book of Genesis."

"Yea! Yea! Yea! If you want your affections taken care of them do some bidding and show me that I am important,"

"You are always important and I most of the time do as you ask until I think it is my turn to be the master of the house and this family."

"Well master come and tell me what you would like me to do. I am not your child so you have to come to me every once in a while."

Don went and took Sue into his strong arms and held her for a long time then he released her and looked up to look into her eyes. After a while just watching he saw her eyes glass over and knew she was going to shed some tears. Then he touched her cheek and said in soft voice.

"I never get over just how beautiful you are. I feel your constant love and power over me. You want to know what I want. I only want you to be there for me and my girls when we need you, and I want you to know that we need you all the time even when we are not by you. We need your prayers reaching out to grab us and get our thoughts back to the most beautiful lady and mother we ever want to be in our lives. That is what I want and everything else that goes with it." Know one said being a mother was easy, but being a dad is more complicated than your job we have to be responsible for everything our family does."

"Go get your girls ready for bed, and I will be ready the dishes can wait between now and whenever."

"Don't hurry I want you to be fresh and invigorating and soft like the first time I met you."

"You mean like on our wedding night."

"We can never replay that night and I want it to be the one that I or we will remember forever. That is the time you were the most beautiful to me."

"I will be as ready as I can."

Don knew she wanted sometime alone she always did he did not know why and it did not matter she was always refreshing and wanting so he took his time with the girls. After reading to them he kissed them and said goodnight.

"Daddy are you going to pray with us tonight?"

"Oh my did we forget?"

"No daddy you never forget I just remembered."

"Yes you did so let's bow our heads and talk to Jesus."

"Dear Lord tonight if you find time to look in on our home to keep us protected from the darkness, and the one who dwells there. We thank you for this day you gave to us. I pray that Gabby and her new friend are willing to keep this happiness of my daughter alive, and it will be good for both of them. I pray for healing and happiness in our lives and let the Holy Spirit come into us and bath us with our love. We ask this in your son's name. Jesus we love you and ask you to remember us in all things. A-men."

Don went to get ready for bed and as he entered the

room Sue was standing there in the low light behind her and all he could think about was the night they had gotten married. He went forward and took his bride into his arms and let the night do its thing for them, and next the alarm was going off in time to get up and get going again.

"Good morning I wish this was Saturday and we had no children for one day it would be like going back into time like ten years."

"Honey it was okay it was just as good as the night you are thinking of. I need to get Gabby something to eat and ready for school, and you need to get going you still have a job, and we need that so we can keep doing this daily thing we are involved in."

"Daily I don't know but maybe we could try to accommodate some more before it goes away."

"Believe me it is here to stay."

"Gabby time to rise and shine school day."

"Mommy can Betty come after school today I would like for her to see where I live."

"I am not sure I have not met her mom yet."

The morning went fairly fast for Sue she had most of her work done, and when she glanced at the clock it said twelve o-clock and she had to feed Jan and herself and then get ready for Mary by one o-clock when she said she would arrive. Calling Jan to the kitchen to eat she thought about putting on a better dress instead of her normal cleaning clothes.

"Jan would you come and get your lunch mommy does not have much time before we have company."

"Mommy will I have some company too?"

"Yes I believe they have a small boy and he may come with his mommy."

"O'boy, a boy to play with what is his name?"

"I don't know so you and I will have to wait until they arrive and then we will both know."

After lunch was over Jan asked.

"Mommy can I go and set on the front step and wait for them?"

"I think it would be better if you waited in here with me. No use scaring them off before we get to meet them."

"Mommy, I am not scary am I?"

"No I should not have said that you are a very pretty girl and I love you too much so you wait in the living room while I go and dress up. You can look out the window."

"Okay."

"Jan mommy is going to change her dress and do not open the door until I come back okay?"

"Yes!"

There is a knock on the door and Jan runs to open the door.

"Hi my name is Jan come on in my mom is changing her dress and I am not. Oops mom they are here."

Sue came from her bedroom and noticed then standing in the entryway. Jan comes running to her saying.

"Mommy I forgot and opened the door."

"It is okay. Hi, I am Sue Meede and you have met my wild one."

"Yes Mary Taylor and this is Al. do you want to go and play with this nice young girl I am sure she has something to play with that you do not have?"

"Yes Jan, you take Al and go to your play room while we talk and get to know each other."

"Well where should we start would you like some tea and cookies, let me get them and we can set in the kitchen if you like. It is just this way. Would you like sugar or honey for your tea?"

"Yes honey would be great. How long have you been here? We moved in just last week and it has been a mad house over our way."

"We moved in one month ago last weekend and we have been getting things ready for Gabby to start school."

"Well you are a way ahead of me I still have boxes setting in each room."

"You said you worked mornings is it close by here?"

"Yes I work at the library five half days a week. I help the others so they do not have to work extra-long hours, and it keeps me out of the boredom of just setting in the house trying to think where I want to put things. Our house is much smaller than the one we moved from back in Indiana."

"This one is too but I think I am going to like it better because of not having to clean all the extra space, and have more time with my two little girls."

"Yes I suppose that is one way to look at it, but I still liked the bigger place. I don't want to get rid of mine and Joe's mother's things they have both gone and we got what was left and now we have a smaller home so I do not know what to do with all them things."

"I am sorry to hear that both of my folks are also gone, and it was so easy to let all them worldly things go to someone else and just carry the money home. They still had things that they had when we were small kids. Don said all I want is pictures and dad's tools so that is what we took from his side and then when mine passed on we took the same things from them since we were the only siblings in each of our families."

"That's unusual because we are the only siblings from each of our families. Now we have only two aunts still alive, and they are very old and stubborn people."

"We now have no one and our kids are so young to not have any grandparents, but I am sure they will make do."

"So what has your daughter said about this new thing of being sisters."

"My daughter Gabby has talked more last night and this morning then she has in the last six months, and we think that is good to a point, but could upset our quite time each evening."

"Betty has been a question and answer child ever since she could talk and your daughters coming into her life has speeded that up to the drive stage. I shore hope this is going to work they are so high and a letdown would not be good since they both moved from their old friends."

"I am sure you are right so maybe we parents will have to make it go slow to start with."

"I was thinking the same thing do you think twice a week would be okay for a while to start with."

"Sounds good what night or day do you think would be okay?"

"Is Tuesday and Thursday okay or Wednesday and Friday?"

"No, Wednesdays I have Bible Study at night and my husband may not appreciate that choice."

"I will be gone for the first night do you pick Betty up or does she walk. If you do, then you can come straight here from school and bring Gabby so she does not have to walk. I have an appointment at three this afternoon and I need to be getting ready to leave and it has been nice meeting you, and I will be here maybe before you get here if you can wait just a little while for me."

"We will wait in the car until you get here so I will see you then. And it has been great meeting you, come along Al we need to be going."

"Goodbye and thanks for coming over it has been nice to talk to someone besides my kids. I have come to the conclusion that women need each other and maybe that has happened to my Gabby and your Betty let us hope so."

Mary was happy with their meeting and Sue had not

thought much about it she was going to see her new doctor she had missed her monthly and wanted to make sure if she was to be a mother again. After her examination she was told that she defiantly was not going to have baby again, but there was other test that she needed to do to make sure there was no other things that were going on inside. She had to go to the hospital on Wednesday afternoon to take two more test. She was not excited about what might be wrong.

When she arrived home Sue and the two girls were setting in the driveway. When she got out of the car Gabby was waiting to introduce her new friend to her.

"Mom this is Betty and can she stay here for a while and play?"

"Let's talk to her mom and see how long she can stay and then we will know."

"Mom can she stay and eat with us, and then we can take her to her house. Please mom."

"Betty you are a cute one and it is nice to meet you, I hope you two can become really good friends."

"We already are we are like twin sisters except we have different colored hair. Our eyes are not the same color either, but that don't matter to us. Look we even have the same shoes and freckles."

"That is great Gabby you go show Betty around and I will see what time she has to be home. Hi that is quite a girl you have there, and her talking has rubbed off on to Gabby and that is a good thing."

"They seem to be a pair and it happened so quick I wonder if it will last."

"We can pray for their sake that if that is what God wants then it will be a great thing for the both of them, and maybe for us also."

"I know that God is big but I am not so sure that praying is going to make it or break it."

"What church do you go too?"

"We don't go to church there are too many other things out here that people say that God made and we like to go and explore lots of things. Although we talked the other evening that maybe we should start going so our kids will know something about what people are talking about when they hear them words."

"Well we go to the one down by the school and you are welcome to come with us sometime."

"Maybe we will, I will see, my husband thinks that Sundays are to go and have fun not to break it in half just to go to church."

"Well you are still welcome Sunday school starts at nine thirty and church starts at eleven. What time do you want Betty to be home?"

"She goes to bed at eight thirty to nine so any time before that is okay."

"Does she know how to get to your house from here. I have never been there so I need some directions."

"Yes she can tell you how to get herself home."

"That will be great see you then."

When she walked into the house she could hear her daughter Jan talking very loud and sobbing in between. She could make out soft voices but not able to hear or tell what they were doing."

"Jan, come down here to me what is wrong why are you carrying on like that?"

"Mommy they won't let me in Gabby's room I want to play with them and they locked the door on me."

"Jan let them do whatever they want to do when the new wares off then I am sure they will let you play with them then. Why don't you come and help me, and we can do something you like maybe outside?"

"Okay but I want to see what they are doing and why did they lock Gabby's door so I could not get in.?"

"They want to be left alone so let them be just you come and help me or go to your room and play you do that all the time."

"But I can hear them and I don't know what they are doing."

"Does it really matter what they are doing?"

"Yes because."

"Because you want to be noisy. Come along with mommy."

"Gabby your little sister is a lot like my little brother he never wants to do anything with me until I have someone over and you will see it is true as soon as you get to come over to my house."

"Jan wants to be involved with everything if it is her idea, but stays away when she wants to play by herself with her dolls. She never wants to play with me when I ask her to play dolls or school, and if you were not here we would not be seeing her she would be in her room with the door shut."

"That is the way Al is he thinks he is missing something and runs to tell my dad or mom that he thinks I am doing something wrong just to get me into trouble. When we lived in our other house he told mom that we were playing family, and undressing like we were going to bed, and I got into a lot of trouble. My dad grounded me for a whole month and when I would ask Al to play he would say no. Go get your old friends to play with you."

"I hope my sister never does that to me. She is only four years old and runs the house mom and dad always has her with them."

"Al is four also and he is just mean he has these fits and goes into my room and throws things all around and I get into trouble because my room is a mess."

"Gabby, dad is home come and set the table so we can eat."

"I have to go and set the table that is my job."

"I don't have any jobs to do at my house."

"My mom said when I turn six I had to start carrying my own weight and so I got to set the table."

Can I go help you?"

"Sure it will not take long then you can meet my dad. You have to watch him he might mess up your hair, but I find if I don't say nothing he leaves me alone."

"Hi dad, I want you to meet my new sister."

"Hi dad, please to meet you."

"Hi yourself, I guess I am dad if you are the sister of my daughter."

He reached and messed up Jan's hair and then he reached to fluffed up Betty's hair but she moved to the side and back but it was too late and he walked to the table without saying anything."

When they set down to eat Betty reached for the buns and then the dish of corn and was told.

"Young lady if you are a sister around here then you have to know that we pray before we eat can you remember that from now on?"

Betty just looked at him and drew her hands back into her lap.

"Shall we prepare our hearts for prayer. Dear Lord Jesus we are gathered here at this table to bring thanks to you. We want to thank you for the food you have so richly blessed this house for. We want to thank you for this home and the love that you have here for us to enjoy. We want to thank you for this new addition to our family and we pray for her soul to be one of us to be with you also. We praise you for this new gift to us and that it will be a blessing back to you and to us in return. Thank you Lord Jesus for being our savior and king. We love you Jesus and we give our all to you. A-men.

Now we can eat with God's blessings every one-dig in. what have you girls been doing?"

Jan responded with.

"Dad they would not let me play with them."

"Well that was not a sporting thing for you two big girls to do. You should have played with your little sister. I think we can change that sometime soon right."

"Yes dad but this was the first time for Betty to be over, and I just want to get to know her, and you know that would not be possible with mouth and years around."

"Gabby let's be nice God put us all here to get along and now what do you think of your new family Betty is it as you thought it would be?"

"I like Gabby and Jan is like my little brother so I feel right at home here."

"Good does that mean that you are moving in?"

Betty looks at Gabby as if to say what.

"No daddy she is not moving in."

"I thought if you were sisters you would be living in the same house, so if she is not moving in are you moving out to her house?"

"Honey will you quit teasing the girls and let them eat. Betty he is just teasing you to get your goat. Now it is time for dessert. I have a nice big chocolate cake with some ice cream on the side. Do I hear anyone say they do not want any?"

"Yes hon. I will pass you girls have yourself a little cake party I want to go and watch the news."

"Okay soon as we are done we have to take Betty home and while I do that you can get the girls ready for bed it is getting late and this is very important for school. Okay girls let's get our dessert so we can finish up her and get going.  "Mrs. Meede I like what you cooked at our house we carry in most of the time. It is K. F. C. or Pizza Hut.

# CHAPTER TWO

This was going to be a time to remember there were two girls who made sure their families were going to get a long they spent not two nights but almost every school night together. Weekends were different they were separated by church and sport things that Betty's folks did for fun. They were excited with the planning of their short trips to go skiing or mountain climbing almost every sunny weekend all summer long and into the snow fall months. Betty tried to get Gabby to go with them, but her mom and dad did not think she should be traipsing off all over the state with someone other than her family. Gabby's family could not do the same things because her dad had to work about every Saturday, and he was not going to miss his church going. Gabby pleaded with her dad but it was always you are not old enough, and you need to spend time with your family some of the time. When school was out from their first year Gabby came home with Betty and asked her parents.

"Mom can I go with Betty and her family they want me to go to Mexico with them for two weeks?"

"Well I can say no but we need to ask your dad about what he thinks about this trip."

"Mom I really want to go."

"So do I but it is not in the cards we do not have that kind of money to just go whenever we feel like it, and I don't think Betty's folks have it either I know."

"That's okay I never get to go any place just to school and Sunday school and church and bed."

"Oh that is a terrible life for a six-year-old."

"I am almost seven in three weeks will that count?"

"You are still six and as your mom I still have the power over you for your welfare. Now for the time being let's drop this attitude and wait for your dad to come home. He still has the last say in our decisions."

"He always says the same thing. No I don't think you are big enough without us to watch over you."

"Gabby go to your room and stay there until you are called to set the table. Betty I think it best for you to go home."

"Yes mom I am big enough to set the table but not big enough to have any fun.."

"Gabby one more word from you and you will miss dinner along with being grounded for a month do you hear me?"

Gabby turned to go to her room.

"Gabby did you hear me?"

She threw her arms up in the air and kept on walking. In her room she lay across her bed and cried to let her confession go away. She was never going to be big enough for anything.

Later Sue asked Jan.

"Jan will you go and get your sister and tell her it is time to set the table and her dad will be home shortly."

"Okay mommy."

Then she ran to Gabby's room she like it when Gabby was in trouble with her mom.

"Gabby mom wants you to come and set the table so we can eat. She said right now."

Gabby asked. "Is dad home yet?"

"No not yet."

"I will be there in a minute."

"You had better come now or mom will come and get you. I will tell her you are not coming."

"Go away you little brat."

"I am going to tell dad what you said."

"Go away you little brat all you do is cause trouble for me."

"Mom Gabby is being mean to me again."

"Gabby you get down here and get the table set and stop tormenting you sister."

And they want to know why I want another sister.

"Hi hon., your daughter has been a little rude just to say the least."

"What is her problem now?"

"She was told to set the table and she is not down here yet to do so. She is mad or upset because I said no to her about going to Mexico with Betty and her family for two weeks.

"I will go and get her."

"Gabby what is going on, you are not some union worker who can strike because you do not like the conditions around you. You are supposed to be setting the table so why are you not down there doing it?"

"Dad I want to go to Mexico with Betty and I was told I could not go because I don't remember any more."

"I think you need to go and do your job before you get grounded for a long time."

"That is it I am already grounded for a month and I do not even know why."

"Maybe because of insubordination."

"What is that?"

"Not doing as you know or was told by someone who has authority over you."

"Well why can't I go with Betty just once?"

"Because your mother and I have not talked about it yet and maybe your attitude has something to do with it whither you go any place or not, and this may last for a while now go get the table set so we can eat."

"Okay I will go and set the table."

"Good girl just remember dad loves you and so does your mother and sister."

Gabby went to do her job she has still to believe that she would go with Betty and her family on the trip. She could not remember her family going anywhere except the last move to this town. She now had a friend that she loved to be with, her new sister was something that made her happy, and that was all she wanted at this time. When her dad came to the table he said.

"Tonight we pray and Gabby I want you to do the praying. Tell God what is on your heart and ask him if he thinks it is okay."

Gabby set for a long minute before she started very slowly to speak.

"Dear Lord Jesus I am sorry for the way I have acted today and I want to thank you for my new sister Betty and that you are still watching over her and her family. I am sorry for my shortness to my sister Jan and my mom. I just don't understand why I cannot go and do this one thing. You know that I will be good and obey her mom and dad. If you don't think I should go then I will be okay. Thank you Jesus, for this food and that it will bring us closer to you in some way. Jesus in your name I thank you. A-men."

"And ever body said."

"Let's eat, thank you Gabby shall we eat and let us be

a happy family again. Sweetheart you told her no, can you share that with us now?"

"Yes I told her because it has been every other night this whole school year that they have been together and I believe that it should be a separation for the two weeks they will be gone and I don't believe that we have the money to send her with them without knowing how much it will cost."

"That is good and I also believe that the money I get for working should be for the whole family not for just one because of a feeling. To do it any other way should be wrong what do you think Gabby?"

"Betty told me it would not cost anything to go with them."

"Do you feel that you should take from them for you food and lodging and whatever extra it would cost them?"

"I never thought of it like that, but I still would like to go."

"I believe you and we believe that they should go as a family, and we should go as a family, and not be responsible for other children that would just want to go with them or us. Maybe when you are older and we have some extra money things can maybe go your way, but not for a two-week period. Maybe a weekend or a day would be more suited for us to make an easy decision is that a good answer for what you believe as your parents should be concerned about."

"Yes, but why are you asking me?"

"Because I want you to understand we are not doing this to punish you. We are doing it because God gave us you and made us responsible for you not someone else like Betty's parents."

"Gabby is what dad said clear enough for you. We want you to have friends, but remember who are the ones who have you and are responsible for you even to the truth of God."

"Yes I guess so but I wonder why they get to go all the time and we never get to go any place."

"Gabby it is because when we moved here because of my job things changed there is no money to do things like your friends do. We owe too much on this house and the moving expense. Someday things will change. I do not want your mother to go to work just so we can go. I want her here to make sure you and your sister get the things you need to grow with and not from some other person who only cares about the money we pay them to keep you for a short time. I want you to get the knowledge from us not someone else so it will help keep you focused in the future as well as today."

"Okay can I go to my room now?"

"Soon as the table is cleared."

The next morning Betty and her mother came to see what Gabby was going to do about the trip. When they knocked on the door Sue answered.

"Well look here what brings you over today?"

"Good morning we came to see if Gabby was going to be able to go with us on our trip. Betty is so excited and expecting her to be able to go with her."

"I am afraid not this time there are some issues that we as a family have to get through. I am sure they would have a great time."

"It would cost you nothing most of it is being paid for by my husband's company and they would not care if Gabby was along."

"It is not about the cost it is about someone else being responsible for our child when God told us to raise her with the ability he gave us and that is what we are trying to do. I hope you understand that and not be put out with us."

"Oh no, that is okay I think you are doing the right

thing but you have to listen to this, for so long, and soon you want to just throw up your hands and say yes, be gone with you."

"I am sure for seven year olds they do not comprehend or know that. Betty, Gabby will miss you for the two weeks but you and her will survive I am sure."

"I am sure they both will, so we will see you in two weeks or so."

"Okay drive careful and have fun."

Sue shutting the door and returning to the kitchen, her mine took a turn thinking it would be nice to go somewhere for two weeks and get away from the hum drum of this life. Maybe she should get a part time job then they could do like everyone else did. If she did what would she do with Jan and the girls when she was not home, unless she got night job and Don could watch over them. No he would never allow that, if he wanted his wife home. Would I feel okay working a whole year just to get away for two weeks and have something different in our lives? She had to shut this down she had things to do besides daydream of lusting after what someone else was doing.

From that day for two weeks Gabby went back to the way she had been before she met Betty. She said very little if nothing at all unless she was asked something and then her answer was very short or not at all. She would not play with Jan even if she was forced to do so she took the time out penalties as if they were just part of her normal day. Jan was not helping any because she kept up the problem just to see her sister punished for not having anything to do with her. When she was not doing or spending time out she was spending the rest of her time in her room or setting in the corner in the dining room. Every day that her dad came home she was setting in the corner finally after almost two weeks he said no more punishment for her it is not doing any good and she is just being stubborn about it. So let her go her way and Jan can go her way and do her thing. Now if she keeps tattling on Gabby then you punish her for the tattling, and let's see if that will solve the problem of the corner.

"I have been thinking I need to get a night job so we can go like other people do."

"We have talked about this before so many time even before we were married that a woman's place is in the home with the children and then when they are old enough or grown and you want to try the job field then I will bless you for wanting to get involved in something other than the house work. Now what about our family life at night time do we just throw it out the window and wait for something to come along so we can go do it.  Why is it so important to be like everyone else."

"I said I was thinking but I do not want to make you upset or leave my time with you and the girls. I am upset because my daughter is seven years old and wants to go and play with other people."

"She is the child she is not running things around here, and she will get over it soon enough. I bet as soon as Betty comes back she will be just like she was two weeks ago."

"Well I sure hope so I was getting used to the way she has been."

Sunday when they went to church it was a bright sunny day and the kids could play outside. They went out to eat and when they came home Betty was riding her bike around on the drive. Gabby did not see her until her mom said.

"Well, will you look at that we have company?"

Gabby did not say anything but her dad could see a big smile come across her face. After he parked the car in the garage Gaby jumped out and ran to where Betty was setting in the grass on her bike the impact caused her to lose control and the bike and both of them went to the ground. Neither one of them said anything but they were wrapped up in each other's arms and trying to get up from the bike.

"Oh, I am so glad to see you I have missed you so much."

"I missed you too and you have to let me tell you about our trip. It was so hot down there and the dust was terrible such a place I never want to go back again ever the people have nothing they wore rags or no clothes at all the little kids ran around naked. I can't believe my folks took us there. Do you know they wanted to come home with us? Yuck I would run away if I had to live like that."

"If you had been born down there then you would be just like them and know no difference."

"I would too."

"No you would not know anything about us unless someone like us went to where you were."

"I am glad you did not go with us I will never be able to get that from my mind I even have night mares about it now."

"Let's go for a bike ride let me go tell my mom where we are going."

"Mom we are going to ride our bikes up the street and back."

"Okay but do not go very far."

"Okay."

"It is okay we can ride up that way and back and go down to almost the school; and back."

As they rode up the dead end street for the four blocks they talked about what they would like to do the rest of the summer. They never talked about Mexico any more. When they were at the end where the timber started they stopped and looked around finding a path that ran into the trees.

"Where do you think that goes?"

"I think if we would follow it we would come out over by my house, but the neighbor boy told me not to go in there because of the wild animals that were in there and you could be eaten up."

"What kind of wild animals?"

"I do not know he did not say."

"Well I am not going in there to find out. What if there were lions and tigers or wolves hiding in there waiting for their lunch."

"I think we should go before some of them notice we are here. All I see is foot prints of some men or big boys look at that see it is not much bigger then my foot."

"Yea, but did you hear that lets get for home?"

They got on their bikes and peddled as fast as they could for one block where there were more houses on the street before they stopped and looked back where they had been.

"Betty got her wind and asked.

"What do you think that noise was?"

"I don't know and I do not want to find out."

"Me neither lets go down by the school?"

Then they started off at a slow pace as they rode along jabbering about everything, and not much at all. A small dog ran to the sidewalk barking at them. And elderly lady called for it to come back.

"Mitty you get back here you are not going to hurt them two girls now come over here to me. You girls live close around here?"

"Yes I live just up the street we just moved here a year ago."

"What is your name?"

"I am Gabby Meede and my friend and sister is Betty Taylor she lives over there and up that away."

"Mitty thinks she wants to check you out and if you

want you can come up here on the porch and play with her. I was just going in to get me a cup of tea would you like something to drink and maybe a cookie."

"Betty would that be alright with you?"

"If you want to it is okay with me."

"Yes that would be fine."

"Okay you two get to know that little thing so she will not think she has to bark at you every time you ride by."

Both girls got down on the floor, and were playing with mitty when they were interrupted by a man's voice.

"Hey what do we have here you two lost or at the wrong place?"

"No we were just watching mitty while the lady went to get her tea."

"Well, okay, my name is Tom Benson and that lady is my wife and her name is Hedi Benson, and our only child that lives with us is mitty. May I ask who you two pretty little things are?"

Betty opened up by telling him.

"We are not things, we are girls, and my name is Betty Taylor, and this is my sister Gabby Meede."

"How can you be sisters with your last names not the same?"

"We are sisters and the names do not matter."

"But you live in separate homes with different parents right."

"Yes, is that wrong because we want it that way?"

"Oh no, I have lots of brothers and sisters and they do not live with me. We are that way because we are the children of God and Jesus is our savior so we are sisters and brothers."

"What does he mean Gabby?"

As Betty whispers in her ear.

"I will tell you later I wonder when the lady is coming back."

Just then she opened the door with her hands full.

"Oh, hi dear, I didn't know you were out here would you like to join us we are having a morning tea party."

"I think that would be grand."

"Here you hold this tray and I will serve our guest. Here girls your tea would you like sugar or anything mixed in it?"

"Sugar would be fine." Said Betty.

"Yes for me too." Echoed Gabby.

"Here take a couple of these cookies you can have whichever ones you like. You girls are the first ones who have stopped to have tea with us. Don't you think that is nice of them Tom?"

Very nice and they are so pretty maybe we could adopt them as our grandchildren since we do not have any of our own close enough and they live just up the street."

"Very well that would be up to them if they wanted us to be their grandparents."

The girls drink their tea and finished their cookies and said.

"Thank you but we need to be going home before we are missed."

"You come back any time you want to we are always around here except on Sundays and we go to church and then to the grocery store. It has been nice meeting you two lovely girls."

"Nice meeting you to Mrs. Benson and Tom."

"They seem to be very nice girls don't you think Tom?"

"Yes, maybe they will come back so we can get to know them better."

"Maybe they will but we will leave that up to the Lord, and let his hands make that decision for us. I hope he sees that it would do us good just to have them come and see us once in a while."

The summer was rather rewarding for the girls. One of the things that they wanted to do, but was not too sure of was. Taking a walk through the forest as they called it. Knowing that they were not to do such a thing because they knew their parents would not appease the thought. They spent one or two days visiting their new grandparents they enjoyed that special tea and the cookies. Gabby spent a lot of the Saturday and Sunday afternoons helping them around the yard because Betty was almost always gone with her family somewhere up in the mountains. Last weekend they had been to Royal Gorge and this weekend they were doing the Pike Peak thing whatever that was. So when they got back she would hear about that all next week. She had been asked to go but her mom and dad just said when you get older. It would be school time in three weeks and they would be starting the second grade. They had asked if Miss Norcutt would be their teacher, but at the time no one knew but they both had wished that she go up with them. That Sunday afternoon Gabby was riding down the street and stopped when Grandma Hedi called her name.

"Gabby how are you where is that little sister of yours?"

"They went away up to Pikes Peak and have not come back yet."

"Oh that would be nice you know Tom and I have lived here most of our lives and we have never been up top yet. It never gave us too much excitement because they say the air is mighty thin up on the top."

"I will never get to go see it my parents never have any money to do things like that."

"Well it is not the end of the world and I have been told that you can see all the way up to Denver city and then some. Some of our friends went once and told us all about it. They saw some big horn sheep and deer while they were up there. I guess that would be something to see."

"I will have to wait and Betty will tell me all about what she saw."

"I am sure she will not much go around when she is talking."

"Yes I know well I need to get home tell grandpa I said hi."

"I will when he wakes up from his nap he has to have one in the afternoon most days."

Monday morning Betty was knocking at Gabby's door early.

"Well look who is back. Gabby is up in her room and you know where that is so go on up."

"Thank you Mrs. Meede."

"Did you have a good time up on Pike's Peak?"

"Yes you should have been there you can see for ever and ever."

Betty ran up the stairs and opened Gabby's door and said.

"Hello my sister how have you been while I was gone. I sure missed you and you would have been very excited if you could have gone."

Gabby ran to give her sister a big hug saying.

"I am so glad you are here I was wondering what I was going to do today. I hate it when you leave and I have nothing to do except I did go and see grandma Hedi and grandpa Tom two days in a row."

Three weeks later school started and Gabby knew more about Pikes Peak then if she had gone and seen it herself. Betty had a way about her to tell everything she did and some things she did not do. Yet it was all-important to the girls who never let anything go by that they both did not know or was able to remember how they knew.

On their first day of school they walked into the room that they would be in for the whole school year to find out that Miss Norcutt was not going to be their teacher. They did find out that their teacher was going to be a man who did not smile while they all stood in an open area of the room. When the last child was put into the room it was then he said his first words.

"Children."

In his very low voice.

"We are here for one reason and one reason only and that is for me to teach you something more then you know right now. It is going to be things besides how to talk and play. So I want all the boys to line up over here and the girls to line up over on that side. Good you are learning real fast and now I want you to come forward when I call boy or girl. Then you will tell us your name and I will seat you where you are going to be for this school year. Now you young lady with the blond hair will you come forward."

No one moved until Gabby walked up front.

"Well now I believe that I must be color blind we have a girl with brown hair instead of blond, but it is a way to start what is your name?"

"My name is Gabby."

"And you have blond hair right?"

"No you must be color blind."

"Right I am now you go to table number one and set in the first chair. Next please and I want this to be a boy please let him be a boy."

"My name I John."

"Good you go to table number two and take the first chair, next girl."

During the process Betty had it figured out that she knew when she was going forward so she could set at the same table as Gabby was setting. On the third round she went forward.

"Well look here the girl with the blond hair has arrived what is your name?"

"My name is Betty."

"Good you go to table number three and take a seat please."

Betty went to table number one and set across from Gabby.

"Young lady that is number one now go and set where I told you too at number three table."

"Betty was talking to Gabby when she was tapped on the shoulder and told again.

Betty in this class in am the one who is in control now you go and set where I told you too."

Betty went and did what she was told to do and the rest of the children were seated and when the last child was seated the teacher said.

"Thank you all for being so good about where you are setting and I want you to know that my name is Mr. Brown, and you can call me that or just teacher either one will be fine. Now this year is going to be a little harder than the last year was for you. In the next ten minutes you will be allowed to go to your first recess; and that will be done in a straight line by table numbers only, and then you will follow me outside in a quite manor. When you are outside then and only then you can do as you want but you will be very quiet while inside the school hall way. On the playground when I blow this whistle then you will line up as you are right now and then we will come back inside to your tables and take your seats. Now do we have any problems with what I just said? I want you to understand because I want this to happen every time we go and come into this room whither it is out to play or to go home at the end of the day. When we come back and seated your studies will have laid out for you and then I will explain what will happen and when you see then it will be that way until the end of this year. Okay everybody set down and then I want you to line up in a slow not rushing manner so we can go outside. The longer it takes in this room the shorter time you will have outside to play. Great let's go and have some fun."

"Gabby why can we not set at the same table this year?"

"I don't know but I do not like it, looking at that boy who sets across from me."

"I am going to tell him I want to change seats with him."

"Do you think you can do that?"

"Yes or I will tell my mom and she will come and tell him to change me so we can be together."

The whistle blew and they all came running and lined up. Betty told the boy to change places in the line so she and he would be at the right table when they got inside. Once seated the teacher asked one child from each table to come forwarded and be the ones who handed out the supplies to each child at their table. So they started with a pack of materials and gave one to each child. When they were done he proceeded to tell them about how the studies would be handled.

"Children when you look at the materials I want you to put them on your left to start with and when we do a subject then you move that one to the right and at the end of the day we will change them back to the left for the next day. Now on top of your pack there is a piece of paper that has lines on it I want you to take it and put your name on the top and then your mom and dad's name and your phone number and address then you bring it up to me. And while we are just starting I see the girl with the blond hair does not remember where she is to be setting so Betty I want you to get up and go change back with the boy you changed with."

"Teacher I want to set at the same table as my sister."

"I want you to do as I say."

"Then I am going home and get my mom."

"I see are you going to be the little trouble maker this year."

"No! we are sisters and we want to set together and we will cause no problem."

"Very well I will send a note home with you tonight and you will get back into this class when and after I talk to your mom. Maybe she will tell you who is in charge of this class and maybe we can get off to a good start."

"Good she will come and I will set here with my sister."

When school was out and they were on their way home Gabby said as they were at the separating place so they could go their separate ways.

"Betty I don't like Mr. Brown do you?"

"He is okay but he wants to be bossy but my mom will tell him what for."

They split and when towards home when Betty opened the door her mom said.

"Hi sweetie how was your first day back in school?"

"Terrible out new teacher will not let Gabby and me set together at the same table. Here he sent you a note to you and you have to go and see him before he will let me back into class."

"Betty what have you done?"

"She told her mom what had happened and told her that Gabby wanted to set at the same table, and she had to tell the teacher that was the only way.

"Betty I will go and talk to the teacher but if he says you are not to set together then he has a reason."

Call Gabby's mom and tell her so she can go with us to school we want to do just like last year."

"Okay but I don't know if it is going to happen like that for you this year."

"Hello Sue this is Marry and I called to see if Gabby has said anything about school to you?"

"Yes she is upset at the new teacher, and Betty not being able to go to school."

"Well the note says that I have to go and talk to him in the morning so Betty can attend school. Betty said that it is because they wanted to set at the same table like last year and he said no. I was wondering if you would like to go with me to talk to him."

"Yes I would I know how much this means to the girls, and I know that it will make them better students if he will just be reasonable with them. If they are not good, then I would be the first one to tell him to separate them."

"I am on the same page as you are I will see you there in the morning."

At school the next morning they arrived at the classroom to introduce themselves to Mr. Brown. After taking to him they had convinced him that they should be kept together and if they did not behave like they were supposed to then he could separate them as he wanted. He finally agreed and told them that if they did not toe the mark then they would be separated for the rest of the year. Sue and Marry were standing there when he told the girls of their decision and they just said okay."

Gabby you and Betty are going to get to stay where you are but we are telling you at this time that if you are disruptive at any time then you will be set across the room from each other is that an agreement?"

"Yes mom."

They said in unison and looked to Mr. Brown and smiled and then said.

"You will see we are going to be your best students. Mr. Brown we are sorry we caused you any trouble. We are like twins and all we want to do is be together, and you will see we will be good."

"No more will be said if the two of you behave and do your work like I ask you to do."

School was a fun time though as it was with Miss. Norcutt, but their new teacher was a man. School went by fast Gabby and Betty was so close they spent each afternoon after school at one or the others house doing their homework and playing. Their only problem was two kids named Jan and Al.

"Betty why don't we ask our parents to let us stay in one house and let them other two kids stay at the other one."

"Do you think they would do that?"

"My folks would not and yours would probably not want to do it either."

"Well we can dream and make believe."

"Let's go and ride around the block for a while."

"Okay that will get my brother off our backs, and we could go and investigate the forest entryway we have not been there for a while."

"Okay maybe them wild animals will be way back this time. Last time they were too close to the street and I don't want to be eaten by one of them."

"We can ride faster than they can run can't we?"

"I do not know we can ride by and see if there are any tracks like the last time."

"Yes real fast the first time and then we can go back and ride slower so we can look to see if there are any more tracks."

When they got to the opening they rode by as fast as they could peddle and down the block they stopped and turned around to look. Then they rode back at a slower pace and found no noise so they stopped to investigate more,

"Look there are fresh shoe tracks there maybe it is the man who feeds the animals lets go over by my house and see if there are any tracks over there."

"Okay with me."

They rode fast over to the other side and when they got there sure enough there were tracks there also.

"Them tracks look just like the ones that were over on the other side."

"Yes and they are only boy size shoes. I bet they are making them noises just to keep others out of the forest."

"Do you think they have a hideout in there and don't want anyone to find out about it.

"I do not know lets go in and see."

"Okay but let's ride around and think about it first."

# PART ONE

# CHAPTER THREE

After riding around back and forth at the opening they planed carefully, easing up to the opening. There they listened but there was no noise. Then Betty said.

"Let's go in for ways to see what is in there."

"Okay but let's hold hands."

They eased step after step back into the opening and because of the density of the trees it became darker to them.

"Betty it is getting dark in here do you think we should keep going?"

"I don't know but let's go just a little further it gets lighter up there around that big tree."

Rounding the big tree, they entered into a large opening with crud looking doghouses all around the large area. They could see the sky up through the treetops.

"What do you think this is Betty?"

"It must be where the animals come to sleep during the night time let's get out of here."

They heard a noise and jumped and turned and run for dear life back to where the bikes were parked. Jumping on them without saying anything they peddled as fast as they could back towards Betty's house. When they got to her drive they turned to see if anything was following them.

"I am not ever going back there again."

"Me neither." said Betty.  "Let's go inside and get something to drink."

After they got a drink, and telling Betty's mom.

"We are going down towards grandma Hedi house."

They rode down to the street that turned towards grandpa Tom's house they saw a lot of cars parked and a couple of them had flashing lights on them.

"What do you think is going on with all the cars and lights and look there is someone on that roller bed thing."

"I don't know." Said Betty. But let's go and see."

After they had parked their bikes in the grass they went to the porch and grandma Hedi was coming out the door.

"Grandma what is wrong?"

"Girls your grandpa is sick and they are taking him to the hospital to see what is wrong, and I have to go with him. You can come back after church tomorrow and if I am here I will know why he got sick."

They went back to their bikes and getting on Gabby said.

"I am going home so my mom and dad can pray for grandpa Tom to be all right."

"Okay lets go."

When they got to her house Gabby burst through the door and ran into the kitchen saying.

"Mom we just came from grandma house and grandpa is sick and they came and took him to the hospital can we pray for him?"

"Yes we can go and get your dad and lets meet in the living room, he is out back."

"Dad come we have to pray for grandpa he got sick

and they took him to the hospital and grandma is crying and had to go with him."

"Woo! Slow down what is wrong with Tom?"

"We do not know grandma Hedi was crying and they took him to the hospital to see what is wrong."

"Okay lets go and pray. Hi Betty, you two been having a good time until this happened."

"Yes we have."

In the house they all set in the living room and held hands and Don started praying.

"Dear Lord Jesus we lift grandpa Tom up to you to comfort him in his sorrow. We know not what is wrong. We know that he is sick from something, but we do not know of what we pray that you do and you will be looking in on him, as we know you will do. We pray that you will help the doctors as they are now checking him out and that you will show them the problem he has. Also be with grandma Hedi and comfort her in her grief and sadness. Bring them both home when he is better. Let the love of yours surround them and keep them filled with the Holly Spirit your love and joy for you. Let the minds of these two girls not worry about him. Let them understand of the problems that older people have. Let their love flow out through and the Holly Spirit to touch each of their new grandparents at this time. As you know this has been a great thing that you have put together with these two wonderful gifts that you have given not only to us but to others as well. We pray that this day will be a happy one for all. In your name Jesus we pray. A-men."

"Dad, will Jesus let grandpa Tom be okay?"

"Let's put it like this God has his agenda and sometimes it is not the way we want it to be,. But I know this he will do for grandpa Tom as his will has set down a long time ago. He will make him better either here on earth or much better in heaven. It is our wish for him to stay but it is Gods wish for him to spend his life in eternity starting any time. Do you both think that Gods will is better than ours?"

"Yes dad but I will miss him."

"Mr. Meede do you mean he may die?"

"I am saying it is up to God to make that decision and we are to agree that Gods decision is the best one for grandpa Tom. Even though grandma Hedi may not want to be alone, and that is maybe why Jesus brought you two girls into their lives just so she would have someone she could count on to help her get through the stress of her husband not coming home, and if he does come home it is something you might think about just to stop and check on her to see how she is doing. Do you think you could do that for her and to keep you knowing and loving her?"

"Yes we will stop every day after school just to see if she needs anything,"

"Yes we will help her do some work if she needs some help."

"Alright girls, and Betty that would be a great thing now have you told your mom and dad yet if not then you should go home and tell them."

"Come on Gabby lets go and tell them?"

"Wait it is getting late and Gabby you need to set the table so we can eat."

"Mom you told me I could eat over there."

"Betty, have you two told your mom this yet."

"No but I will as soon as we get there."

"I think we should let this day end as it has for now. Betty you go on home and tell you parents what we have done and prayed about and tomorrow after church you come back over and you and Gabby can go and check up on grandpa Tom and Hedi."

"Can I come back after I eat?"

"Tomorrow you come back over, tomorrow after church we will have our family time okay?"

"Yes mam, goodbye Gabby."

When Betty walked out the door it was the same thing every time they both got the down head and the glum look on their faces. Nobody knew why they were so close and needed each other so much. It would be a sorrowful time if anything happened to either one of them. When God does something he does his miracles right.

After church when the Meede's drove into their driveway Betty was setting on the front step. When Don had the car into the garage and stopped Gabby opened her door and the two girls ran to each other with their normal hug.

"Would you look at them you would think that one day was like a whole year for them."

Yes hon. And I think it is great."

"Hi have you been waiting long?"

"No I just got here and I am ready to go and see about grandpa Tom."

"Mom we are going to see about grandpa Tom."

"Girls we will be eating soon and I want you Gabby to go and change your clothes, and then we will eat and then you can go."

"But mom."

"Thirty more minutes will not make any change in what you are going to hear when you get there and grandma has to eat also."

"Betty, have you eaten yet?"

"No."

"Are you going home to eat or are you going to eat a sandwich here."

"You mean I can stay and eat with you?"

"If your mom knows you are here then it is okay with us if you eat here. Maybe you had better call her and let her know to make sure."

"Okay."

After dialing the phone her mom answers to.

"Mom I am going to eat at Gabby's is that okay. Goodbye sees you later. We are going down to see grandma Hedi to find out about grandpa Tom,"

Before any one could say anything on either end of the line Betty had it hung up?

"Mrs. Meede, mom said it was okay I could stay. I am going up to Gabby's room."

"Okay but don't stay long we are about ready for lunch."

After lunch Gabby and Betty got on their bikes and went to see grandma Hedi. When they arrived and knocked on the door it was a long time before she came to answer the knock.

"Well look at what I have on my front porch would you two like to come in or stay on the porch?"

"We came to see about grandpa Tom."

Gabby asked with a serious face.

"Well as of the last time I saw him he could not speak but he was still breathing."

"Is he home and can we see him." as Betty moved closer to the doorway.

"No he is still in the hospital and they do not know when he can come home."

"Can we go to the hospital and see him?"

"No girls he is in a special room and no one can see him except his family at this time. Why don't you come in I am waiting for a phone call from our son? He may be coming to see his dad."

"Where do they live is it far away and if grandpa Tom is our grandpa that makes him part of our family so we can go and see him right."

As Gabby let this out the phone rang. Grandma Hedi was talking and crying on the phone and after a little while she hung up and came back wiping tears from her eyes.

"That was Carl and he is coming tomorrow to see his dad and he will make you laugh just like grandpa does."

"Is he old like you and grandpa?"

"No he is just a young man and they are going to have their first baby who should be here in about three months or so. His wife has a pretty name it is Tonya she will not be coming with him this time."

"When is grandpa Tom coming home we want to see him?"

"Well I should know something by tomorrow afternoon or sooner would that be quick enough."

"No but if we cannot go see him then we will have to wait until he comes home."

"Okay girls I have some peanut butter cookies and some milk would you be interested in trying them to see if they are any god?"

"Well Betty, do you think we should?"

"Yes I think I should and you can if you want too."

"Okay we will try them did you just make them?"

"No I did that on Friday so they still may be eatable today."

"Sure grandma can we have two each?"

"Not bad huh; you can have as many as you want or can eat."

"Grandma is there anything we can do to help you?"

"No not today I am just not wanting to do anything yet."

"Thank you grandma for the snacks and can we stop by after school tomorrow and help you?"

"You can stop anytime or day you want to come and see us old folks we love to have you."

"Come on Betty we have to go?"

"Goodbye grandma see you tomorrow."

"Thank you and you keep praying for grandpa Tom that he will get better."

"We will my family prayed together for him yesterday."

"Thank you and grandpa Tom thanks you too."

"Come Betty I want to go home and ask my parents to pray for grandpa Tom to get better and come home. I want them to pray for grandma so she will not be left alone if God wants him to come to be with him in heaven."

"What do you mean Gabby why would God take grandpa to heaven. What would we do for a grandpa if he left to go somewhere else? We just got him he cannot leave so soon."

"I don't but when God needs someone in heaven he just comes and gets them."

"I don't know if I like your God what if he wants one of us what would we do?"

"I don't know but we are very young and I think he needs older people who can work and know more than young people."

"Then when I lived in Indiana why did he take one of my friends because she got killed in a car wreck?"

"I guess so the old people would have children so they could have a family in heaven like we do here on earth."

"I better go home and tell my mom about grandpa."

"I am going to pray for grandma so she will not be scared tonight."

"See you tomorrow at school."

This being the second year of school had brought them together closer than anyone else had thought it would happen to them. They lived and breathed the same and they were un-separable unless their parents said no to a lot of things. This brought them to a sad time when they were separated and now with their newly acquired grandparents being one in the hospital and one home crying upset them and one wanted to pray all the time and the other wanted to go spend time with them and mom's and dad's were trying to figure out just what happened to their two little girls. They were now seven years old going on twenty and having the same feeling as if they were all grown up. Gabby was working at drawing Betty towards her savior and Betty was trying to draw Gabby towards her families' fun times. They seemed to be trying to go in two different directions leaving a lot of the sad times being alone. This was tearing at the heart of this relationship, and could break the chain that had become so strong around them.

"Mom can we pray for grandma Hedi she is so sad because of grandpa Tom not being home."

"Hi Gabby where is Betty I thought you two would spend the whole afternoon down there."

"We came home because grandma kept crying and Betty went home when I said I was going home to pray. I wish I could get her to become interested in Jesus so we could be closer."

"If you two were any closer you would be the same person and we would not know which one you were."

"Do you think dad would pray with us again so Jesus would let grandpa come home so grandma would be happy like she used to be."

"Well there is nothing more exciting than to pray for someone in need. Let's go get him out of his game and ask him. I bet he will be happy to pray with us. You go and get him and see if he has time I will be there in a short minute."

Gabby goes to the living room to get her dad and finds him sleeping. Setting down beside him she wakes him up and then asked him.

"Dad do you have time to pray with mom and I for grandma Hedi. She is so lonely and just cries a lot. We need to ask Jesus to come and help her to be happy until grandpa Tom comes back home. Do you want to help us do that?"

"I would be happy to help my little grown up girl

to pray for someone so dear to her. Where are mom and Jan?"

"Mom is coming and Jan is up in her room probably asleep."

"Oh I see you have him awake. Dear are we going to pray now or latter?"

"Right now is fine with me."

Sue set down beside her daughter and they grabbed hand to pray.

"Dear Lord Jesus my grandma Hedi is so unhappy and I would like for you to come down and touch her to get her back like she was before grandpa Tom got sick and went to the hospital. She needs someone to help her not be lonely and not to worry so much. Can you do that so I will not be sad for her also? A –men."

"Our Father in heaven you are so powerful and yet so kind I ask that you hear the prayer of a small girl and let it be in your liking your will for those two people who have taken in these two girls as if they were their own. Help Hedi to be closer and let her know that she has you to help her along. And at the same time put your hands on Tom to bring about the problem he has, and let him come back to these three special girls who are so worried for him. In your name we ask. A-men."

"Father God as my husband and daughter have asked I know and believe you have a reason and purpose for what is going on and I know along with my family that you can bring this to and end and let them still live a good life together. Let them grow deep into your love and keep them in a happy state for what they have left to this life down here on earth. Give us the entire gift and fill us all with the Holly Spirit. This I ask of you for our little girl and her new arrived sister of our daughter let her grow into you and fill her so she will not be lost and bring her family to the grace of your love and table that they might feed and grow into the ones you have a long time ago made them to be. We ask all this in your name Jesus. A-men."

"Thank your mom and dad I feel that grandma is better right now."

"I am sure as he knows your heart he has already acted for your prayer for those to old people you and Betty hold so dear."

"May I go over to Betty's now I will not be more than one hour?"

"I guess so but only one hour you know this is our night for family time and school is tomorrow."

"Okay thanks mom."

"Hon. are we going to be involved with the Thanksgiving meal at the church or are we going to do our own thing?"

"I will let you decide since you are the one who will be doing the cooking. And since our family goes to that church I believe we should do the church and let you be thankful that you did not have to cook the big meal for us. It may be the time that we ask Joe and Marry to go with us. It would show them what goes on in our church."

"I think that is a great idea I will talk to marry about it soon."

"Hi mom I am back."

"That was not an hour was it my goodness how time flies."

"Betty's mom and dad were shouting at each other so I just left."

"Well they must have had a little misunderstanding over something."

"I heard him say no more staying home on the weekends it was to boring for him."

"Well it is their problem and we need to forget what we heard."

"I am going to ride up and down the street for a while

maybe grandma Hedi will be out on her porch and I can talk to her and cheer her up some."

"Okay but not too long we will be eating early so we can do our family night thing with Jesus."

"Sweetheart would you like to go with me to ask the Taylor's about Thanksgiving at the church?"

"If you need some back up I will be glad to go with you."

"How about tonight after our family time or do you think we should give them more time to cool down."

"You make the call and you will see if they want any visitors, or we can go for a walk and just stop by and knock on their door."

"I like that idea let's eat and spend time in the word and go for a walk we have not did that in a long time."

"Yea, do us good and maybe them too."

After they had eaten dinner and spent their time together they started out for their walk to the Taylor's. When they knocked on their door and then waited for a long time almost five minutes. Then they knocked again to see if the doorbell worked or not then almost instantly the door opened and Betty with a.

"Oh mom it is Gabby and her parents."

"Well ask them to come in."

"Hi what brings you over this way." Joe asked as he walked into the room.

"We were out for a walk and was talking and decided to stop and ask you something if you are not to busy."

"No come in and have a seat. Marry do we have anything left to drink. Would you like some coffee or tea or water or juice? I don't know if we have any of that but water I am sure."

"Hi Sue, Don I heard you were our walking do you do that much?"

"Not as much as we need to, but it was so nice out we decided to make a run out of it."

"What we stopped for is to see if you would like to go to a special thanksgiving dinner our church is putting on this year as an outreach program. We thought it might be nice if we asked you to come with us."

"Well Joe do you think we might be able to go?"

"I guess we can what night is it and what would we bring?"

"You bring your family and the church is furnishing everything."

"We cannot go just to eat for free that would not be right."

"Well if you would like you can stop by the office and drop off a check for a couple of thousand dollars I am sure they will not turn you away. This dinner is already paid for and it is for anyone in this neighborhood to come and partake in it."

"Well Marry, what day did you say or did I not hear?"

"It is on Thanksgiving Day and it starts at one o-clock and run until six unless they run out of food before then."

"Again Marry do you want to go it is your call I have nothing planned for that day."

"I think it may be what we need. Which church is it and where is it located?"

"Our church it is the one down by the school where the kids go. If it is nice we can even walk. We can plan that at a later date when it gets closer."

On their way home Don and Sue felt good they had reached out to help someone draw closer to the Lord. They walked with a spring in their steps the girls were running up and down in front of them.

"My look at all that energy I wonder what we could do with that much."

"We could try to have more fun nights. Maybe with even the energy that we already have."

"How old are you?"

"Thirty something why?"

"That tape track should be worn out by now."

Don grabbed her and wrapped his arms around her and pressed his lips to hers. For a long time, he held her tight then he released her saying."

"You my dear will hear this tape as long as we are together."

"Do I hear you are leaving soon?"

"Never my vows are as strong today as they were when I gave them to you and God. So woman be ready anytime I am not going anywhere but to work and even then I will always have enough to have fun afterwards."

"So now that you are all wound up I should not be unwinding down, or are you just winding up to get me excited."

"I do not wind up about such things and you know it."

"What if I told you it was not a good time."

"Now we have good and bad times have I missed something that has been going on or are you just testing me."

"Neither just open the door before it is too dark for you to see the key hole. Come girls time to be getting ready for bed."

"Mom why do we have to go to bed at the same time every night?"

"So your body will become accustom to getting up at the same time every morning and be refreshed at the same time. That way you will start to build your own alarm clock in your head when you have the proper amount of sleep."

"Dad you get the girls and I will finish up in the kitchen, and we can rest a while before it is our time."

"Okay girls mom has spoken so let's get to it."

November was just another month except the Thanksgiving dinner. Sue had been helping for two days with some of the preparations at the church. She had been busy and now it was time to go see Marry to see what time they would like to go eat. When she went to Mary's the girls were riding up and down the sidewalk just jabbering their heads off.

"Hi, mom are you looking for me?"

"No sugar I just came to talk to Mary and then I am going home, and you watch as soon as I go home you start that way also."

"Hello Sue I saw you out here what can I do for you?"

"I stopped to see if you were still going tomorrow to the Thanksgiving dinner at the church."

"Why yes what time do you want to go?"

"You can go any time but if you want to go with us we will start for church about twelve thirty. So as not to have to wait so long in line, or we can go about three you pick."

"We will meet you twelve thirty Joe could never last until three without eating something. His tummy works like an alarm clock about eating his meals."

"Okay see you tomorrow and do not dress up just casual clothes will be fine."

"Great is Gabby going home with you if so will you send Betty in so she can help with the table."

When they arrived at the church there was a line of about thirty people waiting for someone to open the doors. Sue said.

"I will go and see what they need and get us a table part of the work force for two days. Don you come with me and you two girls stay with Betty and Mary okay."

"Yes mom."

"Mommy can I come with you?"

"No Jan you stay with Gabby and please try to be good."

Don and Sue went through the side door and soon the double doors opened, and the people were told to start forward and to read the sign at the first table.

"Gabby you get the four of you kids and follow me. Joe you and Mary stay in line and when you get to the tables we will get in line to fill the kid's plates. We are going to save the table while we wait for you."

"Good plan it should not take long but I see the line is growing faster than we are moving."

"The smell is going to get to you as soon as you get through the door so tell Joe to hang in there."

"I am sure he will not die but his self-pride and his tummy is on the same time line."

After they were through eating they set in the entryway and talked before they went back home. Gabby and Betty decided they wanted to walk so they left early. Walking along they talked about the same thing as they always talked about when they were alone.

"Gabby why did God give us brats like my brother and your sister?"

"I don't know Betty but it must have been something our mom's and dad's ordered to keep us thinking about keeping our minds on prayer to Jesus for his help to get us up for each day we have to put up with them."

"I wonder if it is all us, we cannot make them do anything because we are not old enough and my dad told me once that I was the oldest so I could help teach the younger ones."

"Except whenever I go to do something I get into trouble for being to bossy with Jan so I just do nothing and still get into some trouble with her mouth."

"I know Al is telling on me all the time so he can get his way, if I talk back it just gets worse for me so sometimes

I just scream at the top of my lungs to get my folks to listen to me instead of the lies my brother is telling to them, he has the most dangerous mind of any child I know."

"What are you going to do for Christmas this year?"

"I think we are going on a two day skiing trip up north why?"

"Just wanted to know I will be stuck in my room all the time you are gone."

"Why not ask if you can go and learn how to ski it is a lot of fun, and Al and I only get to go on the bunny slope, but it is still fun you can't go to fast like up on the top."

"Would your mom ask mine if I could go with you every time I ask it is you need to be older to go with someone else."

"I will ask my mom to ask yours if we are still going. It would be more fun with you then just watching Al all the time while mom and dad goes up top."

"Don't get excited yet my mom and dad will just say no way she is not old enough."

"What do you mean Al is younger than we are and he goes all the time."

"But I do not have any of them things so I would just get to watch and that would not be any fun."

"Gabby we do not have any of them things either we just go and they give us some to use. They give us the skies and the poles, and shoes and we just dress for the cold."

"Well I don't know; will it work for me."

"I am still going to ask my mom to ask yours to see if they might let you go."

Two days later Mary knocked on the Meede's door when Sue answered the door she was not looking good she had been cleaning and was in a frazzle looking state, but she asked.

"Mary how are you won't you come in how are you. I have just been cleaning all day and I probably look a mess. I am glad you stopped I am to ask people what they thought of the Thanksgiving dinner so they can determine if it was okay and if they would do it again next year."

"It was great and yes next year would be great thing Joe said he never tasted so many great deserts."

"Great may I get you something to drink?"

"Oh no I can't stay long I just stopped to ask you something we are planning a two-day weekend up north to go skiing and was wondering if Gabby could go with us it is only two days and two nights."

"Mary we do not have any extra money to do them things and we do not want you paying for our child. It has been touch and go since we moved here the cost is much more then where we were, but Don wanted to stay with his company."

"Sue it will cost nothing if we did not have the time share that my folks gave us we could not go either. When they passed away we got to pick it up for a few dollars, and it is good for our lifetime. So it cost nothing but a small amount for the food we eat and we take all but the one meal with us and if Gabby could go you could send some food with her. We all sleep in the same room, and at this resort we get free skiing equipment and the use of the lifts, and all we do is dress for the season."

"That sounds nice let me talk to Don and we will make up our minds if she can go or not."

"Maybe we could keep it a secret form the girls so it will not give them a letdown if it does not work out. See you later and do not think about money it is hard for us also."

After dinner and the girls were in their beds Sue came and set down besides Don and told him about what Mary had stopped and asked her.

"Really that sounds like even we could afford that except no one gave us anything up front to start with."

"It sounds okay with me but she is our little girl and I still want to keep her without someone else looking out for her."

"Sweetheart let's let her go this time we need to let her know that even though she is little and only seven years old that we do trust her."

"Okay I will call Mary and tell her of our decision, but we do not want them to know until the last minute. So we have to not let her know is that okay with you."

"You know me tight like a rat trap."

"You mean like a sex trap."

"Well that sounds better just say when."

The next day when Mary got home Sue called her to let her know that Gabby was going with them if it was still okay.

"Mary when you get time would you stop over and tell me what kind of food I need to prepare for Gabby to take with her."

At two o'clock Mary knocked on Sue's door.

"Hi I thought we would get this out of the way so you would have time during the day to get things organized for gabby and we will pick her up on Friday morning at about ten o-clock and we will be back on Sunday afternoon about three or four."

"What about the food what do I send?"

"Just send some snacks that the kids will like. The regular meals are part of the package at this time share it cost us one extra day for this one and we get two weeks anywhere we want to go so don't worry about anything, and they do not know how many kids we have."

"I will give you a piece of paper with our authority and insurance card in case something happens and she needs a doctor."

"That will cover about everything, clothes are just whatever she would ware here at this time of the year with some extra socks and a leotard set if she has any or even a set of panty hose of yours for her legs protection if there is any wind."

"That is fine and thank you for doing this for our daughters."

"You are more than welcome see you later."

On their way home from school the girl's stopped at grandma Hedi's to see if grandpa Tom was home yet.

"Hi girls what a surprise it is good to see you come on in and let me see you."

"Grandma how is grandpa Tom?"

"Well he is better but he has had a small stroke and they will be keeping him for about another week or so before he gets to come home."

"You mean he has to spend Christmas in the hospital?"

"Yes but he needs the time so he can be able to get around here at home he will be in a wheel chair for a long time."

"Well if you need any help we can push him around for you."

"Thank you girls but I need to go back to the hospital so I can learn the exercises that he has to do so I can help him here at home."

"Okay grandma tell him hi for us and we are still praying for him."

"That I will do, you two girls will be the best thing for him when he gets home."

# CHAPTER 4

The day after Christmas Sue had everything that Gabby would need all packed along with her snacks. When there came a knock at the door. When Gabby went to open it, there stood Betty.

"I thought you were going away does that mean that you are not going now?"

"I come to tell you goodbye and my mom wants to tell your mom something, so I will see you in a couple of days."

"Hi, Mary are you ready to go here is the bag I have for you."

"Betty, will you take this to the car for me and have dad put it in the trunk."

"Yes mom, bye Gabby, wish you could go with me."

"Bye, me too."

"Well Gabby, are you ready to go. If so go and get your coat we have to get on the road so we can be there before dark?"

"Where am I going?"

"I thought you were going with us you mean you do not want to go."

"Mom, where are they going to take me?"

"Gabby you have been waiting to go somewhere with Betty so we decided to spring a big surprise on you and let you go with them on their skiing trip. Do you want to change your mind and stay home?

Gabby is so overcome with joy; she just stands there not knowing what to do or think.

"Gabby, they need to get on the road do you want to go, and if so get your coat and gloves and boots and go and get in the car."

"Wow! Does Betty know that I am going?"

"Not yet she doesn't but if you hurry to the car she may know soon."

"Oh, mom! Thank you so much, and dad thank you I love you so much."

"We love you too but you need to go get your coat and things so you all can leave."

Gabby is so excited she cannot think as what she needs to do. Then she asked her mom.

"What am I going to wear while I am gone?"

"Your things are packed in the bad Betty took to the car. This has been a surprise for you and Betty for two weeks. Now get on your things or they may leave without you."

"Mom will you go and tell grandma and grandpa I won't be down until we get back. They will be looking for me."

"Yes, someone will go tell them for you. Gabby, you be on your west behavior and do as Mary and Joe tells you. No funny stuff okay."

"Yes, mom I will be very good."

Gabby follows Mary out to the car and is smiling as they open the door for her to get in.

"Gabby, you come to tell me goodbye one more time."

"No Betty she is going with us; can you scoot over so she can get in?"

"Are you kidding me mom, Gabby are you going with us for real."

"Yes, I am and thank you Jesus for this very special time."

"Yes, I now know that your prayers are working, when did you know about this?"

"About ten minutes ago, after you left with my bag of clothes to put into the trunk."

"I did not know they were yours. Mom why did you not tell us."

"Because we wanted it to be a secret surprise so you could go on as you did instead of wondering or worrying about what was going to happen."

"Okay we are all buckled up if so we are on our way."

"Thank you, Mr. and Mrs. Taylor, for allowing me to go with Betty this time."

"It is our pleasure to have you go with us."

"Gabby I still cannot believe you are in this car with me going to have fun. This is going to be the best trip I have taken yet."

"Me neither, this is one big surprise and I hope mom will go see Grandma Heidi. She needs someone to help her and I prayed last night that he would let grandpa Tom come home soon."

"You are really going with us aren't you?"

"Yes I am right here beside you."

"Do you know how to ski?" Al asked

"No but I can learn."

"You will probably ruin our trip when you fall down and break your neck."

"Al you do not talk like that what is wrong with you, any more and I will have your dad stop and tan your back side. Is that clear?"

"Mom what if she gets hurt then we will have to go back home?"

"Al no more or you will not get to go skiing when we get there."

"Poof to you."

Joe hit the brakes and Al instantly said.

"I am sorry I will not talk anymore."

"Young man next time it will be too late for you to say you are sorry and I will stop."

"Okay dad I am sorry and I will be quite."

Gabby did not know what to think so she just scooted down in the seat. They drove in silence for a long time before any one said anything. Then as they drove along the sun came out, and everything looked so much better that Betty finally said.

"I hope the sun is shining when we get where we are going, it is much better when the sun shine even though it is hard to see without squinting your eyes."

Gabby said in a small voice.

"I will pray that it is shining and we all will have fun. Dear Jesus, thank you for this time and this trip we are all going on. Make it a good time for us all and keep us safe and protected while we are gone. Check in on Grandma Heidi and Grandpa Tom, and give them time. Thank you, Jesus, in your name I pray and we do love you. A-men."

"Thank you, Gabby that was sweet of you, and I hope that your prayer will come true for all of us."

"If you believe it will, it will."

"Okay as of that sign we should be there in thirty minutes and if we are lucky we should be able to go skiing yet today."

"Hon are you sure it is about two o'clock now and by the time we check in it will be about four or after."

"Mom we can check in after we go skiing I want Gabby to learn today so we can go more tomorrow."

"Okay Betty, we can wait or dad can take you all, and I will ready our room for us."

"Dad can we do that?"

"I don't see why not but all has to go right for us to have time, and still be ready for our dinner tonight. We have to eat by seven o-clock or we do not get anything but what we brought with us."

As they let the highway they could see all the signs up about the skiing and around the corner the lodge came into view. Cars were parked everywhere along the road leading up to the front opening.

"Everyone stay seated, I will go and see where to stay."

"Gabby this is so exciting you are going to love doing this."

"I hope all is okay and yes I am a little nervous about doing something I know nothing about."

"After the first-time Gabby, you will not be nervous anymore. I remember the first-time Betty and Al was to go she cried because she was afraid and Al would not turn loose from me or his dad."

"Mom I did not cry did I."

"Yes, and after the first time you forgot all about being afraid. Al took a little longer, but he was only about four at the time. And yes, Gabby it is a lot easier when you start young you will see it is going to be fun and exciting for you."

"Okay everybody out and put all your bags on the cart. Then I will go and park and then come back to go up to the room we are on the top floor overlooking the big slope."

"Oh, that will be nice to see all the people flying down the hillside."

"Gabby I can hardly wait you and I, are going to be having the time of our lives. Oh, mom where is dad I want to get up there soon as I can. We need to teach Gabby all about what she has to do with skies on."

"Here he comes who wants to push the cart through the door while I hold it open."

"Gabby and I can push it, you lead the way dad."

"Come through the door and turn to the right to the first elevator."

When they opened the door, and entered there were two big beds and a coach and chair with tables.

"Gabby look there is even a refrigerator and we want to sleep in this bed by the window."

"I guess I get the coach right mom."

"Well let's try it may be better then one of the beds."

"Then where is dad going to sleep?"

"With you in the bed."

"I will take the coach and television."

"Okay if we are going up then we need to get dressed and go we have about one hour and a half left before we have to eat, and I do not want to miss my dinner."

In the next twenty minutes they were downstairs and with skies in hand and ready for the lift. When the lift came by Joe told them.

"I will go first and then Al and Gabby and then Betty in that order and I will help you off at the bunny slope. Okay here come's four seats Gabby you watch out and Betty you get her lined up."

"Okay dad. Gabby are you ready all you do is grab the pole and set on the seat you just watch dad and Al."

"I am ready I think what if I fall off?"

"You cannot get hurt it is too close to the snow and I will fall with you. The skies feel like two big shoes and you cannot walk only by taking short steps, but you will get used to them before the day is over. Al, it is your turn and Gabby you get in line by moving over for the next chair. Ready now grab hold the pole and just set down"

Gabby does as she is told and off she went with a small smile and a little fear on her face. When she was up a little way she looked back to see where Betty was. She had messed her seat but she had caught the next one. When she; looked back forward Joe was not far ahead of her and he was getting off and then Al and then she was next. Joe took her hand and told her.

"Gabby turn loose and just let yourself slid forward I will catch you."

She did right on the seat of her pants and while she was trying to get back up, Betty and Joe was there to help her. Betty was laughing and Al was cackling like a chicken at her. Gabby finally got to her feet saying.

"Well so funny I did not laugh at you so why are you laughing at me.

"Gabby it is okay everyone does this their first time and even some who has did it a long time. Gabby there is some things that you must do all alone and do it your way. Betty, you can show Gabby all the ways of the skies. I am going on up top and I will be back soon so go slow and show her the angles of the skies and how to use the poles. She is very capable of doing okay. She cannot hurt herself on this almost flat ground just stay up from the edge until she gets the points she needs."

"Okay dad we will be okay I won't let her get hurt. Gabby what you need to remember is who you think you are or going to fall just go ahead and fall. When you have learned the skies, you will have the knack to overcome but until then just fall down."

"Okay I am just going to stand here and watch you guys and then I will see what I am to do."

"Gabby, you just lean forward some and use the poles to keep your balance later you can use them to help you move. Just take a small step like six inches but do not let your feet off the ground just skid them along by shuffling your weight on each foot."

"Like this."

"Yes, but keep the points in towards each other unless you want to move faster than straighten them up."

"You go and have your time I will work on my ability to make these things work for me."

"After spending one hour on the slope and falling more times then she could count Gabby was finally making headway and was growing confident in herself. Betty and Al were racing all over the hill and then Joe came by and said.

"Let's all go down it is time to get ready for our special dinner. Gabby put both poles in one hand and hang on to my hand and I will go down with you this first time. Do not be afraid just keep your points together so we will not go to fast for you."

"What if I fall?"

"I will not let you fall just remember the speed we will go is all in the way your points are separated. If you think you are going to fast, then put the points together and you will slow down."

Gabby almost held her breath as Joe and she went over the brink of the bunny slope. They begin to pick up speed she was too busy being a little bit afraid to remember what she was to do with her skies. Then they were getting close to the bottom and Joe told her.

"Gabby put your points together we need to slow down or fall down so we don't run into the wall that is coming at us."

Gabby tried but her mind would not let her body do anything with her feet. At the last minute, Joe pulled her down and they slid into the wall with a thump. Joe turns over and asks.

"Gabby are you okay?"

"I think so."

"Good let's get them skies off so we can get up and become normal and walk to the club house."

Betty and Al came running to find out if they were okay.

"Dad are you and Gabby okay?"

"Yes we were just going a little too fast to stop and Gabby did not know what to do at the right time so I had to pull her down to stop."

"Dad can we go and change if we have time?"

"Yes we have about twenty minutes until they quit serving so let's go and change and get your mom so as not to be late."

"Gabby did you have fun or do you think you would like to go all day tomorrow?"

"I was okay; I just need to know more about it and in time I may get the hang of it and then it could be fun."

"If you were a boy it would be easy."

"If you were a girl we could be closer and have more fun."

"Al being a boy or a girl has nothing to do with it; it is having time to understand."

"Dad I can ski better then Betty can and she is older than I am."

"Al in your mind you can do anything better than your sister so let's leave it at the slope and go clean up to eat."

"Yea Al you put on them bigger skies like I have to wear and you will not be so good."

"Now, now let's not squabble we are here to have fun and let Gabby try something different in her life. So, let's not ruin it for her by you two bickering at each other."

"Dad."

"I said no more here we are at our room."

"Hi, everyone how was it, did Gabby get to learn

much it was such a short time. Was the top in good shape for tomorrow?"

"Everything is great and Gabby did okay except like everyone else to start with she spent a few times on her back side, but I know tomorrow she will be as good as anyone else her age."

"Yea I will have a sore bottom for sure."

"Okay let's go eat something before they close up the dining room. We need to also get to bed and be able to get up early in the morning so we can be on the slope by nine."

"Kids this is a buffet style dinner so you can eat whatever you like. You get to take your plates to the food then go to our table to eat. You can have as much as you like it is all part of the time share. The rest of the weekend meals will be like eating in any restaurant or at home."

Mary tries to explain to them not knowing if Gabby has ever eaten at a buffet before.

"Gabby do you understand about the meal?"

"I will follow Betty and you that will make me feel good by not knowing."

Gabby enjoyed the meal and the talk about what would take place on Saturday. She was somewhat ready and yet somewhat afraid of the unknown.

"Betty, can you ask your dad to teach me how to stop so I won't be afraid. When we come down the hill tonight I was so scared I was going to be hurt when I got to the bottom and ran into the wall."

"I will show you, and if not I will ask dad to show you."

"I don't want Al to know because all he does is laugh at me."

"If I catch him I will bop him up the side of the head, but he will be doing his thing with the smaller kids."

"Okay did you girls get full it is going to close in a

few minutes. If you want more you had better go and get it soon."

"I am full mom how about you Gabby?"

"I don't want any more it is late to be eating for me."

"For us too, but this is an occasionally thing and you get to break habits here."

"Thank you, Mrs. Taylor, but I am going to have fun tomorrow and not have a tummy ache."

"Okay we will be going to our room shortly. By the time, we all get showered and in bed it will be a lot later so if you two are ready we can go start. We will leave the boys down here for now. That way we can have a little privacy. Are you ready if so we can go?"

"Gabby yes we are ready mom."

"Joe, you and Al can stay down here for a while us girls are going to do our thing alone."

"Okay with me we will give you about thirty minutes and then be up."

"Okay girls let's run and do our thing."

When Joe and Al came through the door Betty and Gabby were in their bed talking and Mary was in the bathroom.

"Betty I am getting very tired it is way past my time and is it okay if I pray?"

"You can do anything that you do at home."

She got out and knelt by her side of the bed and bowed her head into the sheets.

"Dear Lord Jesus, thank you for my friend and sister and her family that let me come with them on this trip. Thank you for helping me from getting hurt today and that you would be with us tomorrow while we are skiing. Watch in on my mom and dad and sister Jan and my grandma Heidi and grandpa Tom as they sleep tonight. Thank you for your love and your word. I am sorry I forgot my Bible, but I remember some of the verses. Keep this room safe for us tonight in you name I pray. I love you Jesus. A-men."

"Good night Betty; my friend and sister."

"Gabby do you do this every night?"

"Do what?"

"Talk to your Jesus."

"Yes, it helps me go to sleep knowing he is watching over me."

"Good night girls it is getting late remember we will be up early in the morning."

They were up and dressed by seven o-clock and ready to go.

"Hey, are you all ready to go and get breakfast and hit the slope?"

"Okay Joe we are all ready and hungry just not as ready as you are to start so early."

"Mary, get the girls I will take Al with me and get us a table."

"Come girls before we get left behind."

"Coming mom Gabby had some trouble getting into her clothes they are not really her size."

Breakfast is over and all head to the ski room to be fitted with their skies. Then to the ski lift, and up and away.

"Mary, are you getting off with the kids or am I going too?"

"I will do it so you can go on up I will come with you on the second trip."

Everyone but Joe gets off at the bunny slope, and Gabby needs some start help. When a couple came over and told them they were here to help with the little ones.

"We come to help so the adults can have fun also so if you want to go on up we will assist your children until they know how to get along with the skies."

"That is nice of you do you work for the resort?"

"Yes I am Thomas and this is Karen so if you want we can help and you can go and have fun."

"Okay you kids pay attention to this couple I will come down shortly to see how things are going. My name is Mary and my husband Joe is up top coming this way soon. You kids pay attention and have fun. Gabby are you okay?"

"Yes Mrs. Taylor."

"Al no funny stuff okay."

"Yes mom."

Mary took off and Thomas and Karen started helping Gabby to get used to the skies Betty and Al are sliding all over the hill.

"Gabby, you are catching on pretty good why don't you try going down and coming back."

"Okay thanks."

"You are welcome. Thomas that blond is the one I want she is so close to the one we lost."

"Yes, so let's get ready and after lunch we will be gone and she will be with us before anyone ever misses her."

"I will go and get things packed and put them in the car so we can leave from the lot at the bottom of the hill."

Thomas watches as Karen leaves and the children are all playing paying no attention to what is going on. Gabby and Betty come up to him and asked.

"Where did Karen go I don't see her?"

"She went to the bathroom and will be back soon. What time are your parents going to eat lunch? It is almost twelve o-clock now."

"They will be along soon I am getting a little hungry what about you Gabby?"

"Yes I am where is Al he needs to stay closer to us don't you think?"

"He can stay as far away from us as he wants to it is alright with me."

"Betty go get your brother I see your mom and dad coming down the slope."

"Al get over here it is time to go and eat.' Called Betty as Al just stopped and looked at her.

"Hi you kid ready for some lunch?"

"Yes but Al is way over there being his normal self."

"I will go and get him." said Joe.

"Us girls will start down and get us a table, don't be to long."

"Okay see you soon."

"Mom there comes Karen she had to go the restroom."

"Hi Karen, we are going to lunch see you in about an hour."

"Okay, we will be here, enjoy your lunch."

"Karen, I know our plan that girl Betty does not like her brother much so all we have to do is get him out of sight and the other one takes her to find him."

"What about the other girl?"

"You leave her to me when Al gets out of sight I will go away and come back while you take Betty to look for her brother. I will stay here for a while and then come to look for you and Betty. By then you should be in the car and ready when I get there. I will leave her standing just in case you come back with the boy."

"I think that will work but it needs to happen in about ten to fifteen minutes' tops do you agree."

"Yes, ten minutes should be enough time and by the time the other two decide what is going we will be gone up the road."

As they discuss the plans the Taylor's come back up from lunch on the ski lift, and drop off the kids and go on up top. Al takes off for where the other boys are that he had meet in the morning and Gabby and Betty start playing around while Thomas and Karen watch. At two o-clock Joe and Mary come back by to check on the kids.

After talking for a while they go on back up top. Karen goes and asked Betty.

"Where is your brother I do not see him with the others?"

"He is okay; don't pay any attention to him."

"Thomas go and see where Al is I do not see him."

"Okay but he is alright he was just here a minute ago."

"You go see and come back."

"Okay."

When Thomas returns he says.

"I did not see him over there where do you think he could have gone."

"Maybe he went down the slope Betty you come with me we will go see if he is down there."

"Gabby you stay here with Thomas or right here just in case he comes back. Come Betty lets go."

"Gabby I will be right back that brother of mine ruins everything for me."

As they get hear the bottom Karen tells Betty.

"We need to remove their skies because they are not allowed on the parking lot with them on."

"Betty, come I will get the binoculars to see if we can look back up to see if we can see him."

When they get to the car Karen gives Betty the glasses and says.

"You look back up there to see if you can spot your brother. I will watch the building to see I he comes out he may have went to the bathroom."

"I don't see anyone I know am I looking in the right direction?"

"Look straight up there can you see Thomas and your friend, if so then look to the left of them and see if you can see your brother."

"I see Gabby but I do not see Thomas maybe he has gone to get Al or something."

"Keep watching until you see him. Here give me the glasses you set in the car I will start the engine and we can warm up while we watch."

"Why do I have to have a brother like mine he causes trouble for me all the time? Karen here comes Thomas maybe he has found Al and we can go back up."

"We will have to wait and see when he gets here."

Thomas opens the door and gets in and puts the car in gear and they are off.

"Where are we going let me out of here?"

"Stay put we are going to report your brother missing and then we will come back."

"You go but let me out I want to go back where my friend is and wait for my dad and mom to come down."

"You are going with us so set back and be quite so we can think what to do next."

As they drove west as fast as the speed limit would let them Gabby was up looking and waiting for someone to return to tell her what was going on. She could not leave because then they would all be lost so she stayed and kept looking until she saw Joe and Mary coming down the slope to where she stood.

"Hey Gabby where is every one?"

"I don't know first Al was gone and they went looking for him and then Betty was gone with Karen, and then Thomas was gone and here I am all alone."

"Joe, go see if Al is over there with the other boys. I will stay with Gabby until you return."

Shortly Joe returns with Al asking.

"Gabby which way did Betty go?"

"They went down that way."

"Did all three of them go that way?"

"No just Karen ad Betty they thought Al was down there, but Thomas went this way down towards the buildings."

"Let's go and see what we can find out take the children down the lodge and I will go down this way towards the parking lot to see what I can see."

"Don't take too long I am starting to get worried this is not like Betty."

"I know just you go down and see if you can find any of the three, I will be along as soon as I can."

As Joe nears the parking lot he sees two pairs of skies lying by the fence by the gate one small size and one larger pair. With finding this he removed his skies and started towards the parking lot entrance to the lodge as fast as he could go. Nearing the door Mary and Gabby are standing just inside. Al is looking out the window. Then he asked.

"Have you seen anything of Betty or the other two?"

"No and I asked if the two Thomas and Karen worked here at the resort and so far no one knows them. Joe I am very scared that they may have taken our daughter and left."

"Let's go and talk to the management and see if we need to call the law and start a search for them."

After telling the management and security people their story that they had went through and then deciding about the time spent for how long they may have been gone. They called the police, and they in turn called the F B I because if it could be a kidnapping then they would be the entity who would be in charge. The security people have returned with two pairs of skies and have checked the guest list to fine that there was no Thomas or Karen that had checked in or out during the last seven days. By the time, the F B I arrived and the same story told to them it had been two hours as close as they could tell. That meant the couple had to be somewhere within one hundred plus or minus a few miles, and they could be almost anywhere by this time. They checked the security films and found no one that Gabby or Al could say was the two people.

The only thing they had was a small wallet size picture of Betty to get out on the news. Nothing was adding up to the family or the law as of what could have happened and it did not look good at the time unless someone saw them and reported them to the law.

Mary had cried until she had no more tears. Gabby was withdrawn and not speaking. Al was about the same as always except hanging very close to his mom. It was as if the world had rushed on forward into some place that was unaware of when the people had just been.

"Joe what do we do now?"

"I don't know I asked if we could go home but they said to wait until tomorrow so I guess we stay until they let us go."

"Gabby, do you want to call your mom and dad and let them know what has happened."

"I don't know I guess so."

This was all she could get to come out.   "Okay I will call but they may want us to bring you home tonight, and we have to stay here until the police let us leave."

"Maybe we should wait and call them in the morning that way we may be able to leave"

"Is that okay with you Gabby?"

"I guess so."

"Why don't we all go up to our room and take a bath so we can be ready to eat. We need some time to calm down. I don't believe that this has happened to our daughter. Why us?"

"I want to go to our room so I can pray for Betty."

"Okay dear, lets you and I go and Joe you and Al can come up later that way we will be through with our baths and you can take yours."

"Dear Lord, please look out for Betty she needs you really bad right now. I am praying that those two people will bring her back. She is my sister and I need her. Please change the minds of Thomas and Karen and let them do the right thing and let Betty come back home to us. A-men I love you Lord Jesus."

"Thank you, Gabby, for your prayer for Betty and I am asking the same thing so our family will come back to the whole as we were before this happened.

# PART THREE

# CHAPTER FIVE

"Mom something dreadful has happened. We are starting home as soon as we get
packed."

"Are you alright? Gabby."

"Yes I am not hurt."

"What dreadful thing has happened?"

"Mom I cannot talk about it now."

Gabby starts to sob into the phone and hands it to Joe.

"Hello, Gabby what is wrong? Hello Gabby can you hear me?"

"Hello Sue, this is Joe and everyone is broken about something we cannot figure out. The FBI and the police are working on it, and have told us that we could go home, and wait for them to arrive and maybe by then they might know something."

Joe what are you talking about that Gabby said was so dreadful that happened. Joe please tell me what is going on."

"Sue Betty is missing and they believe she has been

kidnapped by a man and a woman who we thought worked for the resort, but now they know that they had not been registered to be here. No one knows how they got up on the slope, and not be noticed. We are starting home Gabby is okay just a little displaced at this time. We are taking good care of her. We should be home in about three hours or so please do not worry and we will talk to you when we see you."

"Joe let me talk to Mary or Gabby please?"

"They are not with me at this time they went for the last potty stop before we leave. Please do not worry we have been through a lot since yesterday afternoon we will be careful and will see you when we bring Gabby by your house."

Having said all, he could Joe hangs up the phone. This was going to be a very long drive for the four of them. They rode in silence except when Mary was crying, and Gabby crying and Al telling them to stop. Joe said nothing until Mary told him.

"You should have been down there with the kids and I should have gone more often to see them. It is like we are being punished for not spending more time with them."

"Stop it, it is nobody's fault, it is just this kind of stuff happens. Our problem is that it always happens to someone else. We just happened to be the one of choice this time. They will find them two and then they will pay for this bad thing they did. Don't make me the bad guy, and you the bad woman. Granted we should have paid more attention, but they were going to do this no matter what we did they would have made it happen some way."

"We have been pushing our luck we should have been going to church and letting our kids go to Sunday school like we talked maybe this would not have happened if we had just started when we were asked by Don and Sue."

"This was going to take place no matter what we had

done it was just going to happen and it was our child that happened to be the one they choose. It could have been Gabby or Al just as much as it was Betty. I don't want to start playing the God thing when I know it was not him who allowed this to take place, and if it was him then to church I will never go period."

"Gabby how do you feel about this?"

"I hurt a lot for Betty, I found a good friend and sister and now I don't know if I will ever see her again. I just don't know I have to go and tell grandma Heidi and grandpa Tom what has happened and it will hurt them a lot just to know.  My mom and dad will probably never let me go anyplace again, and I want to hurt them people who took Betty. I know that God did not let this happen and I pray that God will intervene to save Betty from harm while she is away with them bad people."

"We will be home in about twenty minutes and we will drop you off."

As they pulled into Meed's drive way to park out of the door came Sue and Don with Jan bring up the rear end. They could not wait to get the door open on the van so they could hold their daughter and find out more about Betty.

"Oh Gabby we have missed you."

She got hugs from mom and dad. Jan just stood there and watched without much emotion. When Mary slipped out of her seat and into the grasp of Sue they stood and cried for the girl that was missing. Don went to Joe and embraced him with tears for his missing daughter.

"Joe we are so sorry for this time and we have been praying all day and our church has been praying for Betty. We don't understand why this happened but we are going to leave it in God's hands for his love and mercy to bring Betty back safe and without any harm."

"Thanks Don you and Sue are true friends but now

we have to get home and wait there for the feds to show they should be there any time. Later this evening they may know something more about the two people that we think took Betty."

"We will keep praying."

"Don you and Sue have a very strong lady and we are very proud of her. She is so nice just to be around. And we are very thankful for her and that we got to bring her home, but she has not opened up to us since Betty has been missing. So be careful she may break soon or don't let her keep this bottled up inside of herself. She has been very quiet since that time when we knew that Betty was not coming back with us."

"We will and all we can say is we are deeply sorry and thank you so much. If you need anything you know where we are."

The Taylor's left for home and all was quite. Gabby was not talking or answering any question she finally said.

"I am not hungry and I want to go and take a bath and go to bed."

"It is kind of early for bed are you sure you don't want to talk some, tell us about the ski trip and if it was fun or not."

"Mom how could it be fun when my sister and best friend just disappeared."

She then turned and ran to her room and slammed the door very hard.

"Hon let's give her, her space for tonight we have all this week to get her ready to go back to school."

"Don, are you concerned about her?"

"Yes I am but we need for her to open up instead of us trying to pry it out of her. She is just a child and she needs time to think. Tomorrow will be soon enough. We can check on her before we go to bed."

"Can we pray for the family?"

"Yes I will."

"Dear Lord God Jesus, why did this have to happen they were so close. Please keep a watch over Betty and Gabby and let them both come back to us soon. There is a very broken family that really needs their little girl back. Let us all do and say the right things and help them overcome this tragedy in their lives. Let this draw them closer to you and your word and love let the comforter shower them with your grace. In your precious name we pray and lift Betty up to you this evening. A-men."

Gabby was up early on Monday she fixed her breakfast and had eaten when her mom came down and asked.

"Well you are up early. Good morning, how do you feel after the long rest?"

"Okay I guess can I go see grandma Heidi and grandpa Tom they should be up by now."

"If that is what you want to do I think it will be okay."

"Yes I have to tell them what happened to Betty so they can be praying for her safety."

"Make sure you dress warm it is chilly out this morning."

"Mom why did God let this happen to Betty?"

"I do not believe we can blame God for this I think it was a very sinful couple and we need to keep asking God to intervene and not let something happen to her. Even if we pray for her safety God may have something else that will be better for her. Remember it is God's will not ours and he may need Betty up in heaven to help him, or to bring someone or thing closer to his son Jesus."

"Why Betty there are lots of other girls he could have had?"

"Yes it could have been you and then what would you be thinking at this time?"

"It would be different because I know Jesus and Betty

does, but has not accepted him as her savior yet and now I don't know if she will ever be in heaven when I get there."

"Sweet heart we do not know this, and I believe that Jesus has special ways with children. Sometimes they have never heard of him before something happens to them so I do not know for sure but he just maybe let them in."

"But I have told her about Jesus, but she does not get my point, and she is as old as I am so she should have known even before we meet."

"But that may not have been her fault if her parents never helped her to see. She would not have had the chance to hear about Jesus in the same way you did."

"Maybe, I am going to go tell grandma Heidi and grandpa Tom so they can pray they need to start as soon as they can."

After dressing and coming back down Gabby tells her mom.

"Mom I will be back soon as I can let them know all about what has happened."

"Okay Gabby, tell them I said hello and to call if they need anything."

Gabby decided to walk instead of ride her bike. It was not that far, and telling them was not going to be easy for her. When she arrived she knocked on the door gently and waited. Then knocked again only louder. Then the door opened and grandma Heidi was they're rubbing her eyes to wake up.

"My goodness you are here very early this morning. Come on in and let me get my act together set down and tell me about your trip and I will get you some hot chocolate. You must be cold from the walk why did you not ride your bike?"

"I wanted to walk and think before I got here. And it was early but I hoped you would be up." As she removed her shoes and coat and hung it up.

"Okay I am going to get that hot chocolate you just sat there and I will be right back."

"Thanks grandma."

As she followed her into the kitchen not knowing when to start telling her about Betty, and what happened on their ski trip.

"Do you have some of them wonderful cookie, and could I have one just to have something in my hand."

"Yes you may have and yes you can and now will you tell me what is wrong before grandpa Tom comes down for his breakfast?"

"Grandma we were having so much fun and then Saturday after lunch Betty just disappeared, and I was left all alone until her parents came down where we were. Then we could not find Betty and then the police and the FBI came and we found her skies and the ones that Karen was wearing. She and Thomas just took her and left. We do not know where she is or if she is okay."

"Oh that dear child, and you are her best friend and her family what are you going to do?"

Gabby told Heidi that she had been praying a lot since Betty disappeared but nothing has happened so far to bring her back.

"Grandma I just do not know what I am going to do I miss her so much and my heart is broken and I am all alone now."

"I know you two girls were so close I thought you were closer than if you had been twins at birth in the same family. Tom come in here we have some real bad news and we need to pray for our missing granddaughter."

As Tom enters the kitchen he asked.

"What do you mean missing?"

"Tom, Betty was kidnapped from the ski slope on Saturday and no one knows where she is except those two her took her."

"Oh! Oh! My, that is hard for an old heart to hear so let us pray that Jesus will protect her and God will not let her go from his protection."

"Dear great and wonderful Father up in heaven, as you know about Betty and where she is please if it is in your will for her keep her safe. Let those who took her from her family and friends be mindful of her and keep her safe and in good spirit so as she will not be burdened by a difficult time and how she feels at this time. She is as you know just a small girl and some people could do some bad things to her we are asking that you not let anything as this that could happen and stop any attacks upon her. Give her strength and peace while she is being looked for so she can come back home without any mental problems to close up her mind. Save her for your kingdom so she will be a warrior for you and the fight against the cruel one that is responsible for the actions of them two people. Dear Jesus we know that you love Betty and you know we love her and will always wonder why this had to take place so we are asking and praying and crying for your help. Gabby has lost her first and best friend she is like a sister to her so don't forget about the life of these two sweet girls. I close now to your loving kindness and faithfulness to those who want to serve you and are willing to do so. We love you Jesus and want to serve you with happy hearts and minds in your precious name we pray. A-men."

"Dear Jesus thank you for grandma Heidi and grandpa Tom. I ask your special blessings on then during this time. Knowing that they are going to worry about Betty, and our friendship I ask for your special time and touch to be here for them. A-men."

"Thank you Gabby, and now Mrs. grandma can I have my breakfast, and fix Gabby another hot chocolate and some more cookies she is a growing child and needs the nourishment for what she I going through at this time."

"Grandpa, are you doing okay at this time."

"Yes sweet one I am doing as good as I can for the shape I am in. grandma is doing a great job keeping me doing what the doctor tells me to do. in the next hundred years I will probably be sick more than I am well, but my Lord Jesus will see me through this and someday I will see my tomorrow and be truly thankful for the Grace he has given to me."

"What do you mean you will see your tomorrow?"

"Well life is divided up into three different day times. Yesterday is like history it is there so we can remember out mistakes and wrongs and then when we remember them we can correct them to be right on the today day. Then there is tomorrow and that is the mystery we cannot see into it we do not know what is there. We do know that when we do see it Jesus will have come back for us and that will be the first time we will see tomorrow. So today is the only one day that God has given us? That is why it is called the present as a gift from God himself. Yes, I know my tomorrow is coming and so is yours and all the rest and we who believe in Jesus will see our tomorrows in heaven and those who do not believe will see their tomorrows down in the pit of fire called Hell. Grandma and I are enjoying our today's now but we are ready for our tomorrows as soon as God and his son Jesus has our mansion ready for us."

"But you are not going soon are you?"

"We do not know the day for which he will come for us we just have to be ready."

"Well I need you here for a while longer. I have no one else to come and talk with. It is hard to explain my thought to anyone but you. Because you listen and do not over feedback to change my mind."

"That is what grandparents are to do, just listen love you and pray for you. Now think about this when we are both gone to be with Jesus you will find someone else to replace us. So do not give up hope in what God and Jesus has in store for you."

* * * * *

Betty has been crying and screaming to be taken back to her friend and family. She has not slept or eaten in the two days on the road except in short dozes and drinking pop. She has finally succumbed to the weariness of her body and has slept for six hours straight. Now that she is awake and not crying and begin to ask question.

"Why did you take me?"

"Thomas she is awake and not screaming at us."

"Why did you take me?"

"When you are calmer we will tell you our side of this story."

"Where are you taking me?"

"We are on our way home, don't you want to go home?"

"I want to see my mom and dad?"

"Your real mom and dad are setting in the front seat of this van."

"I want to see my friend Gabby?"

"Forget about your friend she is long gone."

"I want to see my friend and mom and dad. I hate you both."

"In time you will change your mind so just set back and relax we have one more day of driving and we will be home."

"I want to go to my home not yours I want to see my friend and family so take me back so I can be with them."

Betty was not getting no answers so see just shut up and watched the sights go passed her window. She was dozing when she seen a sign that said Mexico ahead. She then comes to and said.

"Why are you taking me to Mexico I have been there and I don't want to live there. Why are you doing this to me?"

"Well I guess it is time for us to tell you why we are doing what we are doing so you can understand more and ask fewer questions. So listen well as I tell you our story to you. Karen will tell you all about it."

"As you know our names are Thomas and Karen and we had a beautiful blond girl a long time ago in a hospital over in Dallas Texas. When we were ready to take her home she was not blond but had black hair and we knew that she was not ours and someone had switched babies with us. She was very sick and only lived for eight weeks and then we had to bury her. We have fought all these years to find our little girl. You are the girl that belongs to us. The parents who raised you are not your parents you belong to us. They were in a position and we believe the hospital helped them to switch you babies. We know it is going to take a long time for you with all the love we have stored up over all these years you have been gone from us. Your life is going to be good and you will have everything you will ever need. You will have no little brothers to cause you any grief. We are asking you to give us the chance we always wanted for you so we can be a happy family."

"I do not believe you and I want my friend Gabby and she needs me, so take me back to them. I don't like you and I don't care about you and your story and I don't want to live with you in this dumb Mexico that I do not like."

"In time you will like being where we live and your life will be better than where you were living we ask that you let us prove that you are ours and that we care and have you and your life will be great as soon as you get used to the new life you have coming up. We live out in the country, you will be home schooled and have some friends that live not very far from where we live."

"They are not my friends Gabby is my friend and I want to go home to see her. I want to see my real mom and dad, my brother, and my grandma Heidi, my grandpa Tom. So turn this car around and take me back home.

They drove in silence for a long time and then Betty saw the sign USA ahead please stop at the border crossing. When they came to the guard's station and were stopped by the officer Betty hollered out the window.

"I was kidnapped make these people let me go."

The guard looked at her but said nothing. Then Thomas said to the guard.

"She has these mental fits every once in a while and talks out of her head. We are going to Phoenix to see if they can help her. She is getting much worse as she grows older."

The guard just nodded and handed back the car papers to Thomas and they drove off.

"Betty why did you do that; do you know that we could have been detained for days for that stupid outburst? You have to be smarter than that now set back and relax we will be home in about one hour."

"I don't care I do not want to be here with you two mean people."

"I asked you to be quite please obey and do not speak Thomas she is going to need a lot of patience on our part."

"You two are mad and I will get away some time."

"Betty don't make me punish you when you really do not need it. Now I asked you to be quite and we both want you to do as we ask. If you do things will go much smoother for you. We want you to think about what we have told you, and think how we have felt for so long without you living in our home."

"I am never going to be your daughter. I will run

away as soon as I can. I hate you for what you are doing to me and my friend and my real family."

"Before long you will change your mind so for now talking is just your way of pushing out. So now just sat there and think about what we told you we will be home soon."

Betty does as she is told. Just clamping up and ignoring the front seat talk. Then she heard Karen say.

"Man look there is our house I am so glad to be back seems like we have been gone forever. Look Betty this is where we live."

Betty looks out the front window and lets out a big gasp.

"You have got to be kidding that is nothing but a big junky looking trailer house. I am not going to stay here. Probably got rats running all over. I can smell it now Pugh I am staying in the car."

"Young lady it may look bad on the outside but I am telling you it is real nice on the inside, and you have your own bedroom and bathroom."

"I don't care I don't want to be here. Where are all those people you said lived around here? How many lies are you going to tell me before I can leave?"

"There are three families that live just over that swell over there, and the others live behind us over there. We live in a small indent so you cannot see very far but they are there. Every one lives in a trailer house out here."

"Out here where is out here? There is no grass and no trees and what are those big things standing over there?"

"They are cactus and it is very dry here it very seldom rains so nothing grows here it is called the dessert and is very dry the summers get well over one hundred degrees and stays there day and night. It is not as hot as you may think it is by looking at the thermometer. You will love it when winter comes and it stays warm without snow or very cold temperatures. It is around seventy in the daytime and forty at nights. The closet town is Bisbee and it is about twelve miles in that direction. You have to be very careful walking so as not to step on a rattle snake or poisonous Gila Monsters."

"I am still going to run away so check me out soon."

"You also have to watch out for the Indians who live everywhere out here."

"I am not afraid of no Indians."

"Not until you get caught alone then what would you do?"

"Please take me home I want to see my friend Gabby. I want to let her know I am okay. I want to talk with her and play with her, and go to school with her so please take me home."

"You are home and you need to accept this new life we have for you. Your friend Gabby and the ones you think are your mom and dad and your brother do not exists in your life anymore."

"I will also hate you for this. Gabby if your God or Jesus can hear me I will come and find you some day. I need your help and there's to make this happen I am just a small child and I cannot fight these two grown maniacs."

* * * * *

One whole week has gone by and Gabby is now dreading going back to school without her friend she has prayed and prayed for Betty to come home, but Jesus has not helped her to come home. Gabby has returned to the silence of her past she has no joy in her life. Her family has prayed for her not to go back. They have asked God to bring someone else into her life, but all the prayers of the family and church has not changed anything pertaining to Betty and her return it was as if she just disappeared from this life. The FBI and the police has told them they are still working to find her, but until someone or something comes forward their hands are about tied up tight without no evidence to go forward with. Gabby has been taken to her pastor, school counselor, and the court counseling jet she is still withdrawn all inside, and does not talk to any of them about her friend. She speaks only when spoken to by her family. She will not answer any question when Betty's name is brought up unless it is to her grandma Heidi or grandpa Tom she can talk to them about her hurts for her friend. She has had no contact with Betty's family members and does not want too. Most of her free time is spent at her grandma Heidi and grandpa Tom's place there she can relax and not be bomb bared with questions about her attitude and not being able to go forward and find a new friend.

"Grandma, have you ever lost a friend like I have?"

"No child, but I lost my sister who was very close to me. We were together for over seventy years and it hurt for a long time after she was gone to be with the Lord. Now if we let Jesus help us it does get easier understand and deal with. It took me a long time to protect my thoughts and it will soon happen for you. You will find someone else to take her place but never replace her in your heart. You have to pray and give it to Jesus and he will very slowly help you to overcome your grief. You still have your family and your friend Betty no matter where she is her family is not with her so try to think how she feels, and do not leave her family out of your life. Maybe it is you who will lead them all back or to Jesus. Am I saying anything that is helping you to understand what is happening in your life with the thoughts that are going through your mind and keeping you from being the true you that Jesus wants you to be."

"Grandma I just do not understand why my God and Jesus would let this happen and then make us all feel so bad. Does he still love us or did we do something to make him mad at us? Betty and I did not do anything wrong that I know of. I did not do anything to hurt her mom and dad. I still do not like the way her brother Al acts all the time. He is worst then my sister and I and I even pray for them to change, but nothing happens. Is God doing this to punish us for the way we have treated our brother and sister?"

"No, my child I do not believe that Jesus does things like that. He may bring it to our minds to keep us thinking of that wrong, but I don't believe he would have someone kidnapped to get our attention for such a small item. Although he will let the Holy Spirit keep bring it to our conscience to remind us that we should treat people no matter whom they are as friends and love them as we love ourselves. Then help us to change our attitude about them and pray for their actions that keep us upset all the time.'

"Well look who is here while I am setting in there feeling sorry for myself I have a wonderful, thoughtful, young and beautiful girl setting out here that I miss."

Gabby jumps up and is swallowed in a big hug and gives grandpa Tom a big kiss on his check.

"Good morning grandpa, why are you feeling sorry for yourself when you have everything you need?"

"Well when you get my age and all the things that used to work good for you seems to say I am tried so get someone else to do that job. Then we have the tendencies to start grumbling to ourselves and then we start feeling sorry for the shape we are in."

"Grandpa I can help you if you tell me what you need done."

"Well I wish you could but I think I still need to just give it back to God and not think about it and maybe it will just disappear and let me think about what I have left. Grandma does better at this then I do."

"Oh Tom I have the same things going through my mind but I find other things that help me get all the things I cannot do as I used to do we are just old and do not want to slow down. It is time for us to relax and enjoy what we have left like this young girl setting here in front of us with a problem that we have never had to face in our long lives. She finds time just to come and see us and cheer us up. She is a true gift from God, and a true blessing. We need to pray more so God can help her get through this ordeal that has her so upset and thinking all the bad things, or out of control thoughts that keep her so unset all the time."

"Okay my dear and I don't see any reason to not start right now so let me pray for her."

"Dear Lord God, Our Father in heaven and God over all things. As we set here feeling sorry for all our problems we tend to forget about the love you showed us when you let your only child your son Jesus suffer so much for all the wrongs that we humans do. I ask you to keep reminding us of that love to let us know that there will never be a stronger love then what you felt for your son to come and suffer to take all our sins away. So we could spend time with you by loving him and excepting what he went through just for us. At this time, I ask that you comfort Gabby and Betty even though they are so far apart at this time and that you will protect them during the separation of their bodies and minds. Let them come back together some day even in heaven. Help us two old people to pray more for the one let us feel less about what we are and the problems we now have. Keep our eyes focused on you Jesus and bring happiness to our minds and in the things we do. Let this prayer reach out to Gabby's family and to help her to get through her loss, and to Betty's family that they will turn their thoughts and bodies over to you. Let them fall down and except you as their savior and king. Lord let us all remember you more during the waking hours of our lives. I ask all these things in my mind and let Jesus do as his will is for us. In his precious name I ask. We love you Lord Jesus and we want to serve you at all times. A-men."

"Now young lady I believe that you should be going back home before your mom starts thinking something has happened to you. And tell her that you came come down anytime you are allowed too."

"Thank you grandma Heidi and thank you grandpa Tom for praying for us all the time."

Gabby gets dressed and starts her short walk home. As she walks she keeps thinking about if she should go and talk with Betty's parents or if she should just leave them alone. When she got home and in the house she took off her coat and called for her mom when Jan walked into the room and asked in her over abundant voice.

"Well just where have you been. Does mom know where you were? I think you are in real big trouble wait until dad gets home."

"Go away and leave me alone I do not want to listen to your smart mouth."

"Gabby why did you say that to your sister?"

"Mom it is none of her business where I have been she just wants to cause me trouble. Can I talk to you about something?"

"Yes come into the kitchen I was baking a cake for your dad."

"No I want to talk to you in my room it is something that I only want you to know."

"Gabby you know we do not have secrets around here we can talk in the kitchen."

"Very well then I will go to my room I have something to do anyway."

"Gabby what is wrong did grandma Heidi or grandpa Tom say something to upset you."

"No it is my sister that thinks that she has to have her nose in everything I do and then tries to use it to get me into some kind of trouble. So I want to talk to you in my room."

"Okay I will come up when I get done in the kitchen. Is it about school?"

"No it is about something else."

Gabby starts up the stairs and Jan is thumbing her nose at her. Gabby tells her.

"I wish you were not my sister I hate it when you act like some moron out of some space movie. And remember some day you may want me to help you do something and you will not like it when I just tell you no. Go away and stay out of my life until you grow up and become a responsible person. Why don't you go and talk to Jesus and ask him to steer you down the right path and then go down it a long way."

"Gabby I heard that and I think you owe your sister an apologue. Then go to your room I will be up shortly and we are going to find out just what your problem really is."

Gabby turns and runs up to her room and slams the door. Goes to her bed and lies down and lets the tears flow. After a while she gets on her knees and ask Jesus to forgive her of the thing she feels and the way she acts towards her sister and mom and dad.

"Dear Lord Jesus I am in such a mess and I cannot decipher all that is bothering me and the only place I can get any help is at grandma Heidi and grandpa Tom's place. I need your help so I can get through and go on what am I to do when I cannot figure it out. Jesus I pray for Betty and that she is alright and safe, and if you want her I guess it will be alright but I sure do need her here at this time with school starting and to make me happy again. Thank you Jesus for listening to me and help me to stop complaining so much. In your sweet name I pray. A-men."

# CHAPTER SIX

"Betty I am watching you and I do not approve of the way you are acting now get in here and explain yourself."

Betty does not answer so Karen comes to her saying.

"Young lady I am at my wits end with you. We have explained things to you. You are going to get your schooling and do it as your life is going to get worse then you think it is now. So from now on when you are spoken to, asked to do something, and respect your parents, and I mean right now you will be punished far worse then what you think is happening now. Do you hear me and understand what I just said?"

"I have no other choice at this time, but you can punish me all you want but you will never make me care for you, or love you. You have given me these books and I tell you it is the same thing that I did last year in school. I am not going to do them again. Besides I had a friend to study with and now I have to do it all by myself."

"You can ask me and I will help you."

"Why would I ask you so you could lie to me like you have lied since the beginning. All you two do is lie one after the other."

"We have not lied to you, and from now on I or we do not want to listen to your complaining about your friend who ever she was. She has no place in your life from now on."

"I hate this school work and until you get me something different I am not going to do any of it."

"You will or you will spend your days in your room doing nothing."

"Fine there is nothing I want to do around here anyway."

Betty throws her books on the table and stomps off to her room and slams the door.

******

"Gabby you are going to be late for school so let's get it in gear, let's go."

As usual Gabby does not return anything so her mom just stands and looks at her with disgust on her face.

"Dear Lord Jesus what am I to do? It seems that everything I try does not work. My husband just does nothing just saying she will come out of it in time. I know that she has lost but something has to spur her into living again. She is just a young girl. Please I am asking for your help to put us back together as a family. What I need is, understanding so I can help her get through this time. She can talk to her new grandparents but she will not open up to her mom and dad. So Lord Jesus I give her to you, but she still has to live with us. This has broken up Betty's family and has effected ours as well. Please Lord I need we need your help and guidance to redo this problem we now have. In your lovely name I pray. A-men"

"Mom I am ready to go, are you taking me?"

"Well its is about time. Let's go!"

"Mom why can't you just say okay and not put me down."

"I am sorry but I have a life to and it is to take care of my family not just one pouting young girl. I love you, but you are trying my patience at the least a lot of the time."

"Mom I am sorry but no one but grandma and grandpa seems to care about my loss and how I feel. All you want is answers to all your questions, which is not helping me, but making me feel the loss of my friend. Betty is still out there somewhere and we will find each other again someday, and how I feel about it does nothing to do with you all writing your book."

Gabby leaves and gets into the car and is waiting for her sister and mom to come, and wishing that Betty would be at school when she arrives. It was not going to happen Betty was gone and not coming back. All the praying was not helping. After one month everything was the same even Gabby's grades were falling to b's and c's instead of all a's.

on Saturday morning Don and Sue were setting at the table before Gabby and Jan were up drinking their morning coffee.

"Don what do you think we should do about Gabby. I am a lot worried about her. How do you feel? You know her grades are down and she still does not talk much even though when I talk to Hedi and Tom they say she talks their legs off. I do not understand why she can talk to them and not to us."

"Hon I have come to the conclusion that we have to let her have her space and let her work this out she is young and that is going to be on her side. She has not lost her husband nor any children so I have decided not to ask her anything and let her come to us. I think this will work and let her own her thoughts and be able to open up and share with us. Without us asking any questions. That is what I think at this time."

"Don't you care about the way she is acting?"

"Yes I do but it is not working so we need to back off and let her come out. Let the Holy Spirit work in her mind instead of us asking the same questions over and over."

"I don't know how you can do this, but maybe you are right. I will try."

"Good have you heard anything about the Taylor's or how things are going with them?"

"The last I talked with Mary she said that Joe was staying away a lot and they could not talk with any civil words so she has thought that Joe was going somewhere else for his comfort instead of her."

"Why would he do that Mary is very attractive and smart why would he go somewhere else. I think you must have heard wrong I do not believe he would do such a thing. I know he loved his family very much and has told me so lots of times before this happened with Betty."

"I know but she is very discouraged about it. She is not herself any longer, and I cannot help her because I do not know what to tell her about their relationship, or if Joe is staying with some other woman as she thinks. Why don't you go and talk with him and see if you can get any information from him?"

"Like what do I say? Hey Joe, I hear you are messing around with some other woman. Are you sick or just letting rumors take over your life?"

"No just go and talk with him asking him if you can help with anything, but do not mention anything about his sex life."

"Good morning mom and dad what is for breakfast?"

"Gabby, what would like is your sister up yet?"

"I did not check to see."

"I can fix you some pancakes if you like. I know Jan would eat some."

"Just forget it I will get some cereal. You always fix what Jan likes."

"Say young lady you asked what was for breakfast and your mother said she would fix you some pan cakes. Now you will eat them and if you cannot get up in a good mood then you stay in bed until you can come down here and act hospitable to your peers."

"I am sorry I will eat the pan cakes."

"That is better now go and wake your sister."

"Dad do I have too?"

"What, you're too big to mind."

"No!"

Yes you have too."

Going to the stairs and speaking rather loudly she says.

"Jan! Dad said it is time for you to get up. Mom is cooking pancakes for breakfast."

"I don't need you to wake me up to eat breakfast so go away."

"I told her but she is not coming."

"You set down and fix your plate and I will go and get her."

Gabby thinks to her self-Jan sweetie it is time to get up mommy has pancakes ready for you. Then she will say okay mommy I will be right there. Then she bows her head to thank Jesus for the food she is going to eat.

"Dear Lord Jesus thank you for this food to help me grow. Help me to be more at ease will I am in the presents of my family. Please be with grandma Hedi and grandpa Tom and help then get through another day. Keep looking for Betty and help her to come back home. I ask your help in her family. I hear it is going the wrong direction, and if you don't hurry Betty will not have a place to come home too. I pray for your love to surround then and hold them together in Jesus I ask these prayers. A-men."

"Why are you always praying so long?"

"Why are you such a nosey person?"

"Because I want to know."

"Then leave me out of your knows."

"Mom Gabby is getting sassy with me."

"Gabby it is time to be civil to your sister."

"Yea, be civil to me."

"You don't even know what that word means and if you ever know then you will know just how you are."

"Mom!"

"Girls I don't want to hear any more."

* * * * * *

"Betty come in here I have something for you."

"Whatever it is I do not want it."

"It is your new school books I got you the wrong ones I thought you were in the fifth grade. So I went and got a higher grade for you so come and see if you want to study from these?"

"These books are for the seventh grade. I am in the sixth grade I cannot do these I will miss one whole year of school and will not know half of the problems or answers."

"Well this is what they gave me for your age. This says grade seven age fourteen so this is what you need."

"I am only thirteen and in the sixth grade what is wrong with you if you were my mother you should know this without asking."

"I am your mother and it has been a long time so you have to bear with me in some things."

"Where is this so called dad of mine. He is never here?"

"Thomas has to work and it is a long ways from

here so he does not stay here much while he is working so far away. Maybe sometime soon he will get work closer to home."

"What does he do?"

"He works for a mining company out of Canada, and do not worry your pretty head he will show up when we least expect him too."

"What kind of mines does he work in?"

"Gold, silver and some copper."

"Then if that is true then why do we have to live in this shack of a house out here in nowhere land? Why can he not buy a better house?"

"Because this is where we want to live. Now go check out these books and tell me if you are smart enough to do them."

"I am smart enough that you and Thomas are not my real dad and mom, and you have kidnapped me, and everything you have told me is just one big, big, big lie."

"I have told you enough times that this issue is not up for discussion any more so now go and do as I told you."

Gabby I need you and your God I don't know how to pray like you did, I wish my grandma Hedi or you could feel how I feel and try to help me. This life I now live is so much different than when I was living by you. Jesus as Gabby would say please help me to sort this life out. If this is what I think life is then I do not want to be here. If you are Gabby's Lord and the same for grandma and grandpa and Gabby's family, then why is my family so left out and things happening to me and them. What are they doing, do they exist any longer? I am asking you for your help in the same way you help them. I don't know if you hear me or not maybe not, but I wish you would come and help me get away from this life. Thank you for listening and maybe someday I will be able to truly talk to you.

* * * * * *

"Gabby would you come in here I want to talk to you?"

"Yes dad can I finish my paper first?"

"When you are done, then you come and see me."

"Okay dad I am done what do you want?"

"What I want is for you to be truth fully with me and yourself. I want to ask you a few questions and I want you to tell me just how you feel about each question. First do you care about your future and what God has in store for you?"

"Yes dad why do you ask."

"Since this tragedy with Betty your grades have fallen to just passing instead of at the top. I would like for you to tell me why and when do you expect to bring them back up like they were."

"Dad I am trying but I have no one to study with and that has over whelmed me to not try. I want to do better but I need someone like Betty to help me stay focused I guess."

"Gabby listen to me you and you alone are responsible for yourself and what happens during that life span that God has given to you. Your mom and I along with teachers and friends who care about you and the God you serve are here to help you, but you have to learn to draw your strength from Jesus Christ and let him help you to get information or knowledge from us. That is what we are here for to stand behind you and help guide you through your learning years as we all grow. Now the big secret is not what we have it is that you will listen and do from our experience to help you from the time you were conceived in your mother's womb. Now tell me am I getting into that mind of yours or am I wasting my time?"

"Yes dad I know but it is not easy for me as a child

to reach out when God let this tragedy happen to my only friend. I pray and ask for help but I get none in return so I just don't have the energy to move forward. I know I am hurting myself but I am still in a hole and cannot find a way out."

"Okay I will think about this and get back to you on my thoughts."

"Thanks dad is that all."

"No second I want to know if you care about your family and how we feel and others think when they are here. Does your grandma Hedi and grandpa Tom mean more to you then us who live in this home with you? Why do you confide in them and not us?"

"Dad I just told you, and yes I care about my family I love you and mom and try to be a good sister to Jan., but Jan gets everything she wants and I get into trouble so she can get a high for doing it. I have no problem with confiding with grandma and grandpa because they listen to my problems and then they pray for me. They do not ask questions the way you and mom do they just listen. You and mom want to know things that I cannot tell you and you both get upset when I cannot answer your questions the way you want them answered. I do not want to be this way but you give me no way out. You are asking me the same questions you asked me back when we returned from the ski trip I still do not know what you want to satisfy your thinking so I say nothing. I have a feeling Betty is not coming back and I know that I have to recognize that she is not, but it is like a tooth ache that will not go away, and no one wants to let go because they are not satisfied I am okay with it."

Don gets up and goes to his daughter and puts his arms around her and holes her for a long time and then saying.

"Sweetheart dad is so sorry for what you have gone

through, and I am sorry that I could not see to help you, but what has been a part of this has been hurting you instead of helping and comforting you. Please forgive me and I will talk to mom about this. I know sometimes we let Jan get away with things but now it has become and ongoing thing and we have done nothing to stop it. I promise you this will change she is not the baby any more, but is old enough to know she cannot hurt you to get back, but you have to stop putting her down on things so she will not bother you anymore. Do we have a deal to help get Gabby back to the old self when she was a happy girl?"

"Yes dad I will try, but I need help for the future not the past."

"Gabby I am glad we had this talk."

"Me to dad."

"Can we see some improvement by the end of school? I am so proud of you and love you very much. Can I pray that Jesus will intervene in our lives to help us get through this time?

"Yes dad."

"Dear Father God in Heaven as my daughter and I set here in your presence I ask that you let the wisdom of your son Jesus and the comfort of your Holy Spirit shower down up on us. Let it also happen in the Spirit and soul of my wife and her sister so that all can have the joy back on our lives. Help Gabby with the mind problem she has faced and let her overcome the pain of her loss. Also we ask that somewhere and time you will also comfort Betty where ever she is and whatever she is going through. Let her know that we are still praying for her. Thank you for this day and with the strength you have over all things. These we ask in your precious name Jesus. A-men."

"Thank you daddy for becoming my size for this short time."

"You are so welcome."

With one last hug from dad she darts off to her room to change clothes so she can go see grandma Hedi and grandpa Tom.

$$* * * * * *$$

The school year is almost over Betty has decided she has to study even though she has not been given high marks during her home study, but her test grades were higher. So she would pass into the next year grade even though she was working one year above her should be grade. Her tests were done during the scrutiny of her mom most of the time she really never cheated. Even though she had access to her manuals on the hardest problems. Her kidnapping mom didn't seem to care. When she was done with all her test she had been doing then for one whole week. They were graded s she finished each test page. She had five pages for the six subjects she had not studied. Her final score was eighty-seven out of one hundred, which gave her a (b) average for the year. She had to set until all pages were graded and tailed up before she was told.

"Betty you have done very well your score is a (b) average for the year. I knew all along you could do it if you put your heart into your work. Now how do you feel about this life?"

"I do not like it. I never will like it. I am bored to death and have wanted to die a lot of times. I have no friends and I want to know why we are stuck way out here. Thomas is never here and we go nowhere. Don't you believe there is something wrong with the way we live? Why do you put up with this life when I know it could be better? I need someone to talk to besides you because I never know if what you are telling me is a lie or the truth. I wonder if you know the difference. Do not tell me to go and play with them dirty Indian kids who do not speak so I can understand them. I want out of here if you like this kind of life then you stay, but I want out. Next time Thomas comes back I am going to tell him he is wrong to make us stay out here in this worthless whatever country. You people are sick to want to live like this and not want something better."

"Young girl you are dead wrong this is a beautiful place and Thomas and I like it a lot that is why we stay here. Soon Thomas will have his old job back and he will be gone only during the week and home on the weekends. Living out here is the only way we can save any money for our later years. Is that too much to ask for, don't you care about our old age time or how we will survive when Thomas cannot work any longer."

" I don't care about your old age I will not be here so don't expect anything from me. I hate this life and this place you call a home, and you and Thomas for making me live here. I know you would feel better if I was gone so take me back to my old home so I can enjoy them. Then you can set around here and talk to your self and think about whatever you think Thomas is doing for the two of you whatever that is he is doing."

"One day you are going to be sorry for saying all those mean things to your mother. I care about you and what is going to happen to you. Why can't you realize that and quite being such a big brat? Before long you are going to become a young woman and you will need my advice on how to cope with the change in your body."

"I already know about that my real mom told me about it a long time ago. So I don't need any advice from you about it."

"You wait and see you will need me some day and I might treat you just the same way you are treating me. I let you get away with a lot that if Thomas was here you wouldn't get away with so easy he would not tolerate some of your smart mouth ways. He would punish hard for saying anything back to him like you do to me."

"Yea just like when he comes home every five or six weeks for one day and one night and you two carry on like teenagers and then he leaves so just tell me how tough he is. He never says more than hi and bye to me I don't think he cares about me as a daughter I believe the two of you kidnapped me so you would have someone to stay with you."

"You ungrateful little snip I hope someday you have a child just like yourself and then you will know how I feel about the way you treat me all the time."

"I will never have a child just so someone like you and Thomas can come and steal it away and treat it the way you two treat me. I don't want to talk to you any more so go away and leave me alone."

As Betty was setting they're all alone the front door burst open and Thomas slid through asking.

"Where is Karen?"

"In there."

"As she pointed towards the kitchen. Thomas half ran into the kitchen and then after Karen had said hello they were whispering very low. Betty got up and crept towards the door and heard Thomas say.

"I had to run they almost caught me so now I have to get another job. I did not have time to get my last paycheck."

"How did they find you?"

"I do not know I was working under a different name, but I looked out the door and there they stood with pictures and talking to the Forman, and he was pointing towards where I was working. I ran for two days before I had the nerve to ride the bus. I have been all over five states trying to lose them. I walked for three days to get here. I don't think they can find me."

"I thought you were paying them back."

"I was but since we got Betty I have not sent them any money so I guess they decided to come and get it. We had better drop this until later so as the child does not know why I am home so soon from the last time."

"She will never stop hating us, to figure it out, to know what is wrong. I am glad you are here I have been itching for you really bad, and now I could almost cry that you are here to help me with my problem. Betty finished her test and did really well she got a (b) average and I think she could do better but she still wants to defy us when we are trying to help her."

"I am going into the bath room and clean up I probably smell it has been almost two weeks since I was clean."

"Good I will finish here and come in and wash your back really good if you want me too?"

"That sounds great to me."

Gabby tiptoes back over to the easy chair and goes back to what she was reading when Karen comes in and tells her.

"Thomas has come home and is going to be here for a while so I want you to go to your room and be quite until he unwinds he is taking his bath at this moment and I need to wash his back to get the pores open then I will fix something to eat for dinner. I will call you when it is ready and you had better be extra good so Thomas won't get upset. Can you remember that much?"

"Yes I will be extra good for sir Thomas you had better go and wash his back side so he will not smell."

"You little creep I should slap the snoot out of you, but it would do no good. Now you go to your room and stay there."

"Yes mommy you go and make daddy happy and I will not bother either one of you."

Betty runs to her room knowing just what is going

to happen and slams the door to put on a good show for her lying mom like she did not know just what was going on. She knew just what was going to happen because it was that way every time Thomas came home. He went to the bathroom and then to the bedroom to take a nap and Karen was with him all the time. She could hear them giggling like two little kids. Betty's real mom had explained it to her when she caught them doing the same thing. But to Karen and Thomas they were not smart enough to know she knew. She did know now that Thomas and Karen was in trouble with someone, but she did not know just who, but they wanted money and Thomas was working under a different name for some reason. She now would try to find out what he was doing and try to get to the police and let them know. How she had no idea at this time but she had good ears and quite feet. She would eve drop at their bedroom door and see if she could figure it out. Until then she was going to act just like she had been doing since they kidnapped her.

"Betty dinner is ready in fifteen minutes and you can come and set the table for three people."

"Okay."

Was her accented dull reply.

"Well Betty it is good to see you it has been a rough winter not being able to be here, but I will be around for a while until I find more work. How has you and Karen been getting along?"

"About the same when there is nothing to do but set and study, sleep and study it would be nice to go someplace once in a while just to see if there are other people out there."

"Maybe we can run into town before I go get another job and buy you something special. Maybe I can get a job closer this time. How would you like that?"

"It is not up to me to like or not it is your work and

you have to pay the bills not I. So you can do whatever makes you happy and I wish I could do something besides just set around here doing nothing."

"Why don't you get to know some of the kids that live around here who knows they just might like to play with a white girl?"

"I do not want to play with kids who smell like they never take a bath."

"They take baths I am sure it is what they eat that makes then smell the way they do. Just because they look poor does not mean they do not care. So I want you to make an effort to get to know some of them. You just might be surprised to know they are just like you with different colored skin, and you would turn brown if you spent as much time outside as they do. You would feel better with the sunshine pouring vitamin C into your body."

"I don't need any vitamin C I need to get back to where civilized people live. I want to go home but I know I am just talking to my self and getting used to it."

"If you would quit fighting this life you would be better and much happier so why don't you try harder to like it."

"Because I do not like it and I don't want to like it and I will never like it I just don't want to be held here against my will when I know both of you are lying to me about this whole thing."

"I think you should go to your room and think about this and we will get to more of it in the morning. So good night to you."

Betty gets up and giving him one of her looks and stomps to her room and slams the door. Thomas follows her and opens the door saying.

"If you want this door left on this room then I had better not hear it slam again. If not, I will remove it and your pride will go out to the burn pile. Do you hear me or do I have to make it plainer?"

"I hear you."

"You remember that because wither I am here or not when I come back I will make my word good and this door will come off and you can dress in front of anybody that walks past and I will not care. No more okay end of story."

Betty just stares in disgust to think she has to live like she is. Thomas slowly closes the door until she heard the click of the latch then it was quite. She knew where they had gone and what these talks were all about. It was just saying stay in your room until we are done doing our thing and then it will be okay again.

Her mind starts to wonder around and Gabby came in and she thinks about all the fun they had, had together and wondering if Gabby had found a new friend or not. She thought about Gabby praying and wondered how she was supposed to do it so Gabby's God would listen and help her out of this miserable condition she was in.

She thought about her mom and dad and even her little brother Al even now she would like to see him. Knowing he probably had not changed from his usual attitude towards her. And before she knew it she was asleep even without removing her clothes. She woke later because she had to go to the bathroom and found that her door was not shut like it was supposed to be. She would have to sleep lighter when Thomas was home, and not knowing just what he might do to her when Karen was sleeping. If he wanted to harm her she would only have her voice to scream to stop him.

# PART FOUR

# CHAPTER SEVEN

Gabby had brought up her grades and has had a better attitude since her dad talked with her. She has spent almost six months trying to understand the reason Betty had to go away, and the way it happened. Now that her return will never happen and hanging onto a dream she had, had brought nothing but grief into her life. Until her dad had talked to her. The only one who had a good relationship with her was her grandma Hedi and grandpa Tom. She still spent a lot of time at their house-helping grandma Hedi to clean and do things she was getting to old to keep up with. Grandpa Tom was not getting around very good and used a walker most of the time. Since it had warmed up he spent most of his time setting on the porch watching whatever moved. He was getting to know more about the birds that he had come to know that spent time in the trees and bushes in the front yard. Grandma Hedi and Gabby found a bird watching book at a yard sale for him.

Gabby's parents gave him a pair of binoculars that they did not use anymore. He could now see them better and up close. Grandma Hedi spent a lot of her time making stocking hats for the church ladies missionary work for the Indian children out west. She had made almost three hundred hats during the last school year for Gabby and was going to stop at five hundred hats. Gabby very seldom missed a day going to see them. She liked the time both of them prayed for her and still prayed for Betty and her family.

It is her last day of school before summer break and Gabby got out early and stopped early so she could spend her extra time with the two people she could relied on the most. As she came up the street she saw Grandpa setting on the porch he looked like he was taking his nap so she tip toed up on the porch and set down beside him and waited to see if he would wake up. After a few minutes' grandpa Tom startled her by saying.

"Young lady I am to wise for you to sneak up on me. How long were you going to set there before you said something?"

As Gabby jumped she said.

"Grandpa I thought you were asleep and I did not want to wake you. Then you half scared me out of my clothes because I was not expecting anything. Now I know you were just playing with me. I would have set here all afternoon rather than wake you. Just to be close to you is enough for the day. Besides I was saying a little prayer for you while I thought you were asleep."

"I never sleep I just watch the back side of my eye lids to see if there is anything important written there. Then I think of all the things I have done and all the things I wish I had done if I would have taken the time to do them. After our son grew up and got married then left for Texas to work we became like two old bears and started hibernating for the rest of our lives. Then these two sweet girls came by to help and cheer us up. Now we love the time we get to spend with them."

"But Betty is not here anymore."

"She is still here in our hearts and that gives us time to pray for her, and the other one who is still here. That now makes our lives worth living again. Some day you will know just how much old people need some new young lives to come along and care for us. We may not be here if it wasn't for you and Betty to come into our lives and wake us up out of the deep sleep we were in. you have become our grandchildren because we very seldom get to see our real grand children because we can no longer travel that far to see them."

"Grandpa they could come and see you."

"Yes they could but they are very small and the job my son has he cannot get away too easy to bring them up to see us."

"Well then you will just have to settle for me and only me since Betty is no longer here."

"Right now you are all I need soon I will need Grandma to help me get inside but as long as I can soak up this sunshine I am very happy. God has given me more than I had ever expected. He will see me through until he comes to take me home."

"Grandpa God is so good to us and I wonder why he did not do the same for Betty. I will never understand why he let her be taken away from us."

"Child by the time you are my age you will know more and probably understand what you do not know now. I want you to remember we cannot blame God for all the things that happen in our lives. We are supposed to get wise counsel for everything we do, and say not that Betty had any choice of her own, but since then we are to be responsible for ourselves by asking Jesus to come and set, and walk beside us. When we don't then we cannot blame Him just because he is all-powerful and could have stopped it before it started. We have to be a little bit responsible for our own actions. Let me explain a small idea so you can understand better. When life as we know it started for us we were all born in his likeness. Not that we all looked alike or was all male or female, but in the same common bodies so we all have the same position in this life. As we grow up the things he gave us like brains developed in the same manner unless we did not use the common senses to acquire the knowledge we needed for the next day in our life. That puts some of us a little smarter than some of the others, but we are still in his likeness just not in the same atmosphere level in our thinking. What I am saying some of the blame was Betty's and some of it was her parent's because of their responsibility as her parents. They should have taught her about going anywhere with strangers without asking. So Betty did not have the knowledge she needed when she was abducted and not knowing what to do at the time. The rest of the blame is on the two who kidnapped her and their parents for not raising them in the right realm of living. That puts the evil one the devil in their corner and he resides over their conscience and that over rides their common sense leaving them to be judged very harshly by Jesus when they come before Him. Believe me there will be a day, and time they will not like very well. I hope this will help you in some small way until you can have the wisdom to decipherer this with your Lord and Master. Jesus in your heart is all the wisdom you need but to us we need to keep wisdom we need to keep the common senses and the knowledge all in the same place all the time."

"Thank you grandpa, but where did you learn all this that you tell me?"

"It comes with age and someday you will know all I know and probably more. Just remember in this life God will give you something's and if you use them well, or to glorify Him he will give you much, much more."

"How does he give us things that are stored in our mines?"

"As I say some comes from us going to school, and while we work, but most comes from the word SOHK which means the school of hard knocks. That is where we learn the most. That is by not making the same mistake over and over again. When we make a mistake we should learn one very important lesson. That is to try not to make the same mistake again."

"Thank you grandpa, I love you, and it is getting late and I should be going home. I will go in and say by to grandma. Do you want me to tell her that you are ready to come inside?"

"You tell her to come when you get ready to leave and that will be fine with me."

Gabby goes into the house to talks to Hedi for a while and as she comes back she goes over and gives grandpa Tom a kiss on his cheek, and tells him.

"Goodbye grandpa."

"Goodbye child and thank you for the kiss I thought you had forgotten it this time."

"Never grandpa see you tomorrow sometime."

On her way home Gabby thought about why God had brought grandma Hedi and grandpa Tom into her life when she had no grandparents or even to know what they were for. Now she could not thank God enough for them in her life. They were nothing to anyone else that was close and she delighted that they were there for her. When she arrived home Jan was setting on the front porch and when she saw Gabby she jumped up and was screaming at her sister.

"Where have you been I have been setting here for over an hour? You wait until mom and dad gets home you are going to pay for this leaving me set out here to freeze.

You are one sick sister I wish I had a brother instead of you. Now open this door so I can get inside; you are so stupid."

"Jan I am not your keeper the key is in the same place as it always is, all you had to do is get it and go inside all by yourself. The only person around here that is sick is you, and your attitude about what you believe everyone should be doing for you and you do nothing in return."

"Shut up, you get the key it is not where it is supposed to be so how could I use it to get in?"

Gabby went to the flowerpot and the key was not there.

"Where did the key go?"

"Why are you asking me I did not take it."

"Then mom or dad must have move it and forgot to tell us. You see it is not my fault you could not get into the house."

"So what are we going to do?"

"We set until one of them gets home to let us in."

"I am not going to set here that long with you."

"Good then go around the back and set by yourself because I am setting right here until they come."

Jan jumped up and went around the house mumbling to herself. Gabby instantly set down and started talking to Jesus.

"Dear Jesus what am I to do this is the last day of school and I have all summer to be strapped with Jan who for some reason that I do not know can never be civil to me. I am asking for your help to make her to be of a right and sound mine, and be able to live with. I will do anything you ask of me, but you have to let me know that promises and actions are not something she believes in. I ask for your help so I will not be miserable all summer. If you can't find the time for her then find time for me to be able to hold up under the pressure that she makes me go through. I love you Jesus and I want to serve you some day when I get big enough. Help me to be molded to what you want me to be in my life while I am here. I ask you again not to forget Betty where ever she is. In your precious name I pray. A-men."

When she looked up there was Jan stating at her then asked.

"Were you praying for Jesus to save you from mom and dad well I just do not think it will work. You are going to be in big trouble when they get home."

"Jan please go away and leave me alone."

"Well, well I see mom coming up the street so now it is going to start I hope you are ready."

Jan runs to the car and it talking very loud even before the car door is opened.

"Jan what seems to be the problem why all the hollering?"

"Gabby hid the key and then she left me setting here for hours waiting for her to come home from school. She will not tell me where she hid the key, and I cannot get into the house."

"Gabby why did you do that?"

"Mom I do not know where the key is, it is not where it is supposed to be. When I got here I looked in the flowerpot and it is not there. I have been listening to miss loud mouth for longer then I want to. So why would I take the key so I could listen to all the crap she has to put out by going on and on about it."

"Well I see the key is missing so we will have wait and see if dad knows anything about it."

"I can hardly wait when he knows and he is going to sock Gabby up the side of her head."

"Jan your dad is not going to do no such a thing. We will get to the bottom of this as soon as he gets home so each one of you go to your rooms and change and then come and help me in the kitchen."

Jan has decided that she is going to get Gabby into trouble so she sets by the front window waiting for her dad to come home. When she sees his car coming she jumps up and shouts.

"Gabby you had better come up with that key because dad just drove into the driveway, and I am going to tell him how you hid the key so I could not get into the house."

Jan rushes out the door before anyone could say anything. When her mom got to the porch Jan was waving her arms and talking a mile a minute to her dad. Sue goes to the edge of the porch and calls Jan back.

"Jan you get in this house you have caused enough trouble over this key thing. Don will you come in and talk to me before you get all bent out of shape over what she is telling you."

"Yes hon.! I will be right up.

Jan I have heard enough from you now go and do what your mother said for you to do. Your mother and I will get to the bottom of this without your input on what you believe happened. Sue I will be right in; I do have some things I need to get from the trunk first."

"Dad what are you going to do to Gabby?"

"It is what I am going to do to you if you do not get a move on."

Jan stomps off with a smirk on her face and shuts the door a little hard on her way in. Don get through and enters the house.

"Sue come and tell me what is causing all the ruckus about this key and what key are we talking about?"

"The key that is for the front door that is supposed to be in the flower pot is not there and Jan thinks that Gabby took it so she could not get in the house. Gabby was late because she stopped at Hedi and Tom's. Did you remove the key? If not then we need to know just where it went, or if someone has it that has no reason to have it. If they have then we need to change the lock so they cannot get into our home."

"I did not move the key."

"I did not either and if the girls did not then we have a key snitcher and that could cause trouble."

"I will go out and look around maybe it was misplaced from the day before."

Don goes and searches all around the pot and other pots and at the third one he finds the key. He puts it back where it was supposed to be and goes back inside he says nothing until Sue asks.

"Did you find anything in your search?"

"Yes I did and I want to know who used the key last yesterday after school. Gabby was it you?"

"No! Jan was home when I got here."

"So now it was Jan who stole the key."

"Dad I did not steal the key I know Gabby took it so I could not get in."

Jan I found the key in the pot next to where it is supposed to be, and if I heard right you were the last one to use it. So as of now you are the one miss placed it and was then blaming your sister. I believe that you owe her an apologue for your sharp retort towards her. Then after supper you and I will retire to my study and have a large discussion on what will happen to you. Now if dinner is ready we can eat because I can hardly wait to start this discussion."

"Dinner is serves when you all get seated."

"Dad what are you going to do to me?"

"Jan you have one strike against you about the key and two strikes against you because I have not heard your apologues to your sister how sorry you are for your mouth and actions against her. Now you know when I find three strike against you it is not good now would you like to keep talking or do as you are told."

"Don you do not have to be so hard on her."

"She is old enough to do the responsible thing all the time. This is going to be between Jan and I and I am going to change the plan around here. She is old enough to constantly get her sister into trouble all the time, and I have had all of it I can stand she is going to grow up fast or she is going to have a lot of trouble setting for a while. It is time you and I wake up and see that all the trouble is not caused by Gabby."

"Okay! Okay! I am with you but don't be too harsh on her because you are just a little upset at this moment."

"I am very much in control at this time and I had better hear an apologues very soon."

Jan puts her head down and stares at her plate and then says.

"I am sorry Gabby I thought you took the key."

"Now to show us that you are all grown up go and look Gabby in the eyes and tell her again."

Jan looks at her mom and starts to say something and her mom tells her.

"You go and do as you were told."

She looks at her sister and then starts and stops and then says.

"Gabby I am sorry for what I said to you and about what I said to mom and dad. Will you forgive me this time?"

"Jan I forgive you this time and every time, but it hurts me that my sister does not care about how I feel."

"Okay now that we are done eating let's get to the dishes and when they are done Jan I want you in my office and bring the large wooden spoon with you."

Jan helps with the dishes and knows that she has over stepped the boundaries and now she is going to pay with the seat of her pants. She asked her mom for the spoon and starts to her dad's office.

"Jan, take it like a big girl and let your dad do the talking it will be easier on you."

She goes to her dad's office door and peaks around the door to see her dad staring back at her.

"Dad I am sorry I won't do it again ever."

"Come in and take a seat and I will do the talking, you keep quiet, and give me the spoon,"

"Yes dad, please."

"Quite set down and listen to every word I say because I don't want to do this again. Do you know how hard it is for your mom or me to punish you children? It is one of the hardest things we have to do especially after all the training we have given you. When you do not learn from the training it is then that we have to take to the harsh means to adjust the problem that you so not seem to understand. I am going to tell you a few things that I know you should know by now, and when I am done I am going to take this spoon and set them in your mind from the bottom up. So I want you to give me your full attention. First you are old enough to be a more responsible person. I know that some of that is your moms and my faults, but from now on you are going to be very responsible for the action that you do and you will have to stand the test of punishment at any given time. There are seven reasons I am going to talk to you about. Number one is R for reading. I know you are not trying and you will from now on read more books and papers so you can understand what it means for your life. Number two is R for writing now you do a sloppy job and you do not seem to care if it gets better. But you will because you are going to spend the whole summer preparing your writing. Number three is R for arithmetic I cannot say too much about this because it happens to be one of your better subject. So that R will not be very high upon my list for the summer. Number four R is for religion that is for everyone to have something very solid to believe in. you like Sunday school and church, but you will study the ten commandments until you know them left to right and all in-between until you understand them and I will be the teacher. Number five R is for respect this you are very far down the ladder maybe in the hole under it. You do know the word but you do not understand the meaning. From now on you will respect your sister, mother, and me, and anyone else that you come in contact with. Respecting others will show that you care and then in return they will show you the same respect. I want you to ask yourself if you think Gabby respects you for the way you treat and act towards her. Number six R is for responsibility this is you doing things that you are told to do or have been told to do without constant reminding you of that over and over again. This you do without pouting, complaining, or blaming anyone else because you have to do it. By doing the job whether it is your mother, I or your teachers, which will make you responsible in our eyes and will then trust you to do even greater things. Number seven R is for rendering that means changing something from little or no value into something of great value. Right now that means you and there is going to be a big change in you Jan Meede and it is going to hap-pen between now and when you go back to school. Even if it takes a whole lot of these spoon to get you oriented in the right direction. Now you pull up that dress and bend over my knees."

"Dad."

"Do it now."

"Dad boo, hoo, hoo."

As she sobbed, and then pulling up her dress and proceeded to bend over her dad's knee. The tears were flowing and she could not keep from shaking. Dad took the spoon and broke it in half with his hands and then told her.

"You take this and give it back to your mother. Then

you go and take your bath and go to your room for bed and until in the morning you think about what I have told you. Now and from now on the most important is that you will do all the things you are asked to do and never complain about doing them. I don't want to discuss these things ever again because if I have to you will not get off so easy. If you have any questions about them you ask, and the next time I will not break the spoon but I will ware it out on your little bottom do you understand everything I have said?"

"Yes daddy, and I am very sorry."

"I do not want to hear you're sorry I want you to show all of us just how sorry you are. Now off with you, but first I want my goodnight hug and kiss. I need then because I love you and I need to know if you love me."

He got his hug and kiss and Jan left without looking back.

* * * * *

Betty has come to the conclusion that her life is never going to change. The place and time has edged into her as a waiting place that she is not going to get out of until she is old enough to escape on her own. There is no way for her to get away. Thomas is always going take her into town but he is never around. He shows up for his sex life one or two days each month. They still fight and send her to her room so they can go and do their thing. Karen is like a snail she never wants to go anyplace. She just sets around the house doing nothing. The neighbor man brings the food that she orders but he never stays very long and says almost nothing while he is there.

Karen is up a lot at night and Betty hears her talking to someone but it is so soft that she cannot hear anything but the noise. There is no phone so she has to be talking to herself or someone. Betty hears but is not interested in who and goes back to sleep. It is still a boring place if it was not for her studies she could go mad doing nothing. She has never helped with the cooking but does do the dishes and her laundry. Karen hardly ever talks to her unless she wants some help doing something. Betty returns the favor and asks nothing and says nothing unless spoken too.

Once in a while Karen gets lonely because she gets all dressed up just to talk to Betty. Not too often but every week or so. Betty is always doing her studies and today she is having a problem understanding her math when Karen comes in all dressed up nice and primped and starts to be extra nice.

"Good morning to you young lady you look great are you having a good day?"

"Good afternoon and no I am having a terrible day and this math is not getting any better."

"Well I am not good at math so you will have to wait for Thomas to come home. He will be able to help you he is good with math."

"When Thomas comes home I will be a year older he has not been home for over a month already."

"He is working extra-long hours and six days a week and they are behind on their orders so he cannot take any time off, but he is going to come home soon. I got word from him and he misses me and you a lot."

"Yea, he misses you in the bedroom not me. I am glad he does not come home every time he does I know he comes into my bedroom when I am sleeping. I don't know what for but I know because the door is not shut the next morning."

"He probably is just checking on you he would have no other reason to come into your room."

"I don't like the way he looks at me sometimes he is creepy and that scares me."

"I will have a talk with him when he comes this next

time and tell him to stay out of your room. Can you tell me if he has ever touched you in an un-approving way?"

"No! And he had better never."

"I don't believe he will ever besides I am all his and willing to do as he wishes. You are not built good enough for him he likes his woman robust and free. You are just a little flat and skinny so you don't have to worry."

"Karen you can tell him that if he ever tries I will try to kill him in his sleep. So you want to keep him even though I believe he is with someone else. Because, he is gone too long at each time. Even when he comes he only stays one or two days at the most so why do you put up with him? I don't care if he stays away forever."

"You ungrateful kid he is your dad and you talk about him like he was a criminal."

"Well you have just realized your so called husband is a criminal like kid napping me. He should be in prison looking out threw the bars."

"It is not a crime to take your own children."

"It is when they are not yours."

"Betty you are child you're so called other parents stole you from the hospital and left their sick child for us. So if anyone should be in prison it should be them for what they did to your real parents and family. I do hope that someday you will come to know that we are telling you the truth about this.

"The truth is you took me, and I lost my best friend and sister my brother and grandparents. You have gained a child who hates the ground you two walk on, and I will make you remember it for as long as you live and I am trapped here with you. I don't care what you and that Thomas try to tell me I know it is not true and never will be. If you cared about me, you would let me go back to my real home and friend."

"Betty I don't want to argue with you, I do know that someday you will learn to love Thomas and I."

"Yuck! I would throw up every hour before I would come to love you two. Who could love anyone who lives like you do and are forcing me to live the same way? If I did not still know the truth and that someday soon I will see Gabby again I would try to kill myself. There is nothing around here but you and the snakes and rats, and those ugly kids who live around us and never takes a bath. They smell offal all the time. They are all dumb as a box of rocks."

"That is not true they are just trying to make a living with nothing to make it with."

"Yea right those men set around drinking and let the women or wives do all the work, and most of the time they are running around with no clothes on. How disgusting they are as bad as you and Thomas when he is here.

"We do not run around without our clothes on."

"I have sneaked out and watched you running from your bedroom to the bathroom. I know what you are doing so don't try to lie about it. My mom told me all about what you are doing and I don't care as long as he does not touch me."

"He never would, when two people make love the last thing they need is for one of the two to be a smart mouth like you are."

"Yea just like you get some when Thomas is not here. I see you sneaking out in the middle of the night is it to see one of them men who stink so much how can you stand them?"

"I do not and you had better not be talking to Thomas about anything like that."

"What if I do what can you do about it?"

"I will tell Thomas to attack you and break you in before your time."

"Go ahead and I will kill both of you in your sleep."

"This is going no place I do not want to talk to you anymore."

"Great I feel the same way so go and talk to one of your other men."

"You shut up or I will beat a knot on your dumb head."

"Go away."

"Do you want something to eat?"

"Not if you fix it. If I am going to die it will be by my hands not yours."

"Suit yourself I am going to fix me something."

* * * * *

Gabby felt bad for her sister, but she also thought that she deserved everything she got. Before she went to bed after putting on her nightgown she went to Jan's room. Knocking lightly on the door then pushing it open she saw Jan on her knees at the side of her bed. Then she asked.

"Jan can I pray with you?"

Jan waited for a couple of minutes before she answered.

"If you want to I guess it is alright."

"Jan I am sorry for what dad did to you and I know you feel bad about it, but dad still loves you just as much as before, and I love you too."

"Dear Lord Jesus I am with my sister Jan and I ask for the Holly Spirit to come and comfort her at this time give her wisdom to handle what she has been through. Help her and I to get along better instead of like in the past. I know deep down she is a wonderful sister, and she needs to know to excerpt her feelings in a loving way to all the family and her friends. Help me to less negative towards her and let us be friends as well as sisters. I pray also for Betty wherever she is and that you are protecting her from all harm. Someday Lord would you see if she could come back home. You know how I hurt and miss her. I pray for grandma Hedi and grandpa Tom that they would have a good night's rest and a good day tomorrow. I pray for mom and dad that this evening will go away and that they will be able to sleep through the night and awake with a new beginning along with my sister Jan and I. I ask this all in your precious name Jesus. A-men"

"Good night Jan, see you in the morning."

"Thank you Gabby I really do love you."

# CHAPTER EIGHT

Three years have gone by at this time Gabby will be seventeen years old. There has been no word or news about Betty and she is almost a dyeing dream, but Gabby will not stop praying for her.

Betty's parents, Joe and Mary have been separated for four years, and is now going to start divorce procedures without their girl they have lost interest in a family that is not all there. Al has become one bad boy he is in trouble all the time and he and Jan have become close but her parents are not willing to let her go anyplace alone with Al because of his past records. He and his mom Mary still live in the house by Gabby's folks.

Joe has been gone from their lives and only corresponds by the check he sends each month for his child support.

The life at the Meede's place has not changed much; only that Jan and Gabby do not fight anymore. Jan has changed her attitude a lot since her dad and her had the big talk; so in three years she has grown up to be a better sweeter person. Her and Gabby do some times go to a movie together. The lives of these two girls has been touched by God in the short time they were together. Gabby has never forgot the feeling she had for Betty it will be in and on her mind for the rest of her lifetime.

At seventeen years old Gabby has one more year of school to finish and then she will decide what to do with her life. She has stated many times that she would like to spend time searching for Betty and hopes at the same time Betty will be looking for her. She plans to go to college in Texas where she can stay with grandma Hedi and grandpa Tom's son and family. She would take care of the two children as a setter or nanny while going to school. After that she would start her search and then come back home to live. Gabby has not accrued no new friends since Betty was taken besides her sister Jan who has become close. At this time, she has been chaperoning Jan and Al to the movies. Even though her mom and dad do not approve of Al they do not say much as long as Gabby is involved still hopping that whatever Jan sees in Al will go away soon. The best they have going for them is that they do study a lot together and that is helping Al get through school. His mother says nothing and approves of their relationship so far. Don and Sue and Gabby pray a lot for God to help Jan not go too far with him. Grandpa said to Gabby one day when she was down to see him.

"Gabby you tell that sister of yours to let that boy go. To find someone else who would be better for her. I believe he just might get her into some big trouble someday. He has a mind that wonders off course a lot. Tell her she has more smarts then to follow him around. She should be leading him out of his problem area."

"Grandpa you know about both of them all their lives and they both are strong headed people doing what they want to do. I don't believe they are strong enough to stop anything is either one of them go to do something wrong, the other will follow just to be involved. Mom and dad says that God will have to be there to stop them and they are afraid to do too much because Jan is helping Al through his school lessons. If she did not help him he would fail and that would end whatever he wants to be. She thinks she is doing a good Christian thing for him, but he will not attend Church and has not excepted Christ into his heart, and say he does not intend to do so."

"Grandma and I will keep praying for them that one will see the light before it becomes too dark for either one of them. As a matter of fact, I feel like praying for them at this moment."

"Dear Father God as Gabby and I set here talking I know you are listening and hear us. So we would like to tell you in person how we feel. We love Jan and Al as you love them and have instructed us to do so. We still keep your hand on them so he cannot pull them into some position that will harm them for the rest of their lives. We are asking favor for the family for what they do and who they are in your sight. We ask that Jan follow your will that you established long ago even before she was conceived. Father God we know you love your children we know you have your reward for Gabby and Jan and as we are praying that you get your reward for Al also. We pray for the love you have for Betty, and that where ever she is you are protecting her from all the evil one's ways. Keep those ways from her and the hurt that can come from them. Keep her safe until she is big enough to help herself. Help her to get free from the bonds that hold her today. We ask all these prayers in your son Jesus name who is holly and pure and your righteousness show through him who is all wisdom and grace. A-men."

"Thank you grandpa I need to go and help grandma Hedi and I will bring you a cup of hot tea if you like."

"I would love a cup of hot tea and thank you for our thoughtfulness and kindness."

"Hi grandma I come to help you with something if you need. I also need to fix grandpa a cup of hot tea."

You are such a wonderful granddaughter to us. And yes you can help me with this cookie mixture my hands are not as strong as they used to be and these are your grandpa favorite cookies. If you do this, I can fix his tea."

"Okay it's a deal and maybe I can stay long enough to have one of these hot cookies with you and grandpa."

You go to work and I will fix the tea and start the oven and maybe we can have more than one in a short time."

"I love you grandma."

"Child you are very loved also and at times I wish your sister would come down to see us. She is just as much a part of us as you were when you and Betty first showed up. I just don't know or understand her and why she is so distant from us."

"Grandma you do not need to worry over her she has no time for anybody but except Al, and we pray for her a lot. Matter fact that is what grandpa and I was doing before I came inside. I believe she is going to get hurt and only by the grace of God will she not. Okay the dough is ready and now to put it on the cookie sheet and shove it into the stove and wait. In fifteen minutes we can have cookies and milk."

"Right if you will take this tea out to grandpa I will spoon up the cookies but do not tell him about them."

Here comes your tea grandpa and soon we will have woops I am not supposed to say anything. Is there anything else I can get for you?"

"Yes when the cookies get done you can bring me some with the milk okay."

"Grandpa how did you know grandma was baking cookies?"

"Because she does them every third day and it has been three days since the last one. I can see her putting them in the oven at this moment. Oh thank you Gabby have I told you how much I love you lately, and how you are like a fresh breath of flowery air that blows past me with the wind. I get this feeling every time I see you."

"Yes grandpa."

As she gives him a kiss on the cheek and starting to return back into the kitchen to help with the cookies and milk she says.

"Yes grandpa every time I come to see you."

"Well it is not enough because someday I will not be here to say it to you. So I thought I had better step up the times I tell you."

"Grandpa one is enough but, I can except as many as you want to give. Now I need to go and help grandma with the cookies and milk or is tea good enough?"

"Tea is good but when you have cookies you need milk to go with them."

"Yes and I will be right back."

As they set and eat their warm cookies Gabby asked.

"Do you think, if Betty ever comes back that she would know me or I know her?"

"Gabby I think she is just like you no matter how far apart you become when you return back together you will always know each other. You two were so close I believe that God would not let that time go unnoticed by just a mere adjustment in time spent apart."

"Grandma I wish I could believe that is true, but do you remember just how long Betty has been gone?"

"Yes child I do and it makes no difference in God's time we have prayed daily for this to happen and I believe it will come to pass. You have to ask yourself if you truly believe the same thing, and that God is slow in our thoughts, but he is very dependable in his actions for us to get what we believe he wants us to be or do in our lives here on earth. What I am telling you is until the day he comes for you

Betty will always be on your mind and whither you see her here or in the hereafter she will always be there, and if you believe she will come then God will send her back."

"I hope so I wonder how long it would take us to bring our lives back up to date you know it has been almost ten years."

"Gabby your old grandpa can remember when ten years was a long time like when I was your age, but now ten years is like soft putty in the sun it goes real fast. You listen to your grandma she will be here for a long time yet but I will be here very short and I feel sorry for her as she will be here all alone after I am gone."

"No grandpa I will be here for her just like I am now, but you will still be here after I go to college that is only one and a half years from now."

"I hope you are right but I have this lowly feeling that you could be mistaken. You see this body is telling me to slow down and I am so slow now I don't feel like I am moving and one day is just like the next. I have no motivation left. If it weren't for your grandma Hedi I could not make it through every day. So I know that God is putting this body too sleep slowly by slowly. I think sometimes I am just too tough for him, but in the end I know and hope he will be the winner." Tom you are not going one day before your time so remember to think positively so this special girl will not worry about you and your time. She loves you a whole lot and you are trying to scare her about your time left."

"I am sorry momma you are right and I am sorry Gabby, but when I got older and things don't work as I think they should and I get discouraged and would just as soon not be here. I am only thinking about myself and my self-pride keeps getting in the way. I am going to be here to see you graduate from high school and college and get you married to one of the best guy I know."

"Grandpa I love you and I know you would like to do more, but in my Sunday school class we were talking about a time to grow, a time to work, and a time to rest you are now in your rest period of this life. And you are going to be very old if you wait until I get married because I am looking for a man just like you. So far I believe that God broke the mold after you and my dad was formed."

"It only takes a few seconds when the right one shows up. You will be lost in the clouds and no one will be able to get to you. I know I found mine and she has not been the same since."

"Tom will you quite teasing this girl she has all the time in the world to find a man, and besides the only one who changed was you so tell her the truth. Now because I have to and clean up the cookie mess before I can get dinner for this old man. Come Gabby and you can help me instead of listening to his furry dreams."

"Okay grandma you two are so much fun to be around, and I like who you are. True christen believers and people who walk and talk the same all the time. I thank God for the privilege of knowing you. I can never forget the first time we meet and that is the most important of our friendship."

"Yes it was a God thing the way we meet."

✳ ✳ ✳ ✳ ✳

After three years of insults and horrid attitudes from Karen and Thomas. Betty is counting her days she is very strong willed. She told Thomas as they were eating breakfast after his one nightstand and had not spoken to her in over four months and at that time he only made fun of her because she was still very small breasted. But in the last three months she had begun to fill out and was bigger than Karen and as she sat there and eating her cereal he then spoke to her.

"Hey sis, are you wearing socks to empress some man around here you seem to have filed out in the chest area very nicely.,"

Betty just looked at him and returned to her eating.

"Hey I am your dad and when I ask you a question I expect an answer, or do I check for myself?"

"If you want to die then you just touch me."

"Still just one little smart mouth kid. I just wanted to know you seem to be out growing your mom. and they look nice on you."

"Thomas knock it off if she does not kill you then I will if you touch her."

"Oh yea, all I have to do is pull mine out and you melt like hot butter, and I am still the man around here paying all the bills so you can hide out here."

"Thomas you should have not said that. that hurts really bad, and she could never give you what I do so drop the dumb talk."

"Well someday I may just have to see if she knows as much as you do. Besides I am getting tired of working away from home for so long. I need to be here taking care of my two girls it seems that you are growing up without me. That I am sorry for, but it is too late to buy the ore's now the boat is about wore out. I have to leave this afternoon so I can get back to my job for in the morning. I have to go into town and pay some bills and then come back and get my suitcases so you can pack them while I am gone and be ready for me when I come home."

"Yea, I will be ready and so will your clothes. I need to go and see my doctor for a checkup so don't be gone to long this time. I cannot walk to town and leave Betty out here alone."

"Okay maybe I can get off an extra day next time. What seems to be wrong you look great."

"Nothing except I have lost some weight and I just wanted to see if there was some reason for it. I still eat the same as I always did and I just want to know. Other than that I am fine so go and do your thing so I can get your things ready for you when you return. How long will you be gone so I will know if I should hurry or not."

"Don't ware yourself out I have something that needs your attention when I get back, and you miss smart mouth I may show you some time and you will then be glad when I come home."

"Thomas she is your daughter and you should not talk to her like that."

"Maybe so but she needs to respect me for who I am. I still have control over her, and I am thinking I should exercise my rights, but it can wait until another time."

Betty jumped up from the table running to her room and shouting back.

"I will kill you if you ever touch me."

Then slamming her door and locking it and placing the chair under the knob, and thinking why do I have to put up with this abuse. If I only knew how to get out of this place. Gabby where is your God, please send him to help me get out of this terrible place. I don't know which direction to go or how far it is. I can't ask these people because as before they go and tell Karen. Please help me to stand it for a while longer, or give me the power to go on my own and show me the way. I am so alone in this desolate place. I have no clothes but the ones I wear every day and they are not that good they do not fit me. They are like a big sack and no under clothes. They are my daily clothes and my nightclothes. Karen has lots of clothes but they would not fit me. Gabby, please help me send your God to help me. Why have I been made to live like this?

Why am I here what am I supposed to be? I am lost to the world I was born into and no way to get out of it. Just like it has been for the last lot of years I am going mad talking to my self all the time. I want to run away but there is no one to help me if I did. These people called Indians play like they do not understand when I ask them, but I know they do because Karen slips up when she is reprimanding me on some things. I see people leaving even Thomas and they are going in different directions, and when I walked down the road a ways it splits into two different directions, and then into more directions. I can see nothing vast nothing less. Today after dinner she wanted to tell me something but had to get to the bathroom to throw up I think something is wrong with her. When I asked her later she said that Thomas was coming home to take her to the doctor but that was over two weeks ago. I think she is down to her last time she has no strength to do anything so I have to take care of her and do all her work. She is huffing and puffing like she had ran a mile and yet she had done nothing. I asked if she wanted one of the men to take her into the doctor, and she just looked at me as if I were crazy or something. When I go towards the door she starts screaming for me to stop. Today I just kept going when I can back with the closest man and interred the house she was slobbering and trying to get up from her chair. When she saw the man she said to him.

"I told you never to come to my house if I needed you I would come to your place."

"Karen he came to take you to see the doctor."

"Thomas is going to take me when he comes. You get out of my house and you Betty never do this again. They are not allowed in this house Thomas will be very upset when he finds out that you brought him here."

"Does she ever come to your house?"

"No we go out into the night and talk."

"Talk and oh never mind I know what she does. So go and leave she will be gone before Thomas shows up to help her."

"I will go to town to find him or someone who does."

"Can I go with you?"

"No I cannot take that chance."

"What chance?"

"You cannot be seen with any of my people outside this area. Thomas will be very upset and do us harm."

"Drop me off outside of town and go find Thomas I just want to leave this place and I don't know where too."

"You stay and I will go into town and find Thomas or see if the doctor can come out here to see her."

That evening Betty saw the same truck come back and later a jeep and stopped and a man come up to the door and knocked.

"Yes may I help you if you are lost I can't because I do not know anything about here so I cannot tell you where to go."

"I am a doctor and I was told a lady by the name of Karen needed me to check her out. The Indian man said she has been sick for a while."

"Come in and yes it has been over a month and she is getting worse every day. Karen this is your doctor."

As Karen looks up with a start and noting that the man was not her doctor, and trying to talk but not able to just batted her eyes and moved her arms but no noise.

"Go ahead doctor she will corporate because she cannot reject anything she is to weak."

Betty leaves the room and could hear the doctor asking Karen questions but was sure he was not getting any reply. After almost one-hour Betty went back to see if she was needed.

"Well doctor what do you think is wrong with her?"

"I will not know until I get her blood tests back and

then I will know more. I do think that the big C has gotten hold of her and is not going to turn loose. She may have a couple weeks or a month but not much longer. Do you know where her husband is?"

"No he comes every once in a while but stays a day or so, but he has been longer in-between in the last six months. I have no way of getting in contact with him."

"Okay I will see you in two days after the blood samples have been returned. If she has much pain, you give her a shot of this. Have you done this before?"

"No."

"It is easy I have the shots all ready and you just wash her arm with this solution and give her the shot and make sure you give it all to her. There is ten shots here and that should be good until I return. Keep giving her plenty of liquids. I am going now are you going to be alright?"

"Yes I guess so."

"Great I will see you in two days."

"Doctor if she dies will you take me out of here?"

"How old are you?"

"I am seventeen I was kidnapped when I was eight and have been held here against my will ever since. I do not want to be here when Thomas returns. He looks at me like he would like to do me harm you know what I mean."

"I will see you in two days and at that time we can make a decision for you. But for now you have to care for Karen until I return"

When the doctor left Betty went into the house and Karen was staring at her and trying to say something, but no sounds were coming out. Betty got a pencil and paper to see if she could write something down. When she had finished writing the note said.

"I know I have not always been a real mother to you and I am sorry, but when I am gone do not stay here with Thomas alone."

As Betty read she knew she had to leave soon as she could doctor or no doctor. Two days went by very slow for Betty. Karen was in so much pain all the time. When the doctor arrived three days later Betty was relieved to know that she was almost free.

"Hi doctor I thought you were not coming; I was becoming very scared that Thomas would return before you did."

"I was waiting on the blood work and it is as I thought she has cancer and the blood counts tells me that it is spread through her body and she needs to be in the hospital because soon she will not even know that you give her the shots the pain will be over baring to her. I suggest that you pack some clothes and a night grown for Karen and we will be on our way. I have a van coming to get her."

"Can I go with you?"

"No I have to make two stops before I go back to town. You will be fine with the person in the van she is my helper on most of the town calls. She will take good care of you. Have you heard from her husband Thomas I believe?"

"No he never sends word he just shows up."

"I will leave him a note as to where she will be. You get ready she will be here in about one hour; I have to go now."

Betty is stiff with fear and the doctor leaves and in about twenty minutes she hears a car drive up and a door shuts. Thomas comes through the door saying.

"Hey! Hey guess who's home. Where is my girl?"

As he sees Karen slumped on the coach he hollers for Betty.

"Betty, get in here what is wrong with my wife?"

"She is dyeing you left last time instead of taking her to see her doctor and now she has to go to the hospital so they can care for her. The van will be here any moment now."

"There is no van taking her anyplace she is my wife and I take care of her not anyone else."

There is a knock on the door and then another. Thomas opens the door asking.

"What do you want?"

"I have come to take a patient to the hospital so she can be better cared for."

"You can leave I take care of my family and I will see to it if she needs a hospital or not."

"Very well I am just doing what the doctor told me, and if you don't want her in the hospital that is your choice. I will tell the doctor you choose to keep her here. Young lady are you alright?"

"No I am scared something will happen."

"She is okay nothing is going to happen I will be here."

"Okay I am gone and I am sure the doctor will come with more medicine to help her with the pain.

"Betty tell me what is wrong and why is she dyeing?"

The doctor says she has cancer over most of her body and may have a week at most."

Betty turns and starts to her room when Thomas tells her he is hungry and for her to make him something to eat. When Thomas comes from their bedroom after taking his clothes in he then walks up and puts his arms around her chest and says.

"Betty you have nothing to worry about I will take care of all your needs and you can take care of my home it will be better when Karen is no longer here to complain about everything I do or say I will not hurt you."

Betty is stiff with the pressure Thomas has on her breast.

"Turn me loose or your food will be burnt."

Releasing her he backs up and turns towards the living room to look and talk to his wife. Betty could hear him asking questions and knowing he was not getting any answers. He returns to the kitchen table and sets down with his hands holding up his head. Betty sets his food down and tells him.

"I am going to my room to study I am way behind while taking care of Karen."

"Okay go."

Betty shuts and locks the door and set on her bed and cries fear has overcome her mind and there is nothing she can do about it. She hears the doorknob rattle and then Thomas voice saying.

"Why have you locked the door open it up I want to talk to you."

"Thomas I am changing into my night clothes just a minute."

Thomas bangs on the door.

"Open this door right now I don't care if you have clothes on or not you do not have to lock this door or any doors in my house. How many times have I told you this?"

Bang. Bang. Betty opens the door and steps back in Thomas rushes grabbing her arm and pushing her towards the bed and pushing her down on her back.

"I told you I am not going to hurt you I want to know what I have to do for Karen she is trashing all over the floor."

"Let me up and I will show you."

Thomas pulls her up by her arm and looks at her like he usually does. Betty almost runs to where Karen is and picking up one of the shots and tells Thomas."

"This is what you do."

she washes her arm and gives Karen her shot and throws the needle in the trash basket.

"Now you wait until she does it again."

"Betty come over here and set by me I need your company this is more than I can stand I come home to be with her and she is not capable of taking care of me so I want you to take care of me like she would have.”

"No! I told you if you try to hurt me I will kill you and I mean every word of it.”

"I am not going to hurt you it is my position and desire to show you what life is all about when you are fully grown up. And I believe you are old enough at this time.”

Betty turns to leave and Thomas grabs her arm.

"I said you come and set by me.”

"I have to go and clean up the dishes and the kitchen if you want to talk after that we can set at the table and talk.”

"Go do your work and start me some clean clothes while you are at it.”

"I do not know anything about the washing machine Karen never told me how to work it.”

"Well it cannot be that hard we can learn together.”

Betty goes to the kitchen and cleans up and fines a way to tape a large butcher knife to her leg and returns to her bedroom.

"I am going to bed I am tired if you need me for Karen you knock on my door but do not come in while I am asleep.”

Later in the night Betty wakes up from the movement of her bed. To find Thomas, setting on the edge in his underwear with his hand on her hip. Jumping sideways she scorns him by saying.

"Get your wicked self out of my room and get your stupid hands off of me.”

"It is okay I need you to help me with Karen. I gave her a shot but it has not helped. What do I do now”?

"Get out of my room I told you to knock don’t you hear anything I say?”

"Get up before I yank you out of this bed. I said I need help with Karen now.”

"Leave and I will get dressed and be right out."

Betty lays there until Thomas leaves then she gets up and dresses, and goes to see what she can do for Karen. When she gets to the living room Karen is lying on the coach very peacefully. Then turning to Thomas she asks.

"Why did you wake me there is nothing wrong with her you have to give the shot time to work I am not going to ask you any more I am telling you stay out of my room."

"I am sorry but I cannot get you out of my mind. You are my family and we are to take care of each other. Why are you fighting me I told you I would not hurt you in any way?"

"Stay out of my room I do not trust you. Your own wife wrote this note to me."

As she handed the note to Thomas and as he read it his face turned red and then looking up at her he said.

"Why would she write this she knew I would never touch you and now that she is out of the picture or soon will be. I will need you to stay here and take care of this home for us while I am at work. I want us to be a family, and you to be friendlier towards me. I do not want to sexually molest you. I am asking for you to corporate with me so I will have a place to come back to. I am getting old and cannot work forever."

"I have never wanted to stay here you and Karen forced me to be here, and now you want me to take care of you and stay here in this wasted place where there is no life only hate and confusion. You have more nerve then a snake why would you think I would stay here especially just to take care of you. I am not going to be some old man's sex goddess every month or so. Even your own wife would sneak out at night to someplace with one of your neighbors to satisfy her own sex life when you were gone for so long. I told you more than once that if you ever hurt me in this manner I will kill you in your sleep. I am not talking here just to hear my self-talk I mean every word of it."

"Okay I will give you time to think about it. I have a lot of money in the bank in town and you can have what you want if you want to change this house then we can do it. I am asking you not to do something that you may regret later in your life. I am a peaceful man and I do care about my family. I need you to stay here and watch out for my belongings that is all I am asking."

"Then go and cover that thing and leave me alone."

Thomas gets up and goes towards Betty with a smile on his face and that look in his eyes.

# CHAPTER NINE

"Mom, dad, you know Betty's birthday is coming up soon, and she will be gone nine years."

"Yes dear why are you thinking of that?"

"I don't know it just came to my mind. Do you think she is in trouble or is it I am just missing her?"

"Could be both but more likely it is the Holly Spirit making sure you never forget about her."

"I think I am going to go and see grandma Hedi and maybe she will pray for Betty she does such a great job talking to God about things."

"You can do that, but we also can pray for her and wish her a happy birthday if you want?"

"That would be great there are times that I know Betty is okay I seem to feel it in my heart. Wouldn't it be wonderful if someday she just showed up?"

"I cannot even think of the happiness that would surround her if she did."

"Do you think she would be upset about her mom and dad, and what would she think about Al and Jan going together?"

"I do not know but it sure would be nice to find out. Come lets pray."

"Dear Father in Heaven as my daughter and I are setting here thinking about a lost friend from some years past. We are wondering if she is still around or has she gone so far that she will never return. No matter what we are praying for your love and mercy and kindness for Betty and that you are still holding her by your side and protecting her from the harms of this world. The most of this prayer is that on the day she was born seventeen years ago and that day she was taken from us that she would know that she is being prayed for and thought about. Please let her have a great birthday on the day she was taken from us. We pray that whatever the case or coarse it is still your will not ours that Betty is living in. Bless her just if you want so she can come back home, and see her dearest friend. We ask this in your son Jesus name. A-men."

"Thank you mom. Dear Jesus please listen to our prayers please comfort Betty so no harm can come to her. I feel that she is still here some place and wants to come back, but is still being held against her will. Even as I know that you have full power over her and can restrain anything from harming her facially or mentally. If for no other reason let her know about the peace that comes with you when she ever accepts you as her Lord and Savior. If I never see her again, please let her come to Heaven when I get there so we can have the time we missed here on earth to spend together up there. I want to thank you for the time we got to spend together even so short. I know that your will is still in control and whatever happens is for good. As you know I used to weep every night, but now I just feel week and unable to understand. I love you Jesus and someday when I grow up to be educated and a woman I can go and serve you in whatever capacity you have molded me to do. I pray in your precious name Jesus. A-men."

"Well young lady that is a big promise and in a short time you will be where you just told Jesus you wanted to be. So be preparing yourself for that time and do not forget. I know Jesus has a place for you in this world and the one that will come tomorrow."

"I am ready but right now I am going to run down and see grandma Hedi and grandpa Tom to see how they are doing. Grandpa is not the same he has had trouble remembering what he was talking about sometimes."

"Okay, give them our love."

"Oh mom you tell Jan if she ever decides to wake up that I will go to the movie with her."

"That is sweet of you Gabby, and I will relay your message when as you say she decides to wake up."

As Gabby walks down to her grandparent's house she cannot get Betty from her mind. She even asks God in her mind why was she so strong at this time what could be the problem. She thought she had restored her thoughts to not be as concerned any longer. As she walked up on the porch the door just opened like by magic and from the darkness inside came the voice.

"Please come on in what a pleasant surprise we have this morning Tom."

"What surprise is that so early must be that wonderful young girl that lives up the street? Give me a minute and I will be right out."

"Good morning grandma you two would make any day a blessing. You are so thoughtful and kind. How has your day gone so far is grandpa doing okay?"

"He always does okay in the morning up until he gets his breakfast and after that he loses his momentum until it is time to eat again. If I would let him eat all the time he would set the world on fire."

"Ha! Ha! Very nice mom so if that is true then where

is my morning food. Gabby how are you, have you eaten. Even so you can eat again we always have plenty."

"Yes I have eaten but a cup of hot chocolate sounds great. I like grandma's she makes it from scratch instead of from a box."

"You learn from her and you will be better off because all that box stuff is made to sell, not to be good for you. You know now this stuff we eat is okay if God has made it but I wonder sometimes if man has taken over whither it is good for us or not. You know our government has to watch out for us me may do something to kill ourselves."

"Tom you hush Gabby did not come down here to listen to you go on about the politics of this country even though you could be right at least part of the time."

"Grandma it is okay I want to know everything that grandpa and you know about life. I do believe that something's are not that good for us to eat, but if it was not available we would not have the time to make it like you and your parents used to do."

"Well thank you and by the way what is going on in your mind today that we can turn into a blessing."

"Mom and I spent time praying for Betty and since I woke up she has been on my mind very strong, and that is unusual so I came to get the advice of the experts because of your age and wisdom."

"Well that could be something of a lot of reasons but to me it may be that her spirit is calling out to you through the angels of protection and you did just what you were supposed to do pray."

"Grandpa you may be right and us old people are still good for a prayer or too. Gabby do you feel anything special while this has been on your mind?"

"No not really but she has not been this strong for a very long time."

"Well then let's let the angels know that we know and

let them carry the message to Betty to let her know that there are still people who care about her and let them do the work."

"I would like that very much it is so heavy that I want to cry but have nothing to cry about because I do not know the why of it."

"The why of it is God's problem we just need to let him know that we still miss her? Do you want to go first my lovely wife my dear?"

"I would be happy too. Dearest God our Father up in heaven we ask you to listen to our prayers let us praise you and your kingdom. We are here with a friend of Betty Taylor her first given name not knowing where she is or if she is in need. We ask for your sovereign power to surround her in protection. We ask that through these prayers over the years that she has been taken care of so she in time will be able to enjoy your Grace and Mercy and in time glorify you in her actions. We are also asking for comfort and release for Gabby so she will know that you have taken care of her friend and helped her to be satisfied that Betty is in your hands. We will keep up the prayers for that is our wish to you and to Betty. I pray this in your Son's matchless name Jesus we know you are here with us today. A-men."

Grandpa Tom had started one of his coughing spells and that stopped the prayer time it was just one of his morning things until he got the lungs and the baronial; tubes cleared so he could breathe normally.

"Grandpa are you okay do you need something to drink?"

Between the coughing he answered.

"Yes and what, what I really need is for you to jack this body up and pull a new one under me in its place. Except my brain and then send the old one on its way. Thank you dear one for this water maybe I can get this taken care of and then I want to pray for my two most precious girls one here and the other somewhere else."

"Dear Lord God it is not good that we get old and have all these problems, but it is a lot worse when someone is so young and has her heart so burdened over the ache of pain of someone she still loves so much. Would you come and ease that pain for her and at the same time let her very best friend even know that she is still thinking and praying for her where ever she is at this time. Let her someday be able set herself free and come back this way even if she is can let us know and we all can help her get back. The burden on Gabby's heart is real to her and that may be that Betty is in dire need of prayer and your help. Let these prayers awaken the life you want for her. She is not a bad girl that we know of. She still needs to know about your Son's wishes for her to be able to except him as her only way into heaven. So she can spend eternity with you and with us who love her so much. You are a God of many miracles and the hope of this world through your son's terrible death on the cross, and with the love you have showed us let this same momentum carry our friend to the same place you have promised us all. I am old and I would trade my life, that which is left for her safe return. So open up the floodgates of your love Grace and Mercy so Betty still has that chance to except Jesus and live a life of hope joy and happiness that she has waiting for her. Lord Jesus we love you and are not asking much because your strength and power over all things even the evil one can overcome all the problems we could ever have. We ask this from you and your will for Betty this morning so in your name we give you our thoughts and our love back to you. A-men."

"Yes Lord all for my friend come into her life in some way. I feel she is still out there and needing our help. I can pray but you can comfort her and protect her from any and all harm that the evil one can put into her life. I ask that you also stay close to my sister, Al, Betty's mom and dad their lives have been turned upside down over this and if for some reason you can see it clear for the two that kidnapped Betty and let their hearts be humbled to realize what they have done to so many other people. That they may be punished for the crime they have committed. Jesus I love you and I know that Betty would too if she ever gets to know you. So we ask and will obey in your precious name, A-men."

"Is it time to eat yet my tummy is saying it is a way past?"

"You wait and I will fix your breakfast. Gabby, keep his mind off food for a while would you."

"Yes and thank you both for inspiring me every time I come to see you. Grandpa in your life how many times have you prayed for someone else besides grandma and your family."

"Well more than I can count maybe two or three or four times a day so could be upwards toward eighty or ninety thousand times. Maybe if I speed up I could make one hundred thousand in my life."

"Does any one or all of them mean more than if you had only said one or two?"

"That would be like every time you come to see me and your grandma I would not say anything to you for a very long time. Prayer is talking with God and Jesus sometimes just to have someone to talk too. And that time spent keeps the evil one from cluttering up your mind with his evil ways."

"Grandpa you are cool you have all the right things to say I hope that someday I can say and do the same things that you and grandma do."

"Well you have the brains and the looks but I believe you need to tax your mind to speak freely and open up your mind that all boys or men soon are not going to hurt you if you get to close to them. God has some one for you, but you have to do that man the same way you did with Jesus. You know Jesus knocked on the door of your heart for a long time before you opened it up to him. You have to let Jesus and the Holly Spirit help you, to open up your heart to some boy or man just like you did for Jesus. God has made a special man for you a long time ago. You are going to be eighteen before long and you have no idea how it is to be or fall in love with someone who is the opposite sex as you are. I want to see you married to the man God has for you, but if you don't get started soon I am not going to be here to see if you ever see how that feels."

"Grandpa I may never get married."

"Is that to say that you do not want the happiness that God has laid out for you?"

"No it is that I want to enjoy what I have and am not ready to commit my life to just one person yet. Someday maybe but my first reaction to your question is my schooling then my friend and then if God still has some one for me. Well then I will think about it. You know kids do not get hooked up any more just because older people think they should or are old enough. Grandpa there is so much out there for us to do and I want some of that before I get settled with a husband and kids struggling to make ends meet, and getting old or to old to go and do them."

Okay I was just letting you know that when you are young you are ripe and when you get old you are rotten. Young you are full of life and old you have no life left. It is okay to enjoy life as a young person but all the worldly things are not even close to the things that God has set forth here and in the hereafter so enjoy all things before you decide you do not have the time."

"Is there things that you never got to do that you could do now or are not able to do now?"

"Yes I could talk for hours of the things I have heard about that I never got to do or go see. And now the old body cannot do them. But the things I enjoyed most were the times and places that grandma and I got to do together."

"Yes I am sure of that but I can do most things faster now then I could back then."

"How true but remember fast means you miss so much as you go by or arrive. There are lots of beautiful things out there that you are going to miss just because you are in a hurry to get to one special place and never see how that place got to be there."

"What do you mean I don't get your drift."

"One example the Grand Canyon when people get there it is oh and owe and so big but do you know where it all started?"

"Yes with the Colorado river."

"Yep but that was three states away, and many years ago. It is like the Mississippi river it starts with a little trickle from a small lake and becomes the largest river in the USA and goes by or through a lot of states, and carries water from the largest area of the United States."

"I see so what has that got to do with me getting married?"

"Gabby it is better to see the whole country together with someone who is special then later just to see one or two of the states. God is special and he has places for us here to enjoy all of his creations even a man or woman, and even children. Go for the big pictures don't miss this making by being laid up in the society of work, work to get by. All the worldly passions are not worth one day, week, month, or year of the beauty of the Heavens and what God put here for us to enjoy together."

"I see so I had better tackle the first man I see that I may like and make him tell me he is the right one for me."

"No! No! girl you do not have to tackle anyone just

open the smile and raise up your head so the guys out there can see just who you really are. Then the right man will stop and back into those beautiful eyes and then he will chase you until you give in to his wishes. Then you pray to God if he is the right one for you. That will be a lot of questions latter, but you will know in your heart if he is the right one. You watch out for the foreigners."

"What do you mean foreigners?"

"The Romans and the Russians?"

"Why them?"

"Just an old saying those guys with roman hands and Russian fingers on property that does not belong to them yet."

"Grandpa you are funny, and I love you. Now I have to go and see if my mom needs some help. Thank you for your time and your prayers."

As always Gabby gets up and gives him a big hug and a kiss on his check and goes to tell grandma Hedi goodbye.

*     *     *     *     *

Again a few days later Betty wakes up with Thomas setting on her bed in his underwear with his hand on her hip patting and rubbing. As Betty comes around she slapped at his hand and rolled to the other side of the bed.

"What I told you never to come in my room again."

As she slid her hand under her pillow to find the knife handle of the large knife she had hid there.

"I need you and I want you to help me."

"Get out I will not do this with you go away,"

"You are going to help me so just get used to it. Now come I need your help with Karen she is not responding to the shot and I don't know what else to do."

"Take her to the hospital and let them take care of her."

"No she is my responsibility and you now come and help me."

"Leave so I can get dressed."

"I want you to get up and come now."

Thomas grabbed Betty's arm and started pulling her towards him. She had the knife and was pulling it out from under her pillow when he finally turned her loose.

"Okay come when you get dressed I will wait in the living room."

"Go and put some clothes on you are disgusting."

"I may be now but some day you will like my looks."

"I meant what I said if you try to hurt me, now leave and the next time I will not wait if you come in my room again while I am sleeping."

"You talk tough but I know better you are a small kitten with the roar of a lion."

When Betty got to Karen she was not moving so she checked her heart beat like the doctor had done. She found no pulse and then turned to Thomas and said.

"I feel no pulse so I believe that she is gone."

"Well that is great now things can return to normal around here."

"That is all you can say when your wife just died. You have no feelings for her or did you ever care for her."

"She was the one who kept my home in order and she took care of you while I was away. Besides that, she was a good lover when I was around. I respected her for that and for that only we will bury her and go on. You will take her place while I am gone working. I will take care of you in the same way I took care of her. You will watch over my property and cook and wash my clothes when I come home. The groceries will arrive just like they have in the past. You learn to like it that way and you will soon understand why it has to be this way. I will get dressed and go and prepare her grave site."

"Where are you going to put her?"

"Just out there by the garage building it will be easier

to dig there. You put on her best clothes and fix her hair while I do the digging. Then we will carry her out and put her away and then start our new life."

"I will fix her up but there will be no new life as I think you are thinking so do not push me into doing your wishes,"

As Thomas went out the door his only words were.

"We will see."

In Betty's mind her thoughts were you check it out and while you are out there you dig two graves because if you touch me or force or hurt me that is where you will be. She then started preparing Karen for her last dress up. As she worked on her hair and changed her clothes she thought.

"It is too bad that you had to live and die the way you did. I will never understand why you stayed with a man who thought no more of you then a cheap slave. Some day he will slip and it will end for him. I feel that he the same as murdered you for not taking you to see your doctor when you asked him to. Then the things he said about you when you were no longer able to hear or respond. Some day he will pay for that, and if I can help then that will be my gift back to you even though you will never know."

Thomas stumbled through the door asking.

"Is she ready yet I want this over with before the neighbors know what or see something."

"She is ready how are you going to get her out to the grave?"

"Easy you grab her feet and I will take her hands and carry her out there."

"I cannot do that she is worth more than that to me even though she was part if the deal of taking me away from my real home."

"Shut up and get a hold of her feet. I don't want to force or beg you to help me."

"Then you do it by yourself."

Betty turned to go to her room and felt his hand up the side of her head and was falling to the floor.

"I said for you to grab her feet and I don't like disobeying people now before I do something else you get up and do as I tell you to do."

Betty got up and did what Thomas told her to do. They carried and dragged Karen out to the gravesite. Then as she lay at the opening Thomas said.

"Pick her up and let's throw her onto the hole so I can fill it in. Betty broke down and started crying when Thomas took Karen's feet and rolled her into the hole and started filling it in. Betty turned and started back to the house when she heard Thomas say.

"You stay here until I am done then we are going into the house and have our little talk about the rest of your life."

Betty stayed with hate in her heart to the point that she wanted to run or kill the worst person she had ever known. When the hole was filled Thomas turned and said to Betty.

"Let's go we have some things to discuss."

Betty walked and was pushed along towards the house and when inside she was told.

"I am going for a drive and when I return I want to see all her things out here and on fire. I want nothing left to remind me of her. I will give you about two hours and then I will be back."

"Why?"

"Do as you are told you are still a minor and you should remember I am in control and you will do everything I ask you to do?"

"You remember I am a minor and if you are thinking of doing what I think you are thinking I will kill you and walk away with no regrets, and the law will not stop me or punish me."

Thomas starts towards Betty and then turns and leaves.

Betty is trying to be brave and this thought comes to her mind.

"Oh, Gabby, I need your strength I need your God I need help and soon what would you do? I am scared to death he will really hurt me and I am not strong enough to stop him."

Betty went to their bedroom and started taking all of Karen's clothes out of the closet not seeing anything she want to keep and took them outside and plied then in a big heap on the burn pile. Then she went to the bathroom and cleared out all of her makeup and threw it on the top. She had taken all the things she could think of keeping only what she thought she would use herself taking it to her closet and hiding it from Thomas. She put Thomas's clothes in the washing machine and went to her room she had to make a plan that she could handle before Thomas got back. Later she heard his truck come back and then the door opened and he was hollering at her.

"Betty get yourself out here when I tell you to do something I want it done. You had better be showing up quick you don't want me to come and drag you out here."

Betty came to the doorway and asked.

"What do you want I did what you told me to do."

"I told you to burn them things and they are still out there now go and burn them."

"I left you the privilege, so you go strike the match and watch your wife go up in flames, I will not do it for you."

Betty had the knife behind her back and watched Thomas look at her in the way she knew what he was thinking and then he stopped and turned to the kitchen and got the matches and went out the door. Betty watched him through the window as he lite the fire and stood making weird gestures at the fire for a long time always looking back at the house to see if anyone was watching him. There was a small explosion and the fire jumped up and the smoke spread way out the heat must of blew up a spray can. The neighbor man can over to see what was going on he was the one that Karen saw a lot of. Betty saw Thomas gesture with his hand for him to leave because he walked away in a hurry. When the fire almost out then Thomas turned and started back to the house. Once inside he went to the bathroom and told Betty.

"You go to your bedroom and I will be right there."

Then he went into the bathroom and she stood frozen to the floor and then getting up her courage she went to her room locked the door and put the chair under the handle. As she set on her bed with tears running down her face to the point that she could not stop them and the shaking of her entire body. She knew that she would have to be ready to do as she had told him she would do. The door handle rattled and then there was pounding on the door.

"You had better open this door I have told you many times there are no locked doors in my house. If you do not, I will break it down and throw it on the fire with all the other stuff in your room and you will have to sleep in my room in my bed. I am going to ask you one more time open this door now."

Betty heard knocking and looked out her window to see the doctors van parked out front. She opened her door and ran to the front door where Thomas was standing in the doorway telling the doctor.

"We do not need a doctor here there is no one sick at this time so go away and stay away."

The doctor being polite asked Thomas.

"Where is the woman Karen is she okay?"

"She is gone and you nor anybody else can help her now go away."

Betty wanting the doctor to know shouted out the door in a loud voice.

"Doctor Karen died early this morning and he buried her out by the shed."

"Did you report this to the undertaker?"

"I do not have to we live on Indian land and we do not have to apply to your rules."

"If you do not report her to the undertaker then I will send the sheriff out here and you will have to answer all his question and they will be just like you murdered her. You need to take that young girl with you so she can answer and tell her side because she was here with her all the time."

"We are not going anywhere and if you do not get in the vehicle and remove yourself from my property then I will and you will not like the way I play."

"Doctor please do not leave I think he is going to molest me in some way. I need someone to help me please do not go unless you take me with you."

"Man is that true what is she saying?"

"She is my daughter why would I molest her. She has been acting strange ever since Karen pasted on. Now I am asking you to leave us alone so we can get our lives back together. I will go and see the undertaker tomorrow but now I have some grieving to do, and you are stopping the process of forgetting my wife. Now please would you leave and let us get on with what we have to do."

"What are you burning out there it smell very bad?"

"Trash that is what everyone burns and I can do it without your advice or saying so."

"If you do not come in by noon tomorrow I will send the sheriff out to get you. Good day."

"Doctor please do not leave me here with him."

"I will wait in my van for you if you want to come."

"She is not going with you or anybody."

The doctor turned and went to his van and getting in and shutting the door he then called the sheriff on his two-way radio. Then he set there like he was doing some paper work. Betty went back to her room and positioned herself under the covers with the knife by her side and waited. Thomas came in and talked to her like nothing happened but yet very firm in his mean way.

"You are going to be very sorry for what you did now you are going to pay for being disobedient to your dad. First you are going to get a belt across you rear-end. Something I should have done a long time ago. Now to make it stick and make you believe I will do it with your clothes off so the skin is shining. So do you take them off or do I do it for you."

Betty lay there being very still and said nothing first waiting for him to touch her she was ready and now knew that she could do what she said she would do. Thomas reached and put his hand around her free arm and started pulling her to the edge of the bed. Betty can up with a loud cry and swung the knife at him cutting a large gash in the arm that held her. Thomas looked surprised and withdrew his arm and holding the cut with his free hand backed up shouting,

"You little good for nothing now look at this now you are really going to get what is coming to you. So stay there and gloat I will be back as soon as I take care of this cut."

When he left she heard knocking on the door and then voices.

"That little worthless thing tried to cut off my arm and she could have killed me. Now I want her to pay so go down that hallway to her room and take her to jail I do not care and I will prosecute her."

The sheriff went to Betty's room and told her.

"Young lady put down the knife and come with me. You have a lot of explaining to do. We will be going into town so get another set of clothes you will be there for a few days."

"I do not care as long as I get away from that mad man. I will tell you a story that will make even you set up and wonder why."

As she got her clothes and put them into a pillowcase she kept the knife in close reach of her until the sheriff came and released it from her hand.

"This you do not need any longer. Are you ready to go?"

"Yes!"

"Then let's get in my squad car and we will go see what is on your mind. I hope you are on the right side because I don't like pulling in young girls and throwing them in the pokey."

Betty was taken and put in a cell for the night without anything to eat but one glass of water.

"Well good morning did you rest well?"

"Yes but I do not like being locked up for something I did not do unless protecting one's self is a crime in the place for a teen age girl."

"No but I had to protect you because of what you said back at the house. Breakfast will be here any moment and then we have a lot of answers for my questions about you and this woman Karen I believe was her name. So get your act in order and I will be right back."

"Before you go will you tell that man to quite looking and drooling at me I am not a piece of meat he is going to eat."

"Okay, hey you get back on your bunk and look at your shoes and leave this girl alone."

After breakfast was eaten Betty was taken to a small

room where she and some lady and the sheriff set around a small table.

"Betty I am going to record everything you say so I want you to answer my questions in as brief an answer as you can. Are you ready?"

"I guess so."

"How long have you been out there in that house where I found you living with this Karen woman and Thomas?"

"Can I start at the beginning and end up at this time?"

"If you wish but make it brief as you can,"

"When I was between eight and nine years old my family and my best friend Gabby went skiing up in Colorado. On Saturday those two kidnapped me and took me to Mexico and then to the place where you found me. I have been held captive until this time. Thomas was not there much of the time. He was there a day or two each month and some time it was more than four months. Then Karen got sick the Indian next door went to tell the doctor and he came and done some test when he came back he told me she had cancer throughout most of her body, and needed to be put in the hospital so the pain could be better monitored, but Thomas would not take her there so I had to take care of her and her shots, she died screaming because of the pain then Thomas dug a hole and dumped her into it. That is when the doctor came back and then you showed up and brought me here. Thomas was so close to molesting me when you came that is why he had the cut on his arm. I told him, if he ever tried to hurt me I would have killed him, and that is what I would have done if you had not showed up when you did. Anymore questions?"

"Look at this couple and tell me if you know them?"

"Yes this is the two that kidnapped me."

"Do you remember where you used to live?"

"It has been a long time, but I do remember Gabby my friend."

"What is her last name and the state where you think she is at this time?"

"Her name is Gabby Meede and she would be in Colorado if she has not moved I have not heard from anyone since that day I was taken. She lived just about two blocks from where we lived. What was your mom and dad's name?"

"Joe and Mary Taylor, and my brother Al."

"This is enough for now I have other business to attend to take her back to her cell, and get her dinner."

# CHAPTER TEN

Gabby has had no more mind experiences about Betty for over a month. She has her mind on finishing her last year in high school and keeping her grade level above three point nine. She needs it high so she can get some scholar ship money for college. She decided to go for a college down in Texas where grandpa Tom's son lived with his family. She would have a place to stay for watching their kids at times when they needed to get out and do something by themselves. If she got in she would only be half a mile from the campus and could walk or ride a bike. That for the weather would be nice to great during the months of winter. Gabby had picked this one out of three others to be the best or have the best curriculum for her schooling. Texas Lutheran university was not a big school even though Sequim was about half the size of Littleton Colorado where she had lived most of her life. One of her and Betty's dreams was not going to happen they would not be going away to college as they had planned in their young life growing up. There whole life had been crumbled at that one small instant long time ago. They would not graduate together or do anything else together.

She had one month of school left, and yet had not heard from the college, it was tempting her to call or write them to see if she had to change her plans. After school she went home first and then to see her grandparents to check the mail each day. Today she was surprised to find a letter and a package from the college. Hurrying into the house she opened the package to find notes of paper that had to be filled out. Then she opened the letter and read it slowly. It was only six lines long. She read it to herself and then she read it out loud.

"Dear Miss Taylor:

Sorry it took so long, but some of the forms you sent us were not readable because the packet had gotten wet. We do know that there is a place here for you, but you need to refill out the forms for us. After that we will send you your admission papers. Thanks and Hurry."

Gabby grabs the letter and goes to show her grandparent's that she got in. When she arrived she noticed that her grandpa was not setting on the sun porch as he usually was. Wondering why she knocked on the door a couple of times; then waiting until it opened.

"Hi grandma I am late but I have good news. I got my letter from Texas and it is late because of the first package got wet and some of the papers they could not read so I have to refill them out and send them back in a hurry."

"Slow down girl and come inside yes that is exciting news and I am glad it finally came now you can come down and be yourself again."

"Grandma is grandpa alright I saw he was not outside like he is every day?"

"Well he has been up and down today says that his body is not responding like it is supposed to do. He is in the den looking out the window. Why don't you go in and surprise him and I will get us our milk and cookies?"

"Okay thanks grandma. Oh! grandma."

"Yes dear."

"Did I tell you that I love you."

"No but with all the excitement I do understand."

"Well I am telling you now. Getting this letter lets me know that it will come soon that I will not be able to tell you every day that I do. The hard part is knowing that I will not be able to come by every day and see you."

"Yes we know but your life must go on."

"Yes I know as I was telling mom just the other day I was thinking that I would put off college for a couple of years to see what or could I find Betty and then we could go together and be able to help you with grandpa Tom more."

"Gabby we will not hear of such talk you cannot put your life on hold because of other people that would not set well with your grandpa so you never tell him you even thought about what you just said. Can you promise me that you will go on with your schooling?"

"Yes grandma I promise."

"Hi grandpa Tom, how are you today? I missed you being out on the front porch it is such a nice day."

"Well my old bones are giving me a small amount of problems today and this chair fits them better."

"Why don't you buy you an easy chair like this and leave it on the porch. It could not be hurt to be out there until winter comes again."

"You know I was thinking about taking this one out there just the other day, and buying grandma another one for in here. Do you think she would mind?"

"I don't know let's ask her and see the worst thing she could day is no."

"Do you want me to go and ask her?"

"Why not you two could go to the store and have them bring out the one she likes."

"Oh grandpa I almost forgot I got my letter from

college today, and I have been excepted as soon as I resend my papers. I can go to help Carl and go to school at the same time."

"Oh how wonderful, I have been praying that this would happen for you."

"Hey you two are you ready for some milk and cookies?"

"Yes grandma we are ready."

"Momma if it were not for them cookies and milk you give me I would have been gone a long time ago."

"You old goat is that the only reason you have stayed here with me?"

"Oh no that is not the only reason but it has itself way up there on my priority list, and besides I am too old to go chasing some young chick and I have no idea what I would do with her if I stumbled and caught her."

"Grandpa you had better watch out you may not get any more milk with your cookies and then you may choke trying to swallow them."

"I am only teasing you two. To be frank about it she is the second best thing that has ever entered into my life. I remember the first time I saw her I knew that she would someday be my wife. I knew that she was a gift from God to share my life with. Funny how it works because my thoughts at that time really happened and came true. Even though we have had our valleys and high peaks she has never entered my mind as to leave her. She has been my rock here on earth and will be until my last breath."

"Thank you honey, that makes me feel young again."

"Grandpa that was very sweet of you and some day when God brings my man I hope that he is just like you."

"Thanks and if I was fifty or more years younger I would be out there chasing you around the block until I either tripped and fell or caught you. That would be some far out dream, or better lets say a miracle to say the least."

"Well I need to be going mom will need me to help her some. She comes home on the days she works and has nothing left. I still tell her she is doing to much, but she just says some day you will see."

"She is a lucky lady to find a job for only three days a week. I never had them luxuries when I was her age and it will help later when she decides to retire with your dad."

"Grandma did you ever work?"

"Yes I worked when the kids were all in high school that helped put them through college, and let us still live a good life style. You know it says in the good book that if you do not work you will not eat. I went to work just to have something to do with my time."

"My mom says the same thing and us girls don't need a maid any longer. I wonder if every family does that same thing."

"Probably but most do not save the extra they just spend it on toys and fancy cars or bigger homes. They, and they wind up worse off. Because of it even though God gives them the extras they tend to overdo and get into a real financial debt and some even lose everything. I am sure your mom and dad will not do such a thing."

"If my dad has his way they will be poor in material things and high in the bank account. He has a fit when mom wants something now and he cannot pay for it without having to pay more later for it."

"That is a wise man and he will be rewarded someday for his actions."

"I have got to go you to have a nice evening, and I thank you for your prayers. Oh grandma, grandpa wants us to go and buy a new chair so he can take this one out on the porch. What day would you like to do that if it is okay with you?"

"Well if he wants that we can do it any time."

"Gabby thank you for being our blessing. You are

one of our best grandchildren and some day you will be rewarded for all that you have done for us. You may never realize what you have meant to us. You go and have a wonderful time no matter where you are. We love you as much or more then if you were of your own blood. You are a very special girl and will always be so to us."

"Thank you grandma and you to grandpa goodbye for now."

*****

Betty has gone through a lot for her age and as she is telling the sheriff about her past she is still not sure if she is going to be set free and if so where would she go. She knew no one and had no funds to get anywhere. As she goes on telling her story with two strangers listening she hoped she was not getting into more trouble.

"When I was kidnapped we lived in Littleton Colorado. I do not remember the address, but you could check it out. My dad and mom were Joe and Mary Taylor. We live up the street from my friends Gabby and her parents' names were Don and Sue Meede."

"We can do that later but for now we need to follow the protocol of our file pages. Now did either one of these two people damage or molest you in any way?"

"Not facially but mentally."

"Did they ever leave you alone for any length of time?"

"No they would not even let me outside unless one of them were with me."

"Did you have anything to do with any of the neighbors while you were there?"

"No but Karen did when Thomas was gone for long times to work."

"Did she ever bring any of them into the house in front of you?"

"No she went out late at night when she thought I was asleep."

"Did she ever expose any sexual things to you in any way?"

"No why are you asking me all of this. Why don't you try to find my folks to see if they are still living in Colorado? And send someone out to find Thomas."

"Because I am in charge here and things have to be done this way because you are implementing things that will open up an F B I and I don't want to get involved with them yet. Now back to the questions there are only five more. Were you ever hungry while staying with them two people?"

"No but I had nothing but the basic foods no fun or snack stuff?"

"Were you ever punished for doing anything wrong?"

"Only by the eyes of Thomas."

"In what way?"

"Like he wanted to see me without any clothes on of which I only had dresses and no under clothes to wear,"

"Did he ever touch you?"

"No, Karen would not allow that."

"Did they ever promise you anything outside of that house you lived in?"

"No and Yes."

"In what way?"

"After Karen died Thomas said it would be me who took care of his needs."

"What was his need?"

"Keeping house doing his laundry and cooking his meals when he was home."

"Is that all?"

"He never come out and said anything but I knew

what he had in mind. That is why I told him if he ever touched me or hurt me I would kill him, and if you had not shown up I would have killed him."

"Did you feel bad when Karen died?"

"Yes and that was when I was scared the most."

"Because?"

"I knew he would have raped me and I would have killed him in his sleep."

"Okay it is time for dinner and I have to process all this information and decide what I have to do. Now you have to go back to your cell so I can get to my job."

"" Why can't I just stay here and eat?"

"Because any one can come in here and no one can get to your cell unless I let them go.

"Sheriff I don't like it back there with that weird man he reminds me of Thomas. I don't know why I am being punished."

"You are part one part of a crime and right now I do not know all the parts so until I to guess what."

"I should have kept my mouth shut and I could have stayed out there with the Indians and Thomas would have been dead by now and I would not be locked up that is my guess."

" Young lady go with this deputy and be good. I am going to get to the bottom of this and until I do you are going to be in that cell. Now go your dinner will be there in a few minutes I will be in, in a few minutes. I will talk to you again very son.

Betty goes back and waits for her dinner and while setting on her bunk her mind is going round and around. Maybe the sheriff is right because if I were outside Thomas would find me then he would get even. Maybe he will try and contact my real parents. Maybe Gabby and I will see each other again. Maybe I will never see them again and then what could I do. Maybe I could go and live with Gabby and my old grandparents. Maybe they are no longer around where they used to be. Maybe with Karen gone I am really all-alone. Maybe I should go back so I can finish my schooling. Maybe I am all I am ever going to be."

"Hello I have your dinner and it sure does smell good."

"Thank you."

While Betty eat her mind went on the wonder again. Gabby I hope you are still at the house you were before and if you ever think of me tell your God to not forget me. But I sure could use some special help from him. Gabby I wonder if you are okay and I sure would like to visit grandma Hedi and grandpa Tom. We used to get the best cookies and milk from them. Now I can hardly remember what they looked like. Gabby I would have never guessed that I would have to live like this in this country. Oh, why am I thinking about all this I know I am going to be here for a long time? Well at least until I am eighteen years old, and that is way next year. This may be the longest year of my life.

"Young lady are you through eating or are you not hungry?"

"Yes but I was day dreaming and forgot what I was doing. Oh, well, I will be done in a little while."

"Okay you call when you are done I have to take them dishes back to the restaurant so they can be washed."

Betty finished eating, but Gabby is still on her mind along with the sheriff and what he is doing and when he will come to get her again to talk. When she was done she hollered for the deputy to come for the dishes. After putting the dishes through the hole at the floor she retires back to her bunk and doses off having nothing else to do. She is startled back to reality when she hears the sheriff voice come booming into her sell.

"Young lady I need to talk to you again. Can you wake yourself up and come with me?"

"Yua coming."

"" Round here we speak English."

"Yes sir."

"Sit down and don't say anything until I ask you too. You must answer to my questions only yes or no if possible. Now I have six or seven more questions and I want you to not answer right away, but you think them through and then a simple answer are you ready?"

"What is going to happen to me?"

"Like I said short yes or no answers. Now are you ready?"

"Yes."

"Thank you."

"You are welcome can I have a glass of water please?"

"Yes but think what I said no answer I am trying to tell you do not convict yourself by talking. Now are you ready?"

"No."

"Hey you this is not a game, now you get ready."

"Okay but."

"No buts about this. Deputy what am I saying that is not right?"

"Nothing sir."

"Alright question number one. Now did you receive any improper treatment while you were staying with Karen and Thomas?"

Betty waited for a long time while looking the sheriff in the eye before she answered.

"No sir."

"Young lady you told me not to long ago that you were abused mentally now you are saying no which is it."

"Yes Thomas abused me mentally."

"I am trying to prepare you for court if you have to

go. I told you to answer as short as you can but you have to stick to the same story okay."

"Yes."

"Number two. Did you receive anything from these two people of monetary value?"

"No."

"Number three did you lie about the kidnapping and the time?"

"No."

"Number four did you ever try to get away during your time with them?"

"No."

"Number five why did you not try?"

"They watched me all the time when it was daylight."

Number six were you ever subjected to be molested even by the Indians who lived out there close by?"

"No."

"Number seven would you like to meet your real family as you have told me about?"

"Yes."

"Why they may not even know you after all these years."

"My friend Gabby would never forget about me."

"Okay no more questions and you can go back to your cell while I go see the courts to find out just what we can do for you."

"I don't want to go back there."

"I don't want to send you back there but as I stated that is your safest place at this moment."

"Then let me go back to my house if you have nothing to hold me. That way I can help myself by going back and taking whatever Thomas wants to give me. I do not want to be locked up like a rat in a cage."

"You have to wait I will be back before I retire for the night."

Betty is getting absolutely out of sorts and gets up and goes to the door saying.

"Open this up and let me go you cannot just hold me like this I want out so I can breathe some fresh air and go my own way and find my old friend Gabby. You do not believe me or you don't have anything else to do."

"Deputy, take this wild one back to her cell and get her dinner and I will see you both in the morning. It is evident she has something to hide so she can wait until I get it out of her good night."

"You men are all alike I am a minor and you cannot treat me like this I want out."

"Deputy go get me that big paddle and maybe that will get her attention."

"You had better not beat me with no board."

"Then you act like a grown up and do as I say."

Betty glares at the sheriff and goes before the deputy to her cell. She gets her dinner and still no bath or anything to clean up with. Then she decides to give in and lies down and while thinking she doses off. When she awakes it is dusk except for a very dim light in the hallway. She starts shouting and the only one who hears her is the old drunk in the cell across the hallway. He answers the call to get back at her.

"Shut up there is nobody her but the two of us to hear or see so shut up and go to sleep."

First thing on her mind was this is going to be a very long night, and her mind is about burnt out with nothing to think about except her friend who cannot help her. Gabby please can you send your God can he hear me when I talk to you about him. Can I talk to him like I remember you did? I know you are there and can tell when I am in trouble but you did not tell me what I had to do. Please God of Gabby, hear me and send help I do not want to stay in here. I have done nothing wrong so why am

I singled out to go through this life like this. I know you cannot hear me Gabby but I still have you to call too. So I am asking you if you ever feel me like I feel you if so then ask your God to come and help me. Betty lays back and the night goes away into a deep sleep. When Betty wakes up she is being hounded by her neighbor and takes a while to recover from her long sleep. She finally hears his voice and comprehends what he is saying.

"Hey sweetie pie if you get out of here today tell them that you are going to come back and stay with me, and they will let me out also."

"Me stay with you that would be like digging my own grave no thank you and leave me alone."

The hallway door opened and the deputy came down the hallway giving her neighbor his breakfast and turned to leave when Betty asked her.

"Deputy where is mine and how long do I have to stay in here without getting a bath?"

"The sheriff did not tell me what to do for you so he will be in soon to attend to your wants."

"Hey all I want is out do you people hear me. I want out! Out! Out!"

"You keep this up and the sheriff will prolong your stay or your out! Out! Out! as long as he can. You want from us and do not respect us for helping you. Now the sheriff will attend to you when he comes in and not until so set back and relax."

The deputy walks away leaving Betty putting her fingerprints in the steel bars of the cell door. Finally, she looks up and staring at her is the drunk across the hallway with the look that Thomas usually gave her.

"Quit looking at me like that it will do you no good there is one thing you will never see is me without any clothes on so put your eyeballs back into their sockets in your dumb face and turn it off, tune it out."

"Hump smart mouth let me tell you something I have seen girls like you without any clothes and they are a lot better looking than you will ever be."

"Just shut up you pervert."

As she spoke the sheriff came through the door asking.

"What seems to be the trouble in here."

"Get me out of here I do not like that bum undressing me all the time."

"Well now unless he has longer arms then he looks like he has he is pretty harmless. And even if he is it is highly unlikely he could do anything about it. Now if you will calm down I am going to take you for a little drive and then a bath and some breakfast then back to the little room for some more questions."

"Really you are going to take me so I can get a bath how nice of you it has been almost three days you must think I stink."

"Never mind let's go."

Outside he puts her in the back seat and shuts the door then get into the front and begins to tell her what she going to do.

"Now young lady do you know what size clothes you wear so we can get some up to date ones?"

"All I know is that I wear only one size and that is called a sack dress like I have on."

"Okay I need the deputy to go with us while you pick out some new clothes that will fit you. She can watch you where I can't. I am going back inside to get her and do not try to get out them doors. They only open from the outside."

"Wow a jail on wheels' whoopee."

They sheriff just shakes his head and go inside thinking if I had a kid like that I would kill a skunk and push it down her throat. When they came back they drove to the department store without saying anything. Betty is ushered inside the store and watched by both until she goes to try on something. Then the deputy goes and checks out the small room. Betty has something to say about that.

"What are you looking for?"

"Nothing you need to know about."

"You watch good I just might decide to steal something. And do not be snooping over the door."

"I snoop at my cat not young girls who do not respect you. Besides you have nothing I do not have so get in there I have things to do besides baby set some irresponsible smart ass."

Betty turns and looks at her and throws the clothes into the room and turns to walk away. The deputy grabs her arm saying.

"Young lady do not push me I can be very nasty if I have to. Now quietly go and try them clothes on or do I have to do it for you so I can go and do my real job."

Betty cools down and get her clothes picked out and then back to the moving jail where they take the deputy back to the station and then the sheriff pulls out and heads down the road. When they get to the out skirts of the town he pulls into a drive way and gets out. Opening the door for Betty he tells her.

"You can get out now we are going to get you cleaned up and feed. This is my home and my wife is going to see that you have everything you need so be extra nice to her."

"I will try."

"Take you new clothes with you."

"All of them?"

"No just one set and what you have on will just disappear. What would you like for breakfast?"

"For real."

"Yes."

"I would like some potatoes, eggs, over and some sausage patties."

"Don't take all day or they will be cold when you get to eat them."

"I would like to soak for a while if I could."

"You have twenty minutes alright."

"Yes."

"Hi baby I have this girl and she needs a bath and if you will help her I will fix her breakfast."

"I would be glad to help her what is your name?"

"Betty."

"Okay Betty you can come this way and I can get you started. Do you want a bath or a shower?"

"Bath if I can."

"Bath it is, come this way. My name is Cora and I will start the bath water while you get undressed and into this robe."

"You can go outside I can do this."

"I know but my husband will not allow me to do that. So just go ahead I will not look."

Betty get is the tube and feels instant relief the water is just right with bubbles and cream. She is going to stay as long as they will let her. After fifteen minutes she is told time to get out. After drying she goes to the bedroom and starts dressing she feels the under garments for the first time that she can remember then she slips into her new clothes, and parades around looking into the mirror with a large smile on her face. Then she is told to set down.

"Come over here so I can do your hair and put on your new face."

Betty sets without saying a word until Cora is done then she turns to look in the mirror and is startled to see what she has been reformed into.

"Oh my would you look at me. I don't believe it is me I look so different."

"You look lovely now let's go show the sheriff and get your breakfast."

When they enter the kitchen the sheriff looks up as they walk through the door saying.

"Well who do we have here?"

"This is the new Betty dear. Doesn't she look stunning in her new outfit."

"If I do say so myself and just maybe this will change her attitude somewhat so we can enjoy her."

"I don't know how I can pay you for all this, but I do feel better about myself and I thank you both."

"That is enough for the time being now just you set down here and eat this breakfast I fixed for you. Then we have to go and do some more work."

# PART FIVE

# CHAPTER ELEVEN

GABBY is almost done with her schooling. She has all her paper work done for college and most of her tuition money in hand or at the college in Texas. At the Lutheran University. She has only two months left of high school and is the class valedictorian, and she has her speech ready. She is moving on and has set a good example for her sister to follow.

Jan is still messing around with Al on and off still not sure she wants to be hooked to him or open up and date other boys. Jan talks to Gabby a lot about Al and what she would do if she were her.

"Jan why don't you just level with Al and tell him how you feel maybe he will change the way he treats you. If you do not tell him then you will never be happy. He in return does not know how you feel about certain things so he has no reason to change any or part of his life."

"I know, but what if he leaves and doesn't care about me. What would I do for a boyfriend? I would be talked about and probably never have another boyfriend."

"Would that be so bad to go through two years of school without having some boy grouping all over your body just, or just a object for him to come and brag about to his friends." because you are good looking and well endowed. Does that make you somebody?

"Gabby I cannot be like you I need the things that make me feel good about myself."

"Jan remember what dad has always said to you, you cannot push a rope. So why do you try?"

"I am not pushing my rope."

"Yes you are because you are following after Al and the ways he is doing and you admit you do not like it so why do you keep pushing your rope. Be a leader for a change before you get in over your head and wind up with a belly that is getting bigger. Then see who will be talking about you."

"" Gabby I am not having sex with Al."

"Not yet, but I know how they think and it is coming so you need to listen to your heart and change the way you think about how you feel with Al hanging all over you."

"I have to go and finish my school work thanks for listening and your advice was heard."

"Gabby can you come in here a minute?"

"Yes mom, be right there. What can I do for you?"

"I heard you and Jan talking and I want to thank you for standing by her. She has turned out much better than I thought she ever would. She I think actually cares about you and how you feel about her."

"Well I am going to be gone for a long time and she now needs a big sister to look up to and I hope I have done a good job of letting her know."

"I am sure she has and now how do you feel that school is ending soon?"

"I am okay with everything except at times I really feel bad because my friend and sister is not going to be there as we planned so long ago."

"Well maybe she is feeling the same way where ever

she is. You know that both of you are eighteen and she should be able to go her own way soon."

"Yes but she will not be coming home, too much."

"I know but it still is her home."

"Maybe mom she won't be coming home at all. I just know it has been very hard for me to keep going on without her. We had our lives planned before she was kidnapped. Now I struggle with our thoughts back then because I don't want to go alone, and I do not know if she will ever get what we wanted."

"It will all work out the Lord has planned yours and Betty's life way before either one of you were born. You and all of us has prayed for her safety and care for all the days she has been gone, and I believe the Lord has taken care of her in some way. Soon she will be free to come back home even if it is not a real home any longer.

*  *  *  *  *

"Hon what are you going to do with this beautiful young lady you cannot keep her locked up forever?"

"I know I was thinking she could stay here with us until the courts decide or made a ruling even through it is against what I stand for."

"Yes I know but you take a good look at her before you make your decision."

"I have now young lady what do you think about staying here with us. Knowing that soon you may be set free or held for safe keeping until that Thomas guy shows up."

"Then when you are eighteen you can go on your merry way unless he is waiting for you. You still need to finish your school work and I presume all that is still at the house where I found you."

"Yes it is all in my bedroom on the table by my window, and yes I would like staying here,"

"You would still so be locked up. You cannot leave the house without someone with you at all times."

"I can do that."

"Tomorrow I will go out and get your books."

"Can I go with you so we get all of them?"

"Maybe, maybe not I will think about it you two have a good day and Cora keep the door locked."

"We will because we need time to get to know each other."

"Cora what do I do what can I do to help you?"

"You join in the doing what you feel needs to be done if in doubt then you ask. I will not stop you from helping. There are the same things going on here as there is in most homes where people live."

"Can you show me where you put the dishes and I will wash and put them away."

"Here we put them in the dishwasher after the clean ones are put away. So you watch me this time and then you will be able to do it later."

"Where is my sleeping room going to be?"

"Down the hallway last door on the right it is across from our room. Now I have to tell you so there will not be any surprises later on. All the doors and windows in this house have alarms on them so do not go through any of them without permission until you know what to do. Your bathroom is off the hallway next to your room. We need to go and prepare the bed and put things so you can find them and have the necessary items in the bathroom. We do not use it much since our kid left home and moved away and very seldom comes back home."

"What do you do all day do have a job?"

"Yes I do, I raised our child and kept my husband's home in order so when he came home there would be no turmoil while he was here. That is what women are supposed to do take care of the home. I make my husband feel loved by doing it. He in return provides for us and my husband has taken very good care of me and this home."

"When I was with Karen and Thomas. Thomas did nothing but use Karen and she did everything he asked of her. He was never there when she needed him. I never want to be around a man who treated his wife like that."

"There must have been something wrong for her to live like that. There could have been something hidden that never came up that you know of or was sleeping when it did. Good men would never abuse his help mate but always hold her up for his prize."

"I do not know only I want no man in my life unless he is like my real dad. He did so much for my mom. They were so happy they went everywhere together. Even though my mom worked part time to catch up some of the bills she never worked long hours."

"He sounds like a good husband and father do you know where they are at this time?"

"I remember we lived in Littleton Colorado not far from my sister and friend Gabby. I have missed her more than anyone else."

"So you do not know if they live there any longer?"

"No the sheriff said he would try to contact them as soon as he got time."

"So as of yet you do not know."

"No and if I had been more open and less mad at him for holding me for something I still do not know he may have tried before now. he told me a kidnapping has F B I written all over it and he wanted to do what he could before called them in, or maybe just to let me know that he was the sheriff and he would do it his way."

"I am sure that is true and if I understand right it has been a long time am I right."

"Yes about ten years."

Well that takes a lot of digging to recover all the

information someone has, but my husband is good at his job and you being a minor has more priority then a ten-year-old crime. Give him time he will do a thorough job on his own before he will let the F B I come in and run rough shod over his position and territory. By the way we need to get some lunch ready he will be home before long and he has his best meal at lunchtime. By the way have I told you are sure a pretty young lass?"

"Thank you but as my friend would say when we were just little ones that beauty was on the inside and anything could be on the outside. She always prayed and talked about her Jesus I never could understand what or who her Jesus was. Gabby would talk to him all the time, and she would say someday I would be able to do the same thing. I still do not know who she was talking to it seemed like he was just some imagination she had, like some invisible things."

"Betty as far as you know you have never accepted Jesus into your heart, and if not then you will never get the feelings that she had of the Holy Spirit dwelling through your good and bad times you will go through."

"No I guess not Gabby told me I had to tell him that I knew I was a sinner, but I could not believe something that I could not see or feel. Even during this long time, I used to talk to Gabby and tell her too send her God to help me, but I know she never heard me because she was too far away."

"Betty she did not hear you but I believe she could feel that you were in trouble and was praying for you as soon as she felt the Holly Spirit prompting her to do so. Have you ever gone to church?"

"No we talked about it when I was young but we never got around to going."

"You are welcome to join us if you want too."

"Maybe I should, can you help me to feel or talk to

Gabby's, Jesus or help me to understand more about what she used to tell me about."

"It is not like that you have to be willing to accept that belief when the Holly Spirit put that burden on your heart. Jesus is alive and he is knocking at the door of your heart, but it is up to you to open it up and let him come inside. Think of it like this do you remember your mom and dad even though you have not seen them in what over ten years. Do you remember Gabby I believe you said was her name, and do you remember other things and people when you lived in Colorado?"

"Yes but I don't know if I would remember them if I saw them because they would be older and grown up different in looks."

"But you still remember them by the name."

"Yes."

"Well that is the way it is with Jesus Christ he died a terrible death on the cross to save you and I along with everyone else from the terrible sins that we commit. He is the bridge between the life of being in Heaven, or the life of being in Hell. You will live the life of sin in the grasp of the devil or in heaven with the glorious Father God. Even if you never saw him as you see me. That does not mean that you cannot accept him for what he did for you. When you have heard the gospel or read it then and only then can you understand what Jesus is all about. Hey we need to get to work or the old sheriff will not be happy when he gets here and he is still alive and flesh and bone and hungry."

"Hi I am home is lunch ready?"

"Not quite but will be in ten minutes."

"I cannot believe this with two women and lunch is late."

"You be nice we have been getting acquainted and

Jesus and your lunch is not on the same page so wash up and get seated."

As he set at the table watching his wife through the kitchen door he had not realized that Betty had walked into the room behind him until she spoke.

"Hi sheriff your lunch is late because of me and I am sorry for that."

Betty walked into the kitchen to help Cora and as they came back into the dining room her looks took him by surprise.

"Wow who is this? Oh you sure do clean up looking good. Momma you sure did a great job on the girl or I mean young lady she is stunning to look at."

"Put your eyes back into your head she is not looking for a man she is looking for Jesus. Now will you pray so we can eat."

"Wow yes I can. Dear Jesus this girl has entered into our presence and you did a great job of creating her. I now pray that all she has told me is correct and it will not take much longer to get her back into the life you started with her. Thank you for my wife and her hands that do the work in this home. Thank you for this food you have provided for us to eat and enjoy. Help it to mold us into the people you have made us to be in your oh so precious name. A-men."

"How is your day so far dear?"

"It has been good I have an all-points bulletin search out for this Thomas guy. I also found a bank that has an account in it in his name. It has a large sum of money in it. If he tries to access it they are going to get me the information I asked for and then we can wait and nab him when he arrives. It has a no withdrawal sheriff impoundment on it so he has to come to the bank to get anything from it he just does not know why. So in time we will get him while he stands in line waiting for the president of the bank to explain to him the why of it. Then he has a lot of questions to answer. Now when I do get him, you young lady will be behind the window watching and listening and hopefully then I can get to the real truth. Not that you are not telling me the truth, but I have to do this because you told me that he and his wife kidnapped you. So until then you are under my care and will be here in my home and that I am glad we need someone around here to spruce up this home we are both getting old and wrinkled and need a new face to remind us that we are getting old. Thank you for lunch and now I am going to get your schoolwork so I will see you both tonight. Do not go anyplace he just might be out there watching. If anyone knocks on the door does not open it unless you know them."

"Yes dear and your deputy will be in town just in case we need her?"

"Yes she is watching in plain clothes along with my part time deputy you will be safe."

Betty and Cora had a wonderful time talking and sharing the afternoon went very fast. Then it was time to get dinner ready for the sheriff would be there on time as always. If everything went well he would bring her books so she could finish her courses. She was ahead of other students so she had almost finished her studies so she could get her diploma and graduate from high school.

She was beginning to like staying with the sheriff and Cora, but something soon could happen to make that a past tense in her life. When the sheriff arrive it was time to eat, but he had to bring in the boxes of books that he had gotten at her old place. After bring in the five boxes of books into the house he set down so they could eat. When they were through eating Betty went through the boxes and told Cora who was helping that she did not need or want a lot of the things that were in the boxes. What she needed was the one box that was under her bed that held all of her records of school and that would be needed to get her diploma. When all was put back that was to be discarded Core went to the sheriff and told him.

"Hon we need to take Betty out there so she can get all that she needs to complete her schooling. Can we go out tonight so she can be ready to start tomorrow?"

"I do not want to go out there, but since she is in my care I suppose I have to do so. When I got out there I knew that I should have taken her along with me. Okay you both get ready and I will take you out to the old house."

"Betty the sheriff is going to take us out to your old place so you can get what you need so get ready."

"You need to cover up your head he may be out there watching and you can help me watch to see if anyone is fallowing us."

They climbed into the squad car and drove out to the house where Betty had spent almost half of her life. Arriving they opened the door and noticed that things were not the same. Betty ran to her room and looked under the bed to find that her box was still there. Looking around she took things that meant something to her. All in all, she had three small boxes and then they took them to the car. There they found two flat tires on the squad car. Now the sheriff was very upset and told them to get back so he could check under the car to see if there was something out of the ordinary under it. Finding nothing he opened the door to find it full of smoke from a smoke bomb that had been discharged inside. After clearing the car of smoke he radioed the deputy to bring out more tires. After replacing the tires, they drove home to see if everything was okay at the house. After arriving he went into the house to see if everything was okay finding nothing he returned to get the girls. And at that time he turned and asks Betty.

"What kind of vehicle does Thomas drive?"

"He had a different kind almost every time he came,

but most of the times he drove his old pickup truck, then a van and a car."

"I figure that this man is and has been up to no good for a long time. We have to be extra careful as to what we do."

"What did he drive most a truck, car, or a van?"

"He drove each of them but mostly his truck."

"What color was that truck?"

"Sometimes it was blue or green but mostly it was a dirty brown red color."

"Were the cars the same color?"

"No they were a lighter color towards somewhat grey."

"If I showed you some different cars and vans and trucks could you remember what they looked like so I could get a year built on them?"

"I think I could maybe. I do remember he had one like the Indian did that lived close to us, but I never saw the Indian drive his any place. He always went with someone else."

"Betty I want you to keep thinking and if I am not here you write it down or have Cora write it down. If I get enough information I can put out an all-points bulletin on a certain type vehicle for other police officers to look for. Even the Indian nation have their own police force and they are very good."

"Sheriff how long will I have to stay here?"

"I don't know right now."

"Have you tried to find my first family?"

"I put out information to the Littleton police to see if they could find them but no word back yet."

"If you find them can I go and see them?"

"I think that is going to be up to the F B I as to what they want to do about the crime of kidnapping against you and your family. They have only one agenda to follow and you may be put under their jurisdiction until Thomas is found. If you like staying here I may be able to get them to let you stay under our roof."

"How long do you think this will take?"

"Hon why do you not level with her."

"Cora you stay out of this, remember I am the sheriff and I make the decisions about my job and the criminals that I have in my custody."

"Yes dear, but this young lady has to be able to realign her life and not be held in suspicion forever."

"I know and I am working on it as fast as I know how trying to apprehend this Thomas before the F B I send a bunch of people in here and then scare him away. I want this girl to be safe and I believe at this moment she is not, and I happen to be the one who is responsible for her even if I have to keep her locked up in a jail cell to protect her from this abusive man. Now said, I want you to be able to enjoy somewhat of a life as you live here. Your looks have changed and we can do some more to that. You can be our daughter as far as I am concerned and we will protect you as best we can. Is that good enough at this time?"

"Yes sheriff but I need you to tell me about my family as soon as you know something."

"You have a deal."

For the next thirty days nothing changed the sheriff kept checking the house for Thomas to return and the bank had not called. He got word about Betty's dad that he no longer lives with her mom and brother. He no longer lived in Littleton or in the state of Colorado this ended in a dead end for Betty as far as her dad. But, what about the rest of her family and her friend Gabby.

She had finished her schooling up early and had her eighteenth birthday with no one knowing. Cora and her had become great friends and loved being around each other. The sheriff came home with a different idea and at dinner he asked.

"Betty there is no news about your family no one can find any one by the name of Joe Taylor around

"Why would my mom change her name?"

"Well there could be a lot of reasons divorce, death, separation, and disappearance."

"My mom's name is Mary Taylor and my brother's name Is Al. Taylor."

"Good I will get these out on Monday morning to see if there is anyone living there by these names. What did you say your friends name was?"

"Her name is Gabby Meede and her mom and dad is Don and Sue and her sister is Jan Meede. They lived just about three blocks from where I lived at the time back then."

"Good now I want you to know and remember that if your family is found or even your friend's family I will have to call in the F B I. So I want you to get prepared to answer a lot of questions about the past and for the next ten years. I know you can do it but it will be like opening old wounds and it will begin to hurt. Those guys are not sensitive to any one. I was hoping I could find that Thomas guy and then just hand him over to them and you could be free of this past of your life and go on to something you would like to do and be."

"Thank you sheriff but I think with you and Cora's help I can get through it. Just knowing that there would be someone who loved me and was concerned about me would be a big help and comfort I am an adult now, but still need someone, and right now you two are the only ones I know who care."

The next week a lot of things happened. First the sheriff got news about Betty's mom. And about her family. His thoughts were how would he tell Betty about what he found. Arriving home for dinner early Betty and Cora were baking a cake for dinner. They were surprised when he walked into the kitchen.

"Hon why are you home early we do not have dinner ready it will be some time before the cake is done?"

"Well I missed the two most beautiful girls in my life and I wanted to come and see you. And I can come home any time I feel like it. I am my own boss and today I felt like it."

"But your lunch is not ready."

"That's okay I am not that hungry yet, and I have some good news for you."

"Well give us a minute to get the cake into the oven, and we will be ready to share the good news with you."

"I will wait in the living room."

Cora says to Betty in a louder voice.

"I wonder what he has this is very unusual for him to come home early."

"I don't know but I like good news lets hurry and find out what it is."

"Okay Betty you wash up this pan and I will attend to the cake and put it in the oven."

"I wonder what the sheriff has that may be good news because he did not even smile when he said it."

"Let's go and see. Okay you have our full attention so lay it on us."

"It is about Betty's family. We were looking for your dad but he has moved on or something and your mom and brother are still living in the same house. The authorities confirm that your friend's family is still just down the street. They do not know that you are here, and I cannot let them know without telling the F B I, or getting into a lot of trouble from them. I need to know if you want me to pursue and go forward. I want you to know that the F B I will not bring them into it unless you are safe. Right now

I will say that you are not because Thomas has not been located as of this moment. I for one and I presume that Cora for two are very concerned about your safety. If I call the F B I you will be no longer in my custody but there's and no telling where you will be taken. I would like to wait and see if Thomas comes back for his things or money from the bank. I cannot tell you the time that something will come of his show up. I for one want you to know that I am getting used to having you around. Cora has become a lot more energetic since you have been here. I want you to think about what I have told you, and give me your answer tonight and Monday I will do as you wish."

"Hon, that is a lot for this young girl to remember. Can we talk more about this so she is sure she knows of all the ins and outs before you go and do something."

"She can have all the time she wants the longer is more in you and I 's favor. Remember as long as Thomas is out their Betty is in trouble and until he is caught I will be sure Betty is very well taken care of. At this time, I have called in two more deputies so she will be watched around the clock. I still say remember do not open the door to any one unless you Cora know them. If someone comes that you don't know the special alarm you know will bring one of us as in a hurry. Now you two lovely ladies can I have my lunch so I can go back to the old grind."

"It will be ready in a short call you get washed up and get to the table, and do not forget to tell us if anything is coming down."

The sheriff goes to wash up and his pager is calling him. After drying he calls the office dispatch to find out that the bank had called and he needed to go pronto.

"I have to go see you tonight."

"What about your lunch?"

"Got to go see you later."

# CHAPTER TWELVE

Gabby is on her last week with test to complete and then she will be gone from her young life into a life of adult hood. She has been eighteen years old for about six months, and has every ting pretty much her way for a long time. She has enough scholarship money, and the only thing she need is money for food and personal items. She has two months to get all her stuff ready and tell everyone goodbye. She is going to miss her family and her grandmas Hedi and grandpa Tom. Tom has been going downhill for about one year and is now having trouble with his food and getting it to stay long enough for it to nourish his body. His doctor has said he is living on God's Grace not on his own strength. On Gabby's last day of school, she stopped by to see her grandparents and check to see if Tom was doing okay, and Hedi still has enough strength to take care of him. He is spending most of his time in bed and getting weaker all the time. He needs help just to go to the bathroom. Yet with all his problems he is still a happy man.

"Hello grandma how are you and is grandpa seeing any one today?"

"Gabby if you did not come to see him he would be very upset and that would cause me more trouble than I can take care of. He is resting so we can talk for a while before he wakes up."

"That is fine I wanted to tell you about the two new scholarships that I received today. They came to enough to supply me for all my school needs and my personal ones too. I was so excited that they came to only two students in our school so the two of us are set for all four years."

"That is so wonderful that God has looked out for you. Remember Gabby you are a gift from God himself, and you and your parents have given him back his reward. Now you make sure that you tell others what you have done so they in return can do the same thing so God will get their reward also. Let them see what you have done and be able to see the Glory of your Savior and Lord Jesus Christ in all you do and say. I hear a noise from Tom's room so he may be awake. You can go on in and I will get his medicine to help him get through this awakening time."

"Okay."

Opening the door to Toms room she sticks her head through and asks."

"Grandpa, are you awake and can I come in?"

"Yes you can and thank God for this beautiful awaking to see such a lovely young lady who thinks I am worthy of her presence."

"Grandpa you are the lovely one you and grandma have taught me so much through all the years I have known you."

"Did we teach you or did you just observe what we do and the way we did it."

"Both and it has made a big input on my life. One is that I want to be a teacher and that is my way, and if God has another then in time he will show me the different one someday, but to be a teacher and know that God is around and be able to help kids in school to know who they are and who they need to be. That is my goal and I know that it is going to be tough because in our school systems. But if I am to do this I believe that God, Jesus, and the Holly Spirit will guide and protect me during all my encounters throughout my lifetime. I can only pray that all I do and say will honor my Lord at all times."

"That's my girl stick to that and through thick and thin, or mountains and valleys God will never leave you."

"Grandpa do you know that in less than two months I will have to leave here and be far away, and I will hurt for that and I will pray for you and grandma every day."

"Gabby, God has and will keep taking care of us and it is nice to leave you with great inherence God has told us to give to our grandchildren. I hope that it will be with you always even when we are gone to be with our Lord Jesus Christ."

"It will, how could I ever forget the times we have had together we prayed and laughed and cried, and had grandma's wonderful milk and cookies. I will never forget what you and grandma has done for me."

"Hey you two what are you talking about I heard my name mentioned, and I have your medicine so open up and take, but be careful and do not swallow it down the wrong pipe."

"Hon I am so sorry that I cause you so much trouble it is not what I want, or have in mind but my mind and body is two different things at this time."

"It is okay I enjoy taking care of you, you took care of me and our child for a long time and now it is your turn to be taken care of."

"Grandma that is sweet and I do agree with you and I keep wondering when I have to leave who will take care of you when you need help?"

"I don't know child but God will send someone just

like you. Do you remember when you and your friend Betty showed up at our door so long ago? Well if you do, we took a liking to you two that same day. And God will send someone else just like he did you two girls only I hope that someone will be a little older and a little wiser then you two were."

"Oh grandma. I have wondered why we just stopped by that day. Somehow until now I have never put it together, but if Betty was here I am sure she would be willing to stay just like I am. As I think back I have almost forgotten why we ever got together little lone just why we stopped by to see you and all that has happened in our lives is still a mystery, but it has been a good one to remember. Now that we have thought about it I wish Betty could be here to celebrate with us. Have you ever thought about how many cookies and glasses of milk we have eaten and drink?"

"Well it must be close to twenty thousand cookies and hundreds of gallons of milk. I would not want to start baking them all over again. But come to think about it they may be something to be eaten I will be right back."

"Gabby what is the most remember-able time that you can remember coming to our house. Something that you will always remember throughout your life?"

"Grandpa there are a lot of things, but I suppose the most helpful are the one liners and the ideas that you shared with us and mostly me."

"Give me one or two of them."

"Let's see one is, if you bought something for a nickel and you did not need it you paid to much for it. Two would be, I can do anything I want to do unless Jesus Christ has said no."

"You do remember."

"Yes everyone you told us I went home and wrote them down. I have pages full of them."

"That is strange I used to do the same thing when

my grandfather told them to me. I hope that they mean as much to you as the have to me. Sometimes when I think about them, I know that without them I would not be the same man I am today."

"Grandpa I want to thank you for sharing them with us and I am sure that Betty would remember some of them also."

"It was not me it was grandfather who shared most of them with you and Betty and my son which I hope will share them with any grandkids over the years when I will not be here."

"Okay you two open up here comes the cookies and milk. Gabby would you help get him ready so he can enjoy them with us?"

"Yes grandpa I will help you set up which one of these three buttons do I push?"

"Oh no not that one, I cannot eat with my feet up in the air, push the one on the right top. Oh that is better now get me that lap table so I can set my milk down."

"Grandpa can we pray before we enjoy this special gift that grandma brought for us to eat?"

"Yes my dear, what would you like to pray about that is troubling you at this time?"

"Lots, one my leaving to go to college, Two, for my sister who thinks she is in love with Betty's brother Al. three, for my mom who I know is going to miss me a lot. Four, my dad to accept that I am not his little girl anymore and that I will be safe at your son's home. Five, that somehow if Betty is still alive she will find a way to get free from wherever she is. Six, that grandma will have the strength to keep seeing after you. Seven, that no matter what happens that my grandpa will not have to suffer through much pain in his remaining years and that God will have favor on him so he can get the strength to help himself and let grandma rest her strength more. Eight, for myself for Gods wisdom and power and strength will be showered down on me while I am away."

"That is a powerful lot but can I pray for these cookies and milk and after we eat then we can cover the rest."

"Yes that will be okay."

"Dear Heavenly Father we ask that your blessings be over these hands who have prepared this snack of cookies and milk to let us enjoy the fruits of those blessings to our bodies to help us go through what is left of our lives. This is a special time to be here with Gabby as a whole family still missing Betty and knowing that you are still protecting her and will soon help her to be free in your name as precious as it is to us. A-men."

After they had eaten and talked about the normal things grandpa Tom said.

"Now we eat and enjoy this gift to us."

For over five minutes they eat and drink in silence. Grandma Hedi's cookies were the best money could buy or make they were always the same in texture and taste. When through eating Gabby said.

"I want to pray first is that okay?"

Grandpa having the last thought coughs and says.

"Okay now to the more serious things."

"Dear Heavenly Father, through your son Jesus today I am asking that no matter where I am or where I go that I am and will be thinking of my family and these two dear grandparents that I have come to love so much. I ask you to help them get through the hard times even though I will be gone soon and will be so far away. First I ask your patience and kindness for my mom to not worry over me also for my dad, and that you could have the Holy Spirit speak to my sister and help her not to get into trouble with Al.

Help her to trust you and not to trust Al on everything.

I know that Betty is still alive some place and I know you have answered all our prayers for her and that before long she will be back. When she is will you help her to adjust to the difference in her life. My last prayer today is that you can come and put your loving arms around my grandma Hedi and Grandpa Tom and take away the pain and hurt in their bodies. Help them to enjoy the last part of their lives. Keep them happy and knowing that especially I love them and you are their provider of what they need. Help me to be a good reward for you in my studies and the life I will be learning for you. Thank you for being my Lord and Savior, and I ask this same for my friend whom I have not seen for so long. Jesus I love you and will always serve you in all that I do. Thank you for your kindness so far in my life. For your love I pray this to you. A-men."

"Hon would you like to go next or should I?"

"I would love too."

"Dear Heavenly Father for all you have given me over the years I thank you for all and the biggest one I thank you for my husband that you sent to me. Thank you for his loyalty and trust for so many years. Please help him through the remaining time you have for him. keep his minds active and his pains of suffering at the lowest you can. Help me to take care of him as you would and be patient throw off the tiredness I feel in my body. Lord, be with Gabby,s family help them to let go and help her sister who runs a reckless life with the boy she seems so found of. As you know we have missed Betty for so long do not forget her, help her to be safe and be able to know where she had lived before all this happened. Help her not to be angry or upset let her find your son Jesus to help get her through this time in her life set her free Lord. Let her find her your promise so she can be truly be happy. Help her to not be sad about her mom and dad while she was away. Let her be strong and able to accept what has happened in her life. Thank you Jesus for all you have given to us. I pray that we have been good stewards of the gifts from you. In your son Jesus precious name, we want to be good steward to him and to all mankind that touches us in our life here. A-men."

"Thank you my dear you are more than any man could ever ask for."

"Dear Lord God you have heard the prayers of Gabby and my wonderful wife you gave to me. I will ask and please you, and thank you for all these things. Father you have cared for me, and my family for so long. For this I cannot thank you enough. You have brought other people into our lives that have let us grow in our Christian Faith. One is here now and we cannot thank you enough for her presents in our lives. We want to praise you for this good deed and I know it is because of your great love for your people. For all of this I thank you, praise you, and ask of you and your son to be with us until the end of which I am sure is not long in the future. Your Son's return for me will be soon I am sure and you know I am willing to go I just want my wonderful wife you sent me long ago to be in your hands to help her to get through her loss of me and the moving of our dear granddaughter Gabby she means so much to us as you know, and we want no we ask for your protection and guidance for her life. Let her be the best and the most for you in all you want from her. She is one of the most special people we know and our love for her is only by the grace you gave her to us to enjoy for so long. Lord God and through your son I pray for this girl and my wife. Be patient with them and know their thoughts and their love to you. Give them your love and let them meditate on your word. Give them the wisdom of your son through them and let that wisdom flow and your grace be more than sufficient for them. We love you Lord Jesus and please help us in our humanly form to serve you in all that we have until you come for us either one at a time or altogether. Thank you sweet Jesus in your name we pray. A-men."

Gabby gets up to leave for home she goes to grandma Hedi and then to grandpa Tom saying.

"Grandma I love you and I miss you already but life must go on as grandpa says."

She leans down and gives her a big hug and a kiss on her cheek. Then to her grandpa and doing the same only saying to him.

"Grandpa I have known no other man that has had any thoughts towards me but you and my dad you are the greatest for all you have done and given to me. With the knowledge of Jesus Christ and of mankind I know without a doubt in my life there is no room for any man unless he has the creature you do. I know how to be a woman and through you and my dad I now know what kind of a man I want to spend the rest of my life with when the two most important men has gone to be with my Lord and Savior Jesus Christ."

Wow! That is a very high compliment on my part and I will remember to be that man in your life as Jesus lets me. Now before you make me shed a tear of joy you had better get for home to help your mom you know it is after five o-clock."

Gabby looks at the clock to acknowledge and then said.

"I know but she knows how much you two mean to me and she also thinks I made a good choice for grandparents since I have no others alive and never got to know them in this life."

"Gabby you take this to your mother. Tom and I are so very grateful for the time your mom and dad has let you spend with us. You know from what Tom has told you many times being a grandparent to any child is a second chance for us to do a job that we did not have time to do with our own children as they grew up. You remember that when God gives you a family and children, that you spend time with them in more ways than just with shelter and food and clothes. They need wisdom from you and Jesus to go with the knowledge they will get from other trials and mistakes that will hinder them for most of their lives. This will happen as they walk along with others down the path they choose to follow. While walking that path with whoever they pick up make sure they get the right nurturing from you so they will not get the wrong from their so called friends."

"Yes Gabby you cannot push a rope it come out as a follower rather than a leader. Only God has the power to push a rope and that is because he wants you to catch hold and follow him and he want you to be as close to him as possible to know that he is leading you in the right places."

"Goodbye I have to go."

In unison they tell Gabby.

"Goodbye my child."

As she closes the door, and as she is walking home she is talking to God about her leaving and no one to help her grandma with her grandpa. She knows she has to find someone who would want to help every afternoon like she has been doing for about two years. Now she knows that her help is going to be missed. The fellowship that she has had with them will be gone and the loneliness will settle in to help their health tumble more rapidly. She had to talk to her mom about what she should do.

"Hi! Mom sorry I am late but time go so fast when I am at grandma Hedi's. Grandpa Tom is not feeling any better and stays in bed most of his day a sleeping. Can I talk to you about what grandma will do when I am not here to help her?"

"Well yes but there is nothing I can do at this time

and until your sister gets a job to help herself for the next two years I will have to work. So for just something for you to think about you could ask your sister to help some instead of spending all her time doing whatever with Al."

"Mom I think she is a hopeless case of laziness when it comes to working, but I will ask her if she could fine time after school and this summer getting to know them so she would know what to do. I don't believe she will want to it would spend some of her social time with her friends."

"It still won't hurt to ask."

"Do you need anything for supper that I can help with?"

"No I am serving make your own sandwiches and chips. If you see your sister tell her to come and set the table, and if not maybe you could do it instead."

"Okay mom you know I love you."

"Yes and every day I can feel the loss when you go to college, and there are days I want to tell you to wait one more year, but that would not be fair to you."

"It is going to be hard I know, but grandpa Tom says it is hard to let go and I know we have to do that before I leave and not after wards."

"That is wise, but as you know I am the mom and I am the one who has all her heart and soul in you to girls and I know that you are going to be in very capable hands, but it is still going to be on my mind for every day I do not get to see you. And yes I have thought about it for way over a year that your dad and I was going to have to give you totally up to the Lord and not worry if you are okay all the time. It will be easy for you but some day if God blesses you and Jan like your dad and I then you will know how I feel. You are going to a new place with lots of people your own age and you will make some friends and have someone to talk to each day, but we will be here in the same place doing the same things and you will not be coming through that door no matter how long we wait for you."

"Mom I am sorry, but grandma Hedi say's life must go on. Grandpa Tom say's we could hold you back by begging you to stay and help, but in the end they would only hurt themselves because soon or sooner I would leave any way."

"That is true but it still hurts and I will be alone because of the relationship and friendship that the two of us has had for so long a time."

"Thanks mom I love you too."

Gabby looks out the window to see her dad pulling into the driveway.

"Mom dad is home."

"Thanks if you help we can have dinner on the table very soon."

"Hello I am home how is my favorite trio of lovely's?"

"Thank you dear we are fine and dinner is almost ready you get washed up and get Jan from her room and come right back to the table."

"Good for some reason I am starved and it sure smells good. What are we having hot dogs and chili?"

"If that is what you want we can change and fix it for you, but roast beef and potatoes and gravy is what your trio is going to eat."

"I was only kidding be right  back."

After dinner as they returned to the living room was when Gabby had the choice to ask her small family for one lasting favor.

"I am glad we are all here I would like to talk to you about my going to college."

"Sis I have to do some last minute studies I still have to go to school for one more week."

"It will not take long. I want to ask if I could depend on my family to take turns going to see grandma Hedi and grandpa Tom after I leave? They are not in good health and they have no family here to help them. It has just been me for a long time. It is not much just to spend some time with them to make sure they have everything they need. It would not cost anything but a few hours a week. Jan you could do it every day after school, and mom and dad could do some on the weekends."

"Sis you are asking me to give up some of my social life and besides that is the time that Al and I do our studying."

"Jan it would not take more than thirty minutes each day I am sure that would not end your life with Al. think of it as being a servant to them like Jesus wants us all to do."

"Jesus does not take my test for me I am not like you just look and listen and get straight A's."

"Someday, you will be going to college then who will you have to study with. Al is not going to be going away with you. His family has no money for him to go to college. I believe this would be something that Jesus would approve of and take kindness on you for helping not only your sister but also someone who really needs someone for company and a last feeling of mankind in their parting years. It would be a blessing on you if you could open your heart and let God bless you while you were blessing those old folks."

"Mom okay I will think about it."

"Jan as your dad I hope you will make the right decision and your mother and I will also help when you have no time."

"Okay dad I will do it. Gabby when do I start?"

"Any time I leave in eight weeks and you can go with me any time you want to. They are lovely people and lonely because they are almost trapped in their home. You can just run errands for them or whatever you would like. They will appreciate it and you will be loved for doing it for them."

"Not until school it out for me then I will go with you,

but if I can't do it then you have to let me out of this deal is that okay."

"Yes Jan it is okay, but we want your heart in this and not because Gabby asked you to do it for her."

"Yes dad, may I be excused now?"

"Thank you Jan you are a good sister and I love you."

"Thanks mom and dad this has removed a big burden from my mind. I had decided if this does not work I would forgive a year of college and do some correspondence course if they would let me."

"Gabby we have talked about this and you know how we feel. Do not let this ruin your life they will make it some way, and all your prayers and caring will help them get to where God wants them in the coming year."

"I know dad but they are the only grandparents I have and I have learned what grandparents are for. You do not know the joy and love they have given me. They have prayed for me as much or more then you and mom has I have been their inspiration for the last two or more years. I care and I know that someday they will both be gone to be with Jesus and I want what time they have left to full of joy and happiness and love that they have given to each other in their lifetime. I want them to know that I am okay and taking care of myself so they will not worry about me. That is why I have asked you my family to except them as your family also. I know they are old but you are going to be blessed just to get to know them. I am going to miss them almost as much as I am going to miss you both. I know that they are not of your family but in time you will be so blessed just to get to know them as I have. There is never a day that they do not pray for Betty with earnestness and love for her as if she had been gone for only a day. They do the same for me and for Al you my family. I think I am going to retire for the night it has been a very long day for me. I feel like I have been swallowed into a big vacuum.

My day has ended and my life has just been shown a new way. Good night my wonderful parents."

"Good night Gabby it will be a grand new way you will see."

"I will pray for that and mostly thank God for the first years of my life and that the next how many will be not as hard as I have thought."

"Gabby you have no idea what is coming we have taught you all we can and from now on it will be up to you to grab and make the right choices in everything you see and do. All we can do now is pray and hope you will take what you have and increase it with only the wisdom that Jesus can give to you."

"I know dad and I love you both for your time and the trouble I caused in the last eighteen years trying to shape me to be me."

# CHAPTER THIRTEEN

"Betty you have been so good for us and I now feel I am going to lose another child and I don't know all I would like to know about you."

"Cora you are a great mother figure and I will not leave you I have grown to love and care for you and the sheriff. Do you know why he had to leave in such a hurry?"

"No child, I am used to his just getting a page, or a phone call and leaving in a hurry, and when he comes back home if it is of value to us he will tell us and if not he will be back to his old self."

"It is now after six do we eat or wait some more?"

"We will eat he will just have to eat warmed up food. He does that a lot but he is not unhappy because of it. So let's fix something we like and get it over with."

During their dinnertime they talked about what Betty might want to do when her ordeal with Thomas was over. What she wanted to do about college or if she even wanted to go to college. What she thought she might want to do for the rest of her life. Mostly that she had a home for as long as she wanted to stay.

"Betty I want you to be comfortable with us we don't

know how long this is going to last. You will be very safe here with us. In time the sheriff will find out more about your family and you may not get to go see them, but he could arrange for them to come here and meet you. We think them coming here would be the best for you and with less exposure in case you are being watched. I want you to realize that your folks are not going to be the same people you knew before this all started and you need a safe place to get to re-know them as they are today or whatever day this meeting happens."

"Cora, I have been thinking about that a lot and what maybe would be best is for my old friend Gabby and I meet first and she could bring me up to where my family is today since they do not live together any longer."

"That may be wise we can ask the sheriff what he thinks about it."

"He must be on something exciting it is way past his supper time so let's close up, and how about us playing some domino's?"

"Betty I would like that it will pass the time until he gets here."

"Cora do you think something has happened it is almost eight thirty and no call or anything?"

"No he has done this a lot of times so don't you worry. At first I was almost sick when our kid was small because he had not called or showed up. He will be here when he has the work done, and if I call him it will distract him and that will take him longer so I have learned to wait for him to show up or call."

"If I was married to someone like him I would be a mess by now knowing if he was okay or not."

"Maybe someday you will and in time you will be just like me or anyone else in the force. In time you will learn to accept it. If you do not, it will eat you alive and cause trouble in your marriage. So it is their work and our job to stand by them and part of that is worrying and praying that they are okay and will show up as they left."

"Okay I win and we are tied at two games each do you want to play more or do something else?"

"Well we can play one more and break the tie."

"Okay by then it will be off to bed. What time do you go to bed when he is not home?"

"I never stay up past eleven o-clock even if he is not home."

"Okay then if you stay up so will I. I need to be a part of this family and standing for the provider I shall do."

"No you don't have to stay up I am okay with him not being here."

"That is okay but I want too."

"Very well shall we play one more maybe I can tie this up again?"

"Okay your time to start."

"Well her goes and look who just arrived."

"Hello dear, you must be very tired and hungry?"

"Yes it has been a very long and trying day."

"You set down and I will get your dinner while you talk to Cora about your long day."

"I like that girl she seems to know when to go and when to stay, but all in all I am going to miss her when she goes away to stay."

"Me to but maybe we can help her to stay and go on to college this fall. Do you think we could help her in some way with the cost?"

"With the money that is in Thomas's bank account she can go and have lots left over. I just have to find out if it is good or bad money."

"Have you found out anything yet about Thomas?"

"Yes and when Betty comes back in we well all talk about what happened to day."

"Okay here is your dinner and I will go and leave you two alone to talk."

"Betty I need to talk to you can you come and set while I eat?"

"Sure if you want me too."

"Yes this has concerns about you and your future maybe."

"Oh what did I do?"

"Nothing but this will affect you for a while, and maybe change the rest of your life."

"Betty come and set beside me so he can talk to us both without looking over while he eats. Hurry I am getting over anxious to hear what he has to say."

Betty dragged up a chair next to Cora and waited for the sheriff to chew and start talking.

"Betty, as you know you have become, or we have become greatly attached to you living here. I am going to tell you what my afternoon and evening was about. Cora and I will be beside you and help in any way we can. It is going to be taxing on you. I have talked with the F B I and they say you can take your time and stay here with us and they will put out officers to watch all and every move you make, and if someone makes a move towards you. We picked up Thomas this afternoon when he arrived to take the money out of the bank. Right now all of his so call assets are tied up in the court and under my jurisdiction until further notice. Tomorrow first thing you will be asked to sign a legal guardian paper putting Cora and I as the ones you want to be with during this next whatever. You are also a ward of the court until this matter has been resolved and at that time you will be free to go and do, as you want. Am I going too fast for you if so do you have any questions at this time?"

"You really got him?"

"Yes he is in custody and being watched around the

clock until a judge has time to deal with his trial setting, then we will move forward with the F B I and your testimony of what happened. I will make sure you are not rushed. That is if you want us to be your guardians."

"Yes I would like that."

"You need a guardian even though you are now eighteen years of age but since you were only seventeen at the time this started with my department you will be treated as a minor until your trial is over."

"Hon how much money are you talking about and can Betty use it for her college fund?"

"Thousands and that will be determined if it is good or bad money and then what ever the judge will decide. Right now I am leaning towards bad there is just too much in his account and that is tied to two other banks also with money in them at about the same amount."

"So Thomas has been working with illegal people. What was he doing that kept him away for so long at a time?"

"Right now he is not talking, but he will have to open up sooner or later. Nobody can work at a job and collect all that much in a lot of life times. I or we think he was involved in a lot of different things. One of it has to be drugs of some kind. Two we know that money was transferred from California which means he could have been involved in kidnapping children, and put them to work in houses of ill repute or into child sex trade. One of his banks we found out today is in Los Vegas so that could be gambling or he was a booking agent, what we have to do now is wait. Someone will be looking for some of that money and maybe we can get the whole gang. That is why we called in the F B I it was your kidnapping, but that amount of money in different banks and in different states meant that he was in the laundering of money and that is a federal crime. You Betty are going to be at the bottom of the crimes and you are a high priority on their list, and our guess a high ransom subject. So from now on you are under strict orders to go no place without one of them with you at all times. Starting tomorrow there will be a woman move into here with us. They wanted to take you away until I told them we were going to be your guardians. That is why tomorrow you have to sign the papers. I want you to remember that we are not going to let anything happen to you. I want you to not worry about anything one of us will be here with you along with the F B I woman. You are going to be well taken care of and it will not be in a motel or running around the country. This is your home until you are free from this mess that you had nothing to do with. I am thankful that Karen decided to keep you or you could be some place that is not pretty for girls your age."

"Hon where is another person going to sleep in this house. It only has two bedrooms and your home office?"

"That will be a problem we may have a blow up mattress for her and she will be in Betty's room which may be a little crowded, but we have to abide with them. They have the power over us."

"I do not want any other person sleeping in my room with me. Right now I do not believe I can sleep at all. She can sleep in the office across the hallway. Would you let me do that?"

"If she will be okay. Tomorrow there will be several people in here bugging everything so starting tomorrow you have to be very careful of what you say everything will be recorded. It is not for us but for them to be alert to anything that may not be of the normal things that go on in a real home. I have to be up early in the morning so off to bed I go, and you two do not start worrying, everything is going to be okay. Good night this may be the only one we get for a while."

As told the next morning the F B I lady showed up at seven thirty. Betty and Cora were still in their pj's and robes, and then the surveillance people showed and started all through the house. The F B I lady was showed where she would be sleeping, but to their surprise they were told.

"I sleep where I decide and that is in your room and get used to it. I will be like glue and your paper until the investigation is final. Now do you move thing so I can put up my bed or do I?"

"Lady did the sheriff tell you I will not have anyone sleeping in my room?"

"Young lady I believe I was told your name is Betty and the sheriff does not tell me where I am to be watching or waiting now do you move it or do I?"

"Mam this young lady has been through hell and as long as you are going to be in our home you will not be the boss. As long as I live here and this is my home I will decide not you. You were told to sleep in the office den and if you stay here that is where you will stay. There is more than enough room in there for your bed. This is my daughter and this is her home so watch your step. Do I make myself clear."

"You can make it clear all daylong but in the end I will have my way. Nobody answers the door until I say so is that clear. This is not your daughter and you have no jurisdiction over her. She is not a minor and she is going to answer to me is that clear."

"No it is not and if you want control of everything in here then you buy if from us and you can do as you please. Until then you are a guest in our home and that is the way of it. Now you will sleep in the office den room and we will call it the guest room."

While this going on Betty is standing with a glum look on her face waiting for the first to start flying. The sheriff had come in and was waiting when Betty saw him and went to his side. As she looked up to him she said.

"Sheriff I believe they are going to come to blows and I am glad you came home."

"I will settle this but first I need you to sign these papers, and that will make us your guardian until you decide you do not need us any longer."

"I will be very glad to sign them."

After Betty had signed the papers the sheriff brought home the then folded them and put them in his pocket. Turning to go into the living room where his wife and the F B I lady were about to come to blows, and clearing his throat he asked.

"Well hello is this my home or is it some prize fighting arena. Hon what seems to be the matter Betty is half scared out of her head."

"This woman came in here and started telling us what and where and would not take no for an answer, and I was defending our home except she says she is in charge from now on, I was telling her this is our home and if she wanted to be in charge or control then she needed to buy it from us and then she could control the dirt on the floor if she wanted too. Now you tell her so she will understand what I am talking about."

"Sheriff I believe that you know that girl is in our custody until this is over. She will be my responsibility during that time. Your wife does not understand our rules so I want you to tell her what is up."

"Okay ladies I will make the decision and you all will abide by it. These papers here are the court orders for guardian ship for Betty and they happen to have my wife's name and mine on them. This girl Betty is staying in the only home that she knows and you will honor these papers, and our home, if not then you go and see your superiors and tell them to come and see me. You might be in charge of this investigation but you are not this home. You are a guest while you are here in our home. Understood now hon, I do not want you to cause any problems you are still the woman of this house and what you say I will back is that clear. Hon I want you to be with Betty at all-time especially when any one is asking her any questions. You know enough about the law so you can guide her through a lot of it and if not you tell her to not say anything. I will get the county attorney to be the lawyer until some other arrangements can be made. Now I want peace between you two and you will do as my wife says or you can be replaced is that clear before I go and do my job as the sheriff of this county?"

"Yes sir where do I sleep?"

"In the room that my wife told you to sleep. Now I have business to attend to and have to go. One more thing this young lady has gone through more in the past few years then any one ever should have to go through. And from now on I am telling you and you tell the rest of your buddies to go easy on her or you will report to me and I can get very mean if I have to. I will protect her to the fullest intent of the law within this state. I hope this will work because if I had my way you all could go back and crawl under the can you came from, and you can tell the rest of your people that they will respect my family and my home while they are around it. I have said more then I wanted to say and I hope it can be left here. I will see you at lunch dear, and I do not want to come home to anything like this again."

After the sheriff left the three women stood and looked at each other and then they looked at nothing. Finally, Cora spoke up.

"There is someone at the door would you like to answer it?"

"Yes it is probably my clothes and the bed I ordered

but I see it will have to go back and I will get a blow up mattress. I will tell them to set up my things in the office den room is that okay?”

“Yes you go ahead Betty and I will go get into something different we don't want everybody to think we just got up. Come Betty let us go and change and we can then get to our normal things for the day.”

“Thank you Cora I was beginning to think that we were at war or something.”

“Sometimes you have to tell people that no matter what you are of authority and that you are still a human being, and they are not to trample over you. I had a feeling this was going to happen as soon as she arrived it is not the first time I have been confronted by the F B I people who believe that they are the utmost about everything and we who pay their wages and we are the un-most under them. See you in a few minutes and if she tries to intimidate you at any time, you let me know and do not be afraid to tell her no any time you feel squeezed by her pressure to be right and a little above you. She is only human and that is the same as we are so we are equal in what life has for us.”

“Thank you again Cora, I will not take long it is my day to wash my hair, but I will hurry since some of our day has been wasted because of my life.”

The rest of the day went well the F B I woman and her partners did a lot of talking and planning, but they never said anything to Betty or Cora. It was time for the sheriff to come home when the doorbell rang, and every one became very quiet. Waiting for the F B I woman to do the talking to the outside people to find out who was calling. Soon she went to the door and slowly opened it to find the sheriff deputy standing there. After looking at him she opened up with.

“Well what do you want, you know you are not supposed to be here. So speak what are you here for?”

"I have come to bring this message to Mrs. Cora it is from."

Before he could finish the note was swished away from him and the door shut in his face. Turning back, she opened the envelope and was talking the note out when Cora asked.

"Who was at the door and what did they want?"

"One of the deputies with a note for you."

"If it is for me then why are you reading it?"

"Because everything that comes and goes from this place goes through me."

Cora reached and grabbed the note from her hand saying.

"I am not going to put up with you when someone sends me a note or message then how dare you think you are going to read it before I do. I want you out of here until my husband comes home and I mean right now. You don't want me to have to call him. You have stepped on me one to many times, and now out before I throw you out."

"I am not going any place so back off."

"Betty call the sheriff for me please while I read what he has to say."

"I will be happy to do your bidding."

The note was in code that her and the sheriff had used all their marriage life. As Cora deciphered it while waiting on Betty it came to her as.

"Be careful and do not say anything there is a F B I person missing except all their people are accounted for so we believe there is an insider person imposing as one of them."

When the sheriff called and was told of the incident he asked to talk to the F B I woman telling her.

"I am going to talk to your boss because you don't seem to be able to take orders, and you might as well start packing because you are and was told to leave our house and be gone when I get there.”

After hanging up the phone she turned and addressed Cora and Betty.

I am leaving and you will wish you had me stay because the next one will not be as easy as I was.”

“Can we help throw your things out that door?”

Betty looked at Cora with a half-smile on her face. Within fifteen minutes the sheriff was home with him was a younger woman with a large suitcase. After being introduced to Cora and Betty as the replacement she asked.

“Where do I sleep and my name not what I am going to tell you but you can call me Brady while I am here.”

“Okay Brady you sleep in the office den first door on the left. Betty has the room across the hallway from you. The sheriff and I are in the one at the end of the hallway.”

“Okay I will unpack and then we can get to know each other.”

“Cora where did the other lady go?”

“She left about ten minutes before you arrived and I did not see where she went or if she went with someone. Why?”

“This lady Brady came late because of the airline was having trouble with the plane and when she called in she was told someone would take her place and now we do not know which one of them is the real F B I person. So be careful of anything that goes on with her and who she is talking too. I leave you two as the ones who are going to check her out while she is watching you. Cora you know what to watch for and you can tell Betty what to watch for by using the code. Remember write everything down and do not talk unless asked too. I have to go now and I will be home at the same time as always.”

“Well I am in and ready. How are you, and is there anything you need to know about me?”

"Not at this time Betty and I are going to her room and that will give you time to catch up on what you need to know about your home and the way it is set up."

"Good see you after a while and then we can get to know each other."

"Come Betty I want to show you something that you need to know if I am gone some time."

"Great."

In Betty's room Cora puts her finger to her lips and gets a piece of paper and writes down a note for Betty to read.

"Em ma osrry ot have this ahpen ot oyu. Od oyu nuder tsand nay fo this. Handing Betty, the note, and Betty looking at her shaking her head.

Writing down she explains that the first letter becomes the second one and the second one becomes the first one

"Od oyu egt ti onw.".

"Do you get it now?"

"Eys."

Writing more to say this is how we will communicate from now on and destroy each note after reading it. With a smile Cora said.

"See that is simple wasn't it."

"I am sorry I could not get it at first but yes it is very simple now."

"Okay we need to go and get dinner ready and find out if this Brady lady is going to eat with us."

"You go start Cora and I will ask her and be right in."

The evening went very well, the family spent time together and the F B I left them alone even though everything they said was heard and recorded. Except when they wrote down things in their code words. Before they went to bed they all bowed and prayed that God would let things smooth out for them. The next two days were about the same except for the questioning of Betty that did not go well with her. She was not willing to relive the past ten years, and a lot that she had forgotten about. Nonetheless it went on until Cora told them they needed to take a rest and leave Betty alone so she could do some thing for her. This started a small rumble until the sheriff told them that they needed to back off and go reread the papers that were about the same thing as they were asking. Brady came back with.

"We want to know if she knows the truth and if some of her story is made up to make it look bad."

"She is not going to remember all the things you are asking her. She was a small girl and scared out of her mind when this all started you already have the records of that beginning locked away somewhere so go and get them. Now if that is not good enough then I still can ask you to leave just like the last one. This is our home and it is going to be her safe place so let her rest and go out and follow up on the leads I have given you already. If you want them answered then you go to the jail and ask Mr. Thomas about what happened, but you let this girl rest. I believe that will be all for now."

One week later Brady came to the sheriff, and Cora saying.

"I think it is time to confront Thomas with Betty present to get some of these lies into truths. I would like to do it tomorrow at one-o-clock do you have a problem with this. She can have as many present as she feels she needs. There is going to be two questions asked of him. I do not want Betty to know about this meeting. Let me know by tonight so I can let my team know,"

"We will let you know."

Later that evening Cora and the sheriff took Betty aside and in their code writing they ask her.

"There is going to be a meeting tomorrow at the jail

in front of Thomas and they want you to be there are you going to be okay with this?"

"If Cora and you are going to be there it is okay."

"We will be there. I will tell Brady to go ahead and set up what she needs and it will happen outside his cell only."

"Fine with me I will try to be ready."

When the time came Cora and Betty were escorted to the jail where they meet up with the sheriff and two other F B I men and Brady. When they got to the cell area there was a large sheet hanging in front of one of the cells. There were chairs set up and a table with recording devices on it to record all that was said. When they were all seated the two F B I men got up and removed the sheet. Thomas was setting on his bed with his head between his hands and when he looked up there was a surprised look on his face.

"Thomas we have company for you and also we have two questions we are going to ask you is that okay with you?"

Thomas said nothing he was staring at Betty with that look he always used on her.

"Thomas do you know this girl?"

"Yes she stayed at Karen's house a long time."

"She says that you and Karen kidnapped her on a ski trip up in Colorado about ten years ago."

"That is not true we were up there on vacation and she begged us to take her away from the family she was with."

"Betty is that true?"

"No they took me away from my family and friend Gabby, and held me so I could not get away. He and his wife did this to me."

"Karen was not my wife she was a woman who took care of you and my property when I was away."

"Thomas did you take this girl along with your wife from Colorado ten years ago?"

"It was Karen who took her I had nothing to do with it. I may have done some wrong things but I did not do anything to hurt that girl. I was gone a lot of the time working."

"Did you ever try to force yourself upon her in a sexual way?"

"No I did not."

"Betty did he ever try to hurt you in any way?"

"Not until his wife died, and then he told me he was going to do the same things to me as he did Karen and that was to fix his meals and do his laundry when he came by. Then he was in my room in his underwear trying to touch me and that is when I took the knife and cut him., and was running away when the sheriff and the doctor arrived to help me. If they had not come when they did, then he would not be setting in there he would be dead in his sleep. I told him that I would if he ever tried to hurt me in any way. He also helped kill his wife when she needed to be in the hospital he would not take her. You can ask the doctor if that is true or not."

"Thomas is what she just said true or not?"

"I have no more to say."

"Very well your court time is coming soon."

Thomas set there until all was up and walking away when he said.

"Betty I did not have any intentions of ever hurting you. Karen wanted you and I helped her but it was all her idea. I am sorry that you feel the way you do about me."

The F B I man said to him do not say any more it will be held against you in court.

# CHAPTER FOURTEEN

Gabby was having the worst summer of her life. She was torn between her family and her grandparents and leaving for Texas for college. So far she was okay with the college part because she had some place to stay that was somewhat family, because of grandma Hedi and Grandpa Tom's. Their son's place was going to be her new home away from home. She had left her parents and sister behind her to go and get her education so she could become a teacher. Her heart was open and closed because of the condition of her grandpa Tom's health. Her grandma Hedi's strength that was all she could do to help her husband to get where he needed to be and back to bed again. She had talked her sister Jan into going every day to help her grandma Hedi and her mom and dad to help on the weekends, but still she was concerned that she may not ever see her grandpa Tom again after she left for school. When he went to be with Jesus she was going to miss her best friend and counselor of her life she respected him more than any other man she knew. Not as often as usual on her mind was on her friend Betty and why she had not come back home to see her family. But that was God's plan and she had no way of ever knowing until Betty just showed up one day and then she could stop praying for her return.

$$* * * * *$$

Betty was going to get through the six month or so that she was involved dealing with the kidnapping case of Karen and Thomas, or whatever they had been involved with. She also wanted to go to college, but there was no money for her to go on. She had decided that the sheriff and Cora were not there for her to borrow money from for her schooling, and the courts doings she may miss the first semester of college or more. The only thing she had going for her was her new home and that she had learned so much about herself and Jesus Christ by going to church with Cora and the sheriff. Since Thomas's arrest, the F B I, because of what the scare of the Thomas case might throw at her, has held Betty captive in her new home.

She knew little about her old family except that she had been told that her mom and brother still lived at the same place in Colorado that she remembered she had lived before. She still had not heard just what had happened to her dad. She knew that her old friend Gabby was still living with her family. None of these people had been told that she was still alive or where she was. She knew that in time she would be reintroduced to them, but this trial and the closed minds of the courts was going to end first so she could go about life without anyone trying to harm her from the past that she had nothing to do with, or knew anything about what Thomas and Karen had done.

$$*  \quad *  \quad *  \quad *  \quad *$$

Gabby had two weeks before she was to be taken to Texas for school. Her mom and dad were going to take what little she needed to Texas when the time came. Gabby found her mom crying a lot when she thought she was alone. One day when she had come back from seeing her grandma and grandpa she found her mom in her room crying and sobbing when she opened the door to see what was wrong her mom looked up wiping the tears from her eyes.

"Mom why are you doing this to yourself if this is all about me leaving then I will not go. If you keep this up I will stay and do what I can to help grandma and grandpa. We have discussed this many times and you know there is nothing I can do to help you but stay. So what are you going to do about this and the life you still have with dad and Jan? Don't make me feel guilty for leaving to get my education so I can go and do what I feel God is leading me to do. When you do this it makes me smaller and weaker which will hurt me every day I am gone thus helping me to fail in my classed. I want you and dad to be proud of me, and what I am going to be. I want you to pray for me while I am gone. I want to come back when I can to know that you both along with my grandparents are healthy and okay. I do not need for someone to call me and tell me you are sick because I left. I want you to be happy for me and turn your life wholly on Jan so she can have the same relationship with you as I have had."

"Gabby I am sorry but until I don't have you I cannot stop the sadness in my heart still knowing that you are just a phone call away. I know that when you see me it makes you sad and at the same time of giving up, but I am happy for you and what you have accomplished in your short life here. I pray that you will not take my sadness with you that is not my intent. I want you to go happy and knowing we are going to be okay. Someday God willing you will have to go through this as I am and then you will know the pain and suffering women are to go through when God decides to make you a mother. It is built within us to go through this pain for you to understand why God made us the way he did. Giving us the suffering even though our children are grown and can manage on their own."

"Thanks mom someday I hope I get to experience this same thing. By then I will know more about how you now feel."

"I am sure that God had those intentions set aside for you. And though his Grace you will find the one or he will find the one he has planned all along for you to spend a glorious life serving him together. Then you will become the mother of the gift he has for you to share. And at that time he will let you experience a new and different life of love and caring which will be much different then you are going through at this time. Then in your later life I will be experiencing the same things as your grandma has enjoyed with you. And my wish and prayers are that you enjoy those years with happiness and joy and be able to glorify God and his son Jesus during your life.

I believe that is why grandma Hedi and grandpa Tom was placed in your life and you in there's also. So you could have that experience and the pain that goes along with it. God is preparing you and I for the life to come. And with sadness in my heart knowing all this is happening yet makes me sad, but I know in the end you and I will know the peace of Jesus Christ and the Grace of the Father in Heaven to see us through all our happiness and sorrows and end with him in the Heavenly Kingdom he has planned for us."

"Mom you are so wise and thoughtful just like grandma Hedi, and I pray that my sister Jan will also get the feeling I have for them and for herself during the short time she may get with them."

"I hope you are right. Now it is time that you finish your packing and spend your last evening with Tom and Hedi. Tomorrow morning early, you have to be on the bus to Texas,"

"I know and I am almost ready all I have left is my sleeping clothes and I need them tonight. I have my traveling clothes laid out and so I guess I need to go and be back for supper and dad for my last evening for a while. Supper still at six and I shall be here."

"Just do not be too emotional with them."

"I will be careful mom."

As Gabby walked along the street she recalls all the times she had walked to the Benson house in all kinds of weather. Knowing that when she arrived it would be like she had been gone forever. Gabby had flashes of her and Betty walking along and thinking about their future and what they would have done. Now it was a clean picture in her mind. When she reached the picket fence gate tears came into her eyes because she knew that it might be the last time she saw her grandpa Tom alive. Wiping away the tears she pushed forward and knocked on the door. Waiting for the familiar face to be in the doorway when it opened.

"Well look who is here come in it is good to see you. Can you stay long this time or do you have something else to do?"

"I can stay until about six then I have to be home for supper."

"Okay you go on in and see Tom and I will bring in the milk and cookies. I just got them out of the oven so they are hot and soft."

"Thank you grandma Hedi you are such a good hostess when I come to see you."

"Oh dear child that is all I have to do is serve you and pamper that old man in that room tied to his bed."

"Grandma you are such a dear one."

"Get on with you and go and cheer up that grandpa of yours. He has been asking so many times when you were going to show up."

Knocking on the door and opening it just a small amount then asking.

"Grandpa it is me can I come in?"

"Me who? I may not want any company right now."

"Me who. This is Gabby."

"Well I should have known get on in here so I can get my hug. Where have you been I have not seen you for days."

"Grandpa I was here yesterday don't you remember?"

"Yesterday was history; I am too old to live back there. What if I had died then I would not be here today. Oh thank you Gabby you give this old heart a boost of energy every time you show up."

"I am glad I can do that it makes me feel good when I know I can come and see you. it will be a long time before I see you the next time. But my sister Jan will come every day while I am away. If not my mom or dad will come to help you."

"I know but it will not be our Gabby, and she will be the missed one in my mind and heart. That is the only thing I have left that I fear besides leaving Hedi all alone."

"Grandpa is it hard knowing that one's life is almost over?"

"Well when I was young it was much harder than it is now. It is something you do not realize or dwell on when you are young, but now it is on my mind almost daily. Some days, I do not want it to happen and others wishing it was over. But no matter what I think it is up to my Lord Jesus to make that decision. And being afraid, no I am not, I am happy that it is near. Gabby my dear this is a good way of looking at life and death. Each day you go through the process and the longer the days the more it will come to you. I realize that each day I am born again to this life and die from this life that same day. I wake up to a new life each day and at nighttime I go to sleep trusting God that he will let me be born again when morning comes again. If not then I am going to sleep or die that same time. You can be fearful during the day or waking time but when you go to sleep you forget all about the fear and that lets your body rest to be refreshed when you are to be born again the next day. Now that I am old I do not fear much anymore. Does that make since to you?"

"You know what grandpa I have never had it put to me in that way, but it does make some since and have a good feeling about it. That makes me realizes that I should not be afraid for you and grandma even knowing where you will be when you are born again in the light of Heaven."

"Hey you two are you ready for your snack time?"

"Yes mother where have you been I was beginning to think we would not get any. Hum, these smell so good, and hey they are still warm just the way I like them."

"Your grandpa says that all the time he likes them hot or cold or two days old. This man has eaten ten thousand times his weight and more of my cookies and milk. If you could see between his skin, you would find a layer of milk chocolate."

"Grandma Hedi I am sure you are right and just maybe that is why he is so sweet all the time."

"Could be."

"Young lady when are you leaving for Texas for college? Does my son know when you are going to arrive?"

"Early tomorrow morning and Yes he does."

"That soon I knew it was coming up, but just did not want it to be so soon."

"Grandpa I am sorry but time just keeps running along and no way to stop it. I will write you and call when I have the time and the money."

"I know but I will miss that wonderful smiling face that arrives every day."

"How about if my mom bring you one of my last pictures?"

"That will be okay, but I want it to be different than the ones I have now. You know these just stare at me and say nothing. I kind of like the picture that talks to me, and sets in that chair and listens to this old man."

"Grandpa you are going to make me cry and that will make you and grandma sad, and make me want to not go. My mom has a new picture of me, and when she gets them back she will bring you one of them."

"Gabby, don't let this old goat get to you. We have talked about this for some time and yes we are going to miss you greatly, but we know you are going to be in good hands and our prayers will always be out there for you. Now for a happy note lets pray for you and that will take to this new school ad show them what you are made of."

"Thank you grandma who would like to start?"

"I would like to finish." Said grandpa Tom.

"I would like to start."

As they all bowed their heads and took each other's hands grandma Hedi opened up- the prayer time.

"Heavenly Father this is a sad time yet is has all the happiness we can stand. We have to let this young lady go so she can go to college and get the higher learning that you want her to get. She has been such a wonderful and special child and friend to us. We know it is going to be hard not only for us but for her also. So I ask for your loving kindness and love to follow her as she goes her way and always guide her in the things you have for her to do. Let her do good and learn the things you want her to do. She is one of our most cherished children and we do love her so much. Now with your love and your kindness, power, and strength to her to guide and mold her. Help her not to miss this home or the one she lives in or the people that live in them homes. Give her the guided time to learn without the missing of her family and friends. Bring new friends into her life those who you want to be there. We still ask that Betty still be watched over and only you know where she is and what she has gone through. Let her be some day reunited with Gabby and her family. As I now let this girl go I will miss her dearly, but I know someday some way I and we will see her again on this side or the other. So I ask that you keep your hand upon her so she knows that you are there for her. In your precious sons name I lift her to you and to Him. In Jesus name I pray. A-men."

Gabby looks up with tears in her eyes and goes and gives her grandma a big hug then goes and sets down and bows her head.

Heavenly Father, Glorious Father, mighty one, and Holy one. I feel so alone at times since Betty has been gone and this couple who I call grandma Hedi and grandpa Tom has filled my life with so much love and prayers and only you know how much I love them and will truly miss them. They are old weary and sometimes sick yet they are so much full of the love of your Holly Spirit. That it amazes me to know and understand how they do what they do and what they know. Please comfort them in the days ahead. I pray for their safety and health that during these days that they can enjoy their time that you have left for them. They are deeply embedded in my heart and mind. There is and will not be a day I do not pray for them. I praise you Lord God for bringing them into my life they are so important to me as you know. Even though they are not my blood grandparents I know they were sent to me to show me what it can be like to have grandparents. I thank you for them both and the presents they have shown to me during this time. As I pray and will leave tomorrow I will miss them and even if I never see them again on earth or this world I know someday we will be together again. They are special and dear to me and I know they are the same to you. As I finish please comfort them through their pains and support their griefs. I am going to miss them dearly and I ask my Lord and Savior Jesus Christ to be with them always. In your name Jesus I pray. A-men."

The room was quite for a short time then grandpa Tom cleared his throat and hesitated for a little while longer then he spoke.

"Father God hallowed be thy name. I know you are here with us as we are united in this room. Along with us I feel your presences and your touch. I am and old man my life here is almost over. My lovely wife is in the same place and shape as I am almost. Yet here in this room is a young child your gift to us through her parents, and she is leaving in the morning. We will not see her for a long time. Yet she will be with us for as long as you give us. She has brought much joy and happiness into our lives. She is and has been more special than life its self. Only a God like you could have arranged this for us to enjoy. We have so much to thank you for letting her be a part of our lives. Now take her your way let her be what you had planned for her alone to be. Yes, we will miss her, but we know that she is now being lifted up with the hands, the love, and the Grace that only you can provide. Let her not worry, fret, or fear for us. Keep her mind on the things you are going to teach her. We ask that you bless the home of our sons and his family and let Gabby fall into place as a part of that family. Keep her healthy and strong. She has gone through a lot with losing her best and dearest friend. During this time, we ask that you keep Betty in the same prayers that we ask you for this wonderful girl here with us. Gabby is now striking out by herself into a new life. Help her to stay focused on you and the work you have laid out for her to do and be. Keep her safe from the things that the Devil has in store for her. Rebuke him in all things he tries to dump in her path. Give her good health and the wisdom from your Son to keep her on track. I know soon she has to leave and we want our hugs and kisses to go with her and as we pray later that the hugs and kisses will be performed by the Holy Spirit so she will know we are there, and thanking and praying for her in your Sons precious name. We love you Jesus and we all want to serve you for all the days of our lives. A-men."

"Well I hate to say this, but if I eat my last meal with my family I need to be going. You two take care of each other and I will see you some time sooner than later I hope. I am going to miss you and I will write and call when I get the time. I do not know how much time I will have with school and then watching the kids until their folks get home."

"You do what you have to do and do not worry about us we will be fine."

Gabby if you need anything you get back to us. We do not have a lot, but we could do without if you were really in need. Like money for a phone card, stamps, writing paper, or envelops."

"Thank you grandpa but I believe I am set in that field, but food is my biggest worry at this time. I do not want to sponge off of your son and his family. I do not know if the things will cost more down there then up here. I have to go before I start to shed tears and I want to leave on a happy note."

Gabby gave each a big hug and a special kiss on each cheek and then left for home.

"Hi mom I am home. What can I do to help?"

"You make sure you are ready to go this meal is going to be free of your help. I want this to be a special meal just for you. Jan will be back shortly and she will help. Your dad called and said he would be about thirty minutes late. So you go and enjoy your time and checking your luggage.

Then bring it all down so it will be ready in the morning. Dad will put it in the car tonight for you."

"Okay and thanks mom."

Sue had made Gabbys favorite meal and as they set down to eat they all started laughing. Gabby did not get the joke but then her grandparents come with the help of her dad and they were seated.

"Okay this is one special time for one very special girl who is leaving for a while. So this is going to be a time of fun and no bo-bo-bo's just laughter and happiness. Let us pray. Lord this is our time with you so we want this to be of your greatest love and you for Gabby. Thank you for this food and the hands that prepared it for us to enjoy. We ask your Holly Spirit to be over Gabby as long as she is away from us. Let her be careful and keep her safe in your son's name we pray. Thank you Jesus we love and adore you, and care for the time you have with us. A-men."

The meal was just what they wanted it was a big happy time and when it was over Don got ready to take the grandparents' home. This was Gabbys whole family whom she had trusted her life to and wanted them to trust her judgments when she was away. When Don came back the girls were all ready for bed and were setting in the living room waiting for him.

"Well look at you three maybe I should go and get into my p j's and we can have a good old p j party."

"Dad by the time you get them on we will all be in bed five o-clock comes early and I cannot be late for my bus. So good night to my special family."

"Good night dear sleep good."

"You to mom."

"Gabby I know our life's have been on the up's and down's when we were younger but I am going to miss my only sister."

"Jan I will miss you too."

With a big long hug and some tears, they parted and Jan went to her room. Gabby set on the coach in the dim light that filtered through the window from the streetlights. There she spent some time going over the last years that she was now going to give up for another life. Then she also turned in after her longest prayer she had, had before going to bed at any other time she could remember.

Next morning all went well and Gabby was on her bus waving out the window trying not to show her tears. Twenty-four hours later she would be in her new home in a new state with a new family. God help me to be in order so this will be a smooth change over."

*****

Betty was now being prepared by her lawyer for the trial of Thomas, which would start in two weeks. There was still a lot that the sheriff did not know about Thomas. One thing for sure he knew that there was almost two million dollars that had been found in banks with his name on the accounts all was still in place waiting for someone to come and get part of it or all of it, but so far no one had showed. The sheriff and the F B I still had not traced it back to any eligible actives. The thoughts of drug and child prostitution were tops on their list, so far the only thing they had was if they could trick him into saying something about him going to do something to Betty in a sexual way. If they could trick him into saying that he was going to force himself on Betty before she was of age that alone would get him life in prison without parole. The F B I was still watching the sheriff's house even though the woman had left because of no actions upon the house. The bug system was still in place and was monitored from a van outside somewhere close. Betty and Cora had more freedom around and in the house that at one time had become a house prison to them. After a session with her lawyer Betty was escorted home by taxi and when she opened the door she hollered for Cora.

"Cora I am home."

"I am in the kitchen preparing dinner and you are home earlier than usual."

"Yes I am through until next week when the trial starts."

"That is good maybe you and I can enjoy a better time. We need to talk about your future and what do you want to do."

"You know I would like to go to college but I have no money so I probably should start looking for a job so I can support myself. You and the sheriff do not need me on your burden list. I need to become responsible for me. When I look at my future I can only see staying here forever and not becoming anything but a hermit crab floating through life with all these things always stopping me from becoming me."

"You will see Betty that when this trial begins your life is going to start to change into something for the better. You do not have to think about your future until this is over and out of your life. Then you will be able to look forward and start to think about what you want to do and dream and hope for yourself and the life God has intended for you."

"I hope you are right, I look at my life as just one blank space and wonder just why God has let me go through all this and not have helped me to get free a long time ago. Our pastor has talked about how God loves us and I wonder why he loves some people differently than others. You know like me and then you and the sheriff. I have met young boys and girls at church who I would give my life to have been loved like they have been."

"Betty first God loves all of us the same, you have

been in a group that the Devil and you will see soon he is going to have to turn loose of you and Jesus is going to make sure that you will be set free from Satins hold on your life. God wants all his children to be at peace with themselves and those that are around them. You have to know this and we are going to get you through this tragedy that has pledged you for so long. The sheriff and I are not going away we are going to help you to overcome this past life and then help you get started on your way to one and only happy times that you are going to talk and walk with the Grace of God that he has given to you. Then and only then will you forget your past and be able to enjoy your future. When you get to meet your friend and your family and get excited again the sheriff and I will still be there for you to come to any time you need us. You have grown into our lives and we want you to know we are not going away. You are going to be our adopted daughter for the rest of our lives, and you and only you can take that away from us."

"Hello I am home is dinner ready? If so I will be right in."

"Yes it is you go and get cleaned up and join."

"Betty home yet?"

"Yes she is with me in here."

"Good I have something for her."

"Maybe he has more good news."

"It is better then what we had."

As he slipped into the dining room.

"How was your time today with your lawyer?"

"We are through until the trial starts."

"That is good and we caught a woman trying to take money out of one of the bank accounts. She was surprised he was locked up. Said she was his wife and they had two children in high school. We are looking for more than one marriage license so we can get him on bigamy. That will help his cause and we hope she can tell us some of the things we need to know so as to have more to pin on his backing. So far she is smart or just does not know what he did for a living. Like you said about Karen when he never showed up. She is saying the same thing except that she has been married to him for about the same amount of years as when you were kidnapped. So unless we find out more then we just have someone else who depended on his money to get through life. He treated her with respect and always cared for the two children."

"Can I asks what will this do for me?"

"That will be up to the judge, and if Thomas opens up to any of the questions that he is asked."

"Hon, what if he does not, what will Betty have to say to get them all on her side?"

First she has nothing to worry about the lawyers did not like to be brought into a kidnapping trial it is not their thing, and there is no one else available at this time. That is in our favor so you just smile when you need to and do not smile when asked any questions."

"I am not scared but I am a little nervous. I do not want to do anything that will make me stay any longer in this mess then I have too."

"Trust me you are going to be very happy when this is all over. Now can we eat?"

# CHAPTER FIFTEEN

Gabby was now in Texas and has met her new family and called home to her family and grandparents to tell them she was safe and was going to like her new home. She would be very busy for a while getting enrolled in college and planning her new life. The thing's that she has thought about that has changed is more on her part then any of the family members she has left behind. They have to think about one person Gabby and that she will not be there at any time they need or want to talk to her. It is about the people that Gabby has left to go to another part of her life and that they are going to take up a lot of her thoughts. She will have to spend time each day wondering if her mom is okay or still weeping over her loss of a child, or her sister who is doing what they agreed to happen with her grandma Hedi. Her dad that is probably the only one who has given into his loss of a daughter but will still miss her without saying too much about it. And a lot of time about her grandma Hedi and the work that she has to do just to get through each day if no one goes to help her do what Gabby had been helping with for over two years. And most of all the time she will miss talking and cheering up her grandpa Tom who she may never see again this side of Heaven. So the thoughts, before each one is a lot different in their minds.

✳ ✳ ✳ ✳ ✳

Betty was starting her time with the trial and she was very scared because of the way that Thomas looked at her all the time. She had set through three days of talk that she did not understand. She knew that she was sweating on the inside because she had to look at Thomas all the time. On the fourth day Betty, was called by the judge to come and set in the witness chair beside his desk. As she got up she turned to look at Cora and the sheriff, but she could not make her legs walk up to the chair.

Your honor may I talk to her for a moment?"

"Sheriff you know I let no one talk to a witness unless I ask him or her too. The answer is no she is big girl and I have asked her to come forward and if she cannot do it then I will have someone help her. Now Betty will you come forward and take this seat?"

Betty slowly walked forward to the front when she was seated she was asked to swear on the bible to tell the truth. The whole truth and nothing but the truth so helps her.

She answered slowly.

"Yes if I can."

For the next two hours she was asked questions about the years after the time she was kidnapped. She answered all of them to the best she could remember. When asked if she had been molested she could not answer. Thomas was setting looking at her with that look on his face.

"Betty you have to answer the question. Did Thomas this man setting over there ever molest you in any way while you were being held captive in this home where they took you?"

"Yes!"

"In what way?"

"Just like he is doing now."

"But he is over there and you are over here. How can he have molested you like you say?"

"The way he looks at me; the way he came into my bedroom in his under wear. The way he touched me when I stabbed him in the arm."

"Betty did he ever have any sexual time with you?"

"Not like you think but he tried three times without doing the act."

"The act of what?"

"You know I don't have to say it. He is an evil man and I want him out of my life and my sight. I will not answer any more of your stupid questions while he is setting there licking his lips like I was a lollypop."

"Betty did he ever touch your breast or between your legs?"

"Not while I was awake but he tried and I told him I would kill him if he tried. When he got close that day I took the knife and stabbed at him and ran outside. That is when the doctor and the sheriff showed up. My answer is yes."

"No more questions for now."

After a short recess the judge came back into the courtroom and looked at Thomas.

"Thomas will you stand up I have one question to ask you. Thomas did you ever touch or attempt to touch this girl while she was in your home?"

"I could have and I probably should have because I am being blamed for doing it any way. But I still say I had no intentions of doing anything to harm that girl she was like my own child."

"Do you have any other children?"

"No I have never created a child with a woman in my life."

"Thomas we have a woman outside who says she is married to you. Would you like to see her and the two children that is with her?"

"That is a lie. I had only one wife and she is dead."

"Bring in the family."

"Now do you know of this woman and these two children that are with her?"

Thomas said nothing, he just stood there and looked at them.

"Thomas is this your wife and children?"

Thomas lowered his head and said nothing then in a low voice he mumbled something.

"Thomas, are these your family speak up so I can hear you?"

"Yes!"

"Did you ever try to have sex with the girl that lived with you and Karen?"

"Yes!"

"Did you kill your wife Karen who lived with you by not taking her to the hospital when she need to be there even after the doctor said she needed to go?"

"Yes!"

"This case is closed I will make my judgment tomorrow morning at ten o-clock the jury is dismissed to leave we will not need for you to make a judgment in this trial. Take that man away from my courtroom and do not bring him back. I believe he knows what his judgment is going to be. Tomorrow the only people I want to return is Betty, the sheriff, you two F B I men and the two lawyers. This court is adjourned."

It was a quite night at the sheriff's house no one said much. The next morning after eating a light breakfast they all went to the courthouse to hear Thomas's judgment. When they arrived the judge was waiting and when Cora walked in he said.

"Cora you're not supposed to be in here, but because you are the acting mother of this girl you can stay. Where is the two F B I men do they think I am going to wait on them forever? Sheriff while we do wait on them go and get Thomas I have decided to let him come in to hear his sentencing."

When all had arrived the judge remarked by saying.

"This is the worst case I have ever had in my court room and I hope it is the last I will be back in a moment just stay seated."

When the judge came back out he looked at Betty and said.

"Young lady I am sorry for what you have been through and I have tried to make something out of this so you could have a new start in life. God only knows you need it. I know there is nothing any one can say or do to make it all go away. Although I believe I have something that will help you get a new outlook about what life is supposed to be like. I understand that you know, that your parents and original family will be coming out to see you soon. That will be when you are ready not before. I understand that you have a friend that you have not seen also. We are prepared to bring her and your family out here to see you. At this time, we do not know about all the money that Thomas has in his accounts, but he is never going to need not even one penny where he is going. Some of this is being set aside for his wife and his two children. Some of it set aside for the F B I until they determine it does not belong to someone else. I am setting some aside for you to attend college to prepare you for the future. There is some set aside for you after you finish college to start your life with. All of these funds I have not set a figure to yet, but I will have it by the end of next week. There is some at this time I will give to you for your upkeep until you start college. There is some that will go to the sheriff to pay for your expenses since he found you. This is to replace the sheriff and the county and the cost of this court time. Your sheriff will summit to me in writing of that cost to you and the court cost. You the F B I get nothing because you are on the tax roll already. I will give you three months to give me proof of any amount against this fund or it will all be set aside for these children. Sheriff add in the cost of bringing her friend and her family out here and back home. You Thomas will be sent to maxima security prison for the rest of your life without parole no matter how good you are. I would like to offer more for your evil mind but life is just so long and yours is used up. Sheriff take this man out of my court room and you have one week to submit your cost to me. This court is adjourned and you F B I people have three months or less it is up to you. All the funds are in the custody of this court and at my disposal at this time. Betty I am sorry for what has happen to you and what you have been through but you can depend on the sheriff and his wife to help you in any way they can. Now go and get started on this new life."

As they left the courtroom Cora said to Betty.

"You have all the time you need to make your decisions. If you need help I will be glad to help you. We would like for you to stay with us as longs as you need too. What would you like to do first?"

"I do not know I am so over whelmed with the judge's decision I need time to come down and relax. Can I take a week or so to start changing my life time here and for the future, or can I just stand here and scream until I can make no more noise?"

You take all the time you want and if we can help you

then you let us know. And for screaming here it may bring the sheriff and the force out to get us and put us away."

Do you think that would release me of the tension I have built up or just make me hoarse in the throat? I will not make a move unless I talk it over with you and the sheriff. If he and the doctor had not come when they did I do not know just where I would be. So from now on you and the sheriff are going to be in every move I make. I owe you two so much I do not know just how I can ever repay you."

"Betty I am speaking for me and I know my husband we say you owe us nothing. we have been so happy since you have been here. We owe you for that excitement in our lives, and want it to keep going. We have come to love you as our long lost daughter, and we will be happy and excited to meet your real parents and family and your friend. We hope that you will understand if they are not who you have in mind they are it has been a long time and we all change."

"Cora I know and that scares me a lot that they may not want to see me, and if not then you will be my only parents I have, and we will have to make it a lifelong thing. I don't mean it like I don't want you if they are real, and we get along after a while I mean I want you and the sheriff to be my family forever."

"Good let us go home and see if we can fix a Celebration meal for the sheriff and his family."

They were quite as they drove home and when they arrived they noticed that there were no cars around, and that meant that the F B I had left as fast as they had arrived. Cora spoke up saying.

"Look we are here and it looks like we have our home back to our selves again maybe now we can relax and talk like grown up people again."

"That is what I need most at this time to be alone with

the ones who I know love me and care about me. Those who I can trust, and share my life with. I do not know if I can do that with my real family at this time."

"Betty give your self-time and think about if little bits at a time until they arrive. Then you can make that decision as to what you believe and they want for your future as a family. Let's get that happy dinner ready for this family that lives here in the home."

At dinner the sheriff listened to Betty and Cora talk about her family that she did not know then he asked.

"Okay this I will leave to you as to when I make that phone call and by the tickets for them to come. I am sure that they will have the same droughts as you do when they finally know that you are alive and safe. What you tell them about your life is up to you. I would advise you just to get to know them and then plan other visits later as you feel they are warranted. Remember you owe them nothing and they should feel and show only the love they had lost for so long anything else should not matter there is nothing neither of you can bring back or relive so think only forward and go on.

"Betty the sheriff is right and some advice from me is that you should let him know when and then adjust your mind to your future about school and what you want to be or go to school for. It is only one month before the second semester starts or you will have to wait until the next fall to start."

"Yes you are right and I have been thinking about what I would like to do. I do not want to go away too far to start with so I could come home on the weekends to see you. I have heard of forensics police work and I want to help in some way to help children who get caught like I was to have more hope than I did. I do not want to work with the F B I, but for someone like your sheriff so I could get closer to them and not have a big head because of what I was. Do you think I could do that kind of work?"

"We would be very proud to have a child of ours doing that same thing. If you are sure then I will get you some information and find a good college for you to attend. And remember the judge said your college would be all paid for no matter what anyone would do or they try to change even the F B I will not change that part for you. No matter what they find in the next three months it will not change that part of the funds. So go for whatever you want to be we are shooting for this to happen and with our help you can be happy doing what God has put you here for."

"I think this is what I want, but I don't know because of the way I was raised by Karen and Thomas."

"You can change any time you feel you are still wanting to do that particular subject, but you will still get your education for something that you can live with."

"So if I decide that police forensic work is not what I really want I can change and get my degree in something else?"

"Yes!"

The next morning at breakfast Betty had decided that she wanted to see her real mom and dad and brother in two weeks. She also wanted to see Gabby after that. So the sheriff made the arrangements and her mother and brother would come in two weeks. That would give them both a chance to get used to something they did not know, or any of them knew about what it would be like meeting strangers for the first time. When the sheriff told Betty of the time she asked.

"Why is my father not coming?"

"They do not know where he is at this time. Betty your mom and dad separated shortly after you was kidnapped and your dad left and only sent his monthly check to your brother. Your mom said your friend is gone away to college and she will tell her mom and dad that you are okay and want to see her as soon as she can get away from school. That may not be until spring break."

"My mom and brother will be here in two weeks then?"

"I have gotten their plane tickets and they will arrive in twelve days which will be on a Saturday and they will stay here or in a motel if you want."

"I think a motel would be better to start with because it will require two rooms and we have only one. Unless you would like to share your room with your mother."

"I think a motel room for them will be okay. How long will they be here?"

"Because of your mother's job she has only one week of vacation time left so they will be going home at that time. Your brother is also missing school and I understand that your brother is dating your friend's sister, Jan so we should be hearing from her very soon."

*****

After Gabby got home from school Carl Benson asked for her to come to his den office he had some good news for her. When she arrived he was setting at his desk and turned saying to her.

"Set down I have some wonderful news. I was home and answered the phone and it was your mother."

"What did she say the last time she called it was when your grandfather Tom had passed away so this must be very important has something gone wrong?"

"No everything is okay she told me that your old friends mother called and told her that your friend Betty has been found and wants to see you. The sheriff that called and told her said that he needed your address or phone number so he could make arrangements for you to come."

"Oh thank you Lord. Do you mean now, but I cannot leave school now I have all my test to do?"

"No when you have time or are free to do so."

"Can I talk to her what is her phone number? Oh yes Jesus thank you for answering our prayers."

"I have the number of the sheriff and you can call and talk to him."

"Oh Jesus I am so excited that you did not forget you answered all our prayers. I knew you would save Betty and the time does not matter just as long as we get to see each other again. Thank you thank you Jesus I love you for this special time again thank you Jesus. A-men"

"Do you want to call the sheriff now or wait?"

"Yes!"

"Let's do it now."

"Okay here is the number and you can dial the number, but as a word of caution are you prepared to find out after so long a time?"

"Yes I know she has not changed any more then I have."

"Just remember she is not and you are not who either one of you think you are to each other things have changed. You cannot take up just where you left off so long ago."

"I know but I know Jesus set this up and this time and it is for us to overcome the past and go on with the future."

As Gabby dialed the number her thoughts were on Jesus and that he had all things in order and that when someone answered it would be only good news.

"Hello this is the sheriff's office. How may I help you?"

"Hi, my name is Gabby Meede and I was told to call

this number and talk to the sheriff about my friend Betty Taylor is this the right place and may I talk to the sheriff?"

"One moment please."

It was a long moment and Gabby was almost in tears as she set waiting for the sheriff to answer and then the phone brought her out of her thoughts when it talked to her.

"Hello this is Gabby Meede from Littleton Colorado?"

"Yes I am."

"Good do you know anything about Betty Taylor in the last ten years or so?"

"No she has been gone about that long."

"I am going to ask you one question so I will know you are who you say you are. How did Betty disappear?"

"She was taken by a man and a woman on a ski slope in Colorado."

"Okay here is what I need from you. First when can you come, but not before at least two weeks from this Saturday? How long will you stay? So I can make arrangements for you it will be of no cost to you for this one trip?"

"I have about three weeks of heavy end of the semester testing before I can leave."

"You are saying three weeks from this Saturday before you can come.?"

"Yes can I call and talk to Betty?"

"No she is going to be very busy trying to get into college so until you come there will be no words. But I can tell you she is fine and nothing is wrong. She is one smart beautiful girl and she is my responsibility until things change for her. Do you want to fly or take a bus?"

"I can fly if someone picks me up."

"Good I need your full name and your address so I can buy your ticket and send them to you."

After giving the sheriff all the information he needed

he then hung up and Gabby turned and let her tears roll down her cheeks and sobbed into her hands. Carl gave her a small hug and left her to enjoy her happiness. Later that evening she called her grandma Hedi to tell her the good news and then called her mom and dad to share it with them. They all prayed with her over the phone. She went to her room and cleaned up and then set on her bed and prayed.

"Dear Heavenly Father and my Savior Jesus Christ I can only thank you for this day and that I was sure always that you were watching over the safety of Betty for this I can only thank you for never letting me doughty your power and love. I ask for your protection over her and my trip to see her, and that we will be the same yet different because of our ages. Still the hearts that were joined together as children will be the same now that we are grown women. Let me understand her when I see her and that our love back then will shine through. Let our future be together even though we will be separated. I pray that Betty got to know you and has let you into her heart. I pray that nothing bad has ever happened to her to keep her from being the vibrant girl she used to be. I thank you God and through your Son Jesus name I pray. A-men."

Gabby went down to share her excitement with her new family and when she would be going to see her best friend ever.

✳ ✳ ✳ ✳ ✳

When the sheriff went home he told Betty about Gabbys phone call and said.

"Gabby will be flying in here three weeks from this Saturday I sent her ticket off to her this afternoon you are going to be very busy in the next three weeks and I have prayed that all will go good even great for you during this time."

"How long will Gabby be here?"

"I left her ticket open ended so she can stay as long as she needs too."

"Does she have to stay in the motel?"

"Do you want her to is not she can stay here. There is only one of her and we have the extra room she can stay in."

Betty jumps up and gives Cora and the sheriff a big hug.

"You are going to see one special girl when she arrives."

"Do you believe she has not changed or do you think she is still the same?"

"We believed that we were identical twins and was very seldom separated. I believe right now that we are still the same. I now know her Jesus and I now know he protected me for all these years so the two of us could be together and our time apart has not changed us in any way. We are just older and have more to talk about."

"Do you feel the same way about your mother and brother and if we can find your father?"

"Not really Gabby and I were our family we just lived in separate homes. I believe this same will be true when we see each other again."

"Okay now you know about your family and your friend. Now I want to work with you on the colleges and time you can start. We need to tell the sheriff so he can give a report to the judge for the money and how much. Have you thought about a college yet of all that the judge has information on?"

"Some and I know that the college in Tucson has all I need and it is close to here so I could come home a lot. Yet the one in Colorado has the same thing I want to study and it is closer to where I used to live. I do feel more at home here then up there, but my family may want to change my mind. What do you think I should do stay here or go up there?"

"I do not want to say I want you to make up your mind and then you will be the one responsible for the outcome. What we really want you already know and you will always be able to come to this home and visit as long as we are here. If you change your mind later then we will help you in that decision. Remember this is your life and you are big enough, smart enough, and old enough to make your own decisions and choices. I am sure all will stay behind you and abide by your choices. Remember it is your life not ours."

"Thanks Cora I have been praying but nothing has stuck yet so I guess I have to just make the choice I see best. The cost between the two colleges are not that much so I can tell the sheriff to take the high one and tell the judge and if I change my mind later it would not make much difference in the cost. What I need to know does the judge have to pay all the money up front and that would keep me in that college for the whole four years of the time I need to complete my schooling."

"I am sure it will be put into a trust of some kind and paid when the school wants it."

"Okay that is what I want, and now I need clothes inside and out how do I pay for them?"

"I am sure we can do that and then turn in the receipt and the judge will give us back the money. He said we are to turn in a bill for your up keep since you have been here and I am sure the sheriff will do just that tomorrow we can go shopping for your clothes and other things, and do not let us forget the suit cases to carry them in."

"This is going to take a lot of time. How will I know

what the girls at college are wearing? How do I dress to fit in with the rest?"

"First I would choose what I want to wear and not what everyone else is wearing. I am sure the shops in town can help us in that regard. Before we go tomorrow we need to make a list like clothes, personal items, hair and makeup items that way we will not forget anything,"

"That is a great idea will you help me because I have never owned some of them things that you are using and that I use of yours."

"I believe this is going to be fun for both of us."

When the sheriff came home for supper he got the new plans and said.

"Go for it make sure you get enough for at least six months of use. That way I can get these bills turned in to the court and then you will be on your way. Remember Saturday is coming up and your mom and brother will be here so I suggest you spend as much time with them as you can. It will be the door opening for you and them for the rest of your life. They will not look the same or talk the same you are family but you are now a stranger to them, and it will take time to rekindle together again. Don't talk about the past unless you want to they do not need to know at this time."

"I know you two are trying to help me and I appreciated it very much, but I still am a little scared of what to expect. I only remember being close to my dad and he is gone away. My brother and I never got along he was such a bad kid I wonder what he is like now. I now think that maybe this will have to wait and see when they come."

"That is good now I have to go to bed tomorrow will be a long day for me and you girls go do what you do best. Good night."

Good night dear I will be right in."

"Good night can I call you dad?"

"If you feel good about it then it is okay by me."

Betty jumps up and gives him a big hug and a kiss on his cheek saying.

"I have wanted to do that for a long time, but I did not know if you would approve of it."

"I approve and you can do it more often. Only kidding any time, I will accept and tell you it has made my day."

* * * * *

Gabby had talked to her mom and dad about the news and then her grandma Hedi.

"Grandma, are you okay and doing fine or do you need something. I know your time is not as pressing as when grandpa Tom was with you, but I need to ask you something that is going to happen in two weeks and I just need you to tell me it is going to be alright."

"Yes Gabby my time is now much with nothing to do but I am doing fine your sister and folks keep me interested in life. What would you like to ask me?"

"You know about Betty and in two weeks I am flying out to Arizona to see her and I know of nothing to talk about or what to do with her. I am asking for some advice as to what you might think."

"Gabby go and be yourself let her be herself do not press just let the Holly Spirit put you both through what God wants to happen. Remember your grandpa used to say you cannot push a rope so let the Holly Spirit pull the rope for the both of you. That is all I can think of at this time, and you can call me any time,"

"Thanks grandma I love you and I wish you could go with me to see her."

# PART SIX

# CHAPTER SIXTEEN

On Saturday morning when Betty woke up she was very nervous about the time in less than two hours she would stand at the door and see her real mom and her brother for the first time in over ten years.  Now what would she say. The words kept coming back to her mind. Be yourself, be yourself. After dressing in her normal ware she went down to have her breakfast, and finding a note from Cora saying.

"Gabby the sheriff and I have gone to get your mother and brother and will be back about ten thirty or so."

Betty stood and looked at the note and read it again and seeing on the bottom to turn over. There it said remember to be yourself and we will be there for you. We love you.

Betty looked at the clock and noticed she had one hour to eat her breakfast and clean up before they would be back. After breakfast she was walking the floor and watching the clock saying to herself, be myself, be myself and worrying about when the door would open and she would get to look in the face of two strangers standing there that was her relation. Looking at the clock it said ten o-clock and no one had showed so she decided it was time to pray.

"Dear Father God and Jesus what am I to do this is something I am not functioning with and I need your guidance right now as of what I am to do. Please help me to not get to nervous and still have a good time and slowly get to know these people and be not afraid. Thank you so much for this house and the two people who has taken me in. Help me to get through this time in my life. Now help me to get through one more time so I can go on. Thank you Jesus for your love for me at this time in your precious name I pray. A-men."

Betty then heard someone calling her.

"Betty come and meet you mother and brother."

When Betty walked into the living room she saw two people she did not know. She was introduced to them and went to greet them. Not saying anything they set down and Betty was asked.

"Are you okay with this arrangement with us we know we have to get to know each other slowly and that is what we want to do. I am your mother Mary Taylor and this is your brother Al. we want you to know that we had given up that we would ever see you again. Your dad is not here and has been gone since about the time you were taken from us. It was more than he could bear. Your brother and I have lived alone since that time. Someday we may find your father, but so far he is just gone. I want to say you look absolutely beautiful almost as I had expected and want you to know we have still prayed and prayed for you. Your friend Gabby is okay and away at college in Texas. Her sister Jan and Al have been seeing each other for some time now. I cannot tell you how happy I was when the sheriff called and told me you were live and okay. And would be setting here in his home looking at you. Thank you Lord for this day."

"Sis do you remember me?" if not then I want to tell

you even though I was a bad brother I always loved you and am so glad you are okay."

"Yes I do remember a small boy my brother that I did not want. Gabby and I did not either one of our brother and sister. I think because we lived in our own little world and did not want anybody else in it. I have been thinking for the last two weeks about my life before and have remembered a lot of things. I know we traveled a lot and I did not want to go unless Gabby could go with us and the first time she got to go is when I was taken. I want you to know that Cora and the sheriff is my family at this moment and I want it to stay that way. They are the most and biggest blessing I know of at this time. I found the Lord Jesus Christ that Gabby had and now I am happy I will slowly become more interested in my past but my future is all I want to remember. The last years have not been good. The best part I remember besides Gabby is her grandma Hedi and grandpa Tom. I would like to see them sometime. I will get to see Gabby in two weeks and I am looking forward to that day. I am going to college as soon as I can get in. my new family has helped me tremendously and I am going to stay here for college. I am glad you could come I don't want to get any hopes up for you or for me. I want to be friends and get to know both while you are here. If you can find my dad, I would also like to see him. Right now I am well. Nothing has happened to me physically, but mentally I am scorned and hurt, but I am healing so I do not want to go back through the last nine or ten years until I can deal with it sensibly. Again I am glad you are here and can I get you something to drink or a snack?"

No we are fine and we do understand we are here to see you and to let you know we have hurt and still love you even though as you have said we do not know, but your outside and insides were born of us, but in time we do want to know more about the one we lost so many years ago. We want to be a part of your life in any way we can."

"Yea sis you are my sister and I want to know you. I have had a sister all my life but I do not know who she is and I want that to change as soon as it can."

Betty and her new acquainted family spent each day and evening talking about the loss they felt over the last years of their separation. Betty's mom Mary had a lot of crying time, but Betty never broke down once or shed a tear she had become a very strong about any feelings she might have had. Her emotions she felt and had put away in her mind she was nice but not in a loving way she knew whom they were and could remember a small amount of the time she had been in Colorado. The time in Arizona had blocked all the family feelings they were trying to push upon her. As the week was ending she was more ready for it to end. She was not willing to open up because of the pain of the past. The day before Mary and Al were to leave Betty finally asked about where her dad was. It was a simple question, but neither one of them gave her an answer so she asked again.

"I would like to know when I would expect to meet my dad. How can I let him know that I am okay?"

"Dear when we get home I will get in touch with him and tell him to call you. I cannot promise you anything or if he will call when he knows. We do not and have not communicated in many years. I have a phone number at home and it changes a lot all I can do is try for you."

"That is okay but if it takes too long I will be in college and no way for him to contact me."

"All I can do is try, no promises and no hard feelings it is his life and he choose to not let us live it with him."

Those were the last words that they spoke until the next morning at their departure time.

"Betty I know it will take time but you are welcome

to come to our home and to see us at any time. I will help you with your airfare or bus fare, but we live very close. We have very little extra money."

"I do not want to take from you I have nothing no job and I want to get an education first and I do not want to use this man and woman any longer. They have helped me more than anyone else and I cannot accept things from them much longer. I know I am on my own and you can write to their address and I will answer. They can I am sure get your mail to me. I am sorry I cannot express more but for me I want to get better acquainted, but it is going to take time for me. I am glad you came I will write to you when I can and tell you what I am doing."

"Very well we will keep in touch and next week you and Gabby renew your friendship I believe that is what will let you trust people again."

"I will do that and again thanks."

On their way home from the airport Cora stated.

"Betty you have a lot in common with your mother she seems very nice and I know she wants to regain what she has lost. Also I was listening a lot and you did the right thing when you would not talk about your past. I know, as a mother I would want to know and would not think about the pain it would have put you through. All I can say is that we are very proud of you and also to tell you how strong you showed yourself and your feelings you will go a long way. I am sorry that God decided or let the Devil I should say to put you through, but God has won over you and you will be a better person for that raw experience. Yet I know inside you it hurts and will hurt for many years to come. The sheriff and I love you for who you are not what you are."

"Thank you Cora and do you know that the two of you are the only people that I feel any love towards."

"Yes I think we know."

＊＊＊＊＊

"Gabby we have to leave for the airport in thirty minutes so you have everything ready?"

"I think so I am so nervous I cannot think."

"Just you relax this is going to be just as hard for Betty as it is for you."

"Probably so, but well. I can't help this feeling that has come over me and last night I prayed that God would send her angles down to help with this long time reunion of Betty and I, but so far it is not being answered. So I guess it will be up to the two of us to handle this time. Do you think she will accept me after all these years?"

"I think if she doesn't then she has lost more than I can tell you. Gabby since I have gotten to know you I cannot think of another person that I can compare you with you are very close to my wife in the way you handle yourself and that will see you through this next week. Now I have your bags in the car and I need to get you there also or you may not get to go. Get your goodbyes over with and I will meet you outside,"

Gabby does her goodbyes and with tears running down her cheeks she go out to get into the car.

"Carl I am sorry you have to drive this cry baby but I just feel over whelmed at this time maybe I will get it out of my system by the time I have reached Arizona and see Betty."

"Well one thing for sure the plane will fly faster without all that weight of your tears and it is okay. I think they are tears of happiness and that makes it okay."

"Thank you Carl you and grandpa have a sweet nature about you and I love it."

"Thank you now you go and enjoy yourself and let God work on your new relationship with Betty, I believe the two of you will get back together quicker than anybody she uses to know."

"Okay you have my return flight schedule?"

"Yes!"

Gabby waved goodbye and went to get on her plane she had to pray a lot before she was to arrive. She thought about how would she know who was picking her up. No one told her who was to do this how would she know. Then she thought about the sheriff so she would look for a policeman in uniform with a young lady with him. One hour into her flight she was still thinking about who and what would she do if no one showed. Surely they would not do that to her. She was becoming a nervous wreck and she could not stop the emotions she felt. The only recourse she could think of was she had to pray. Bowing her head and folding her hands she started talking to her God.

"Dear Heavenly Father I am so nervous and I need some comfort from you through your Holly Spirit. I do not know why I cannot get my mind off of this meeting. Please I am asking for your help. I feel so lonely right now and I need you to hold me and help my mind relax. Help me to start enjoying this trip and what is shortly going to be the renewing of and old friendship of which I believe you put together when I was younger. Help Betty and I to understand that the time is the only thing that has changed. Even though we are both older and will not know each other and maybe that is the part that scares me at this time. Lord Jesus I have prayed for this for so long not knowing if it would ever come true. Now I am overcome with these thoughts that scare me but yet I want to be myself when I first set my eyes on Betty and need your help to say the right things and be able to know her from her looks. I know she will be different as the same as I am. I just need your spirit to go first to prepare her and I to meet and not be total strangers. Let us know that you are going to be there with us all the way. Help me to know is she has ever accepted you as her personal savior. Help us to understand and know, let me know and except her if she has changed too much. I pray since you have put this friendship back together please let us understand why it was severed for so long. I am asking for your help because this plane is landing and very shortly we will come face to face. That is when we will need you the most. I ask all this in your precious name. Help us to come together, and some day serve you each day in the capacity you have set down for us to follow. A-men."

The walk from the plane to the baggage claims department was the longest walk she had done in a long time. She was having trouble putting one foot in front of the other and then the baggage room opened up and as she stood looking and then started walking towards the baggage belt to retrieve her bags she noticed an officer standing by the belt all alone by the belt she was to get her baggage. He was standing there all-alone and she would have to just walk up and ask him if he was the one would was to pick her up.

"Hello sir, I am looking for a sheriff are you the one I am looking for?"

"I do not know but I wish I was. You are lovely to look at. Do you know his name?"

"No!"

"Well I am not a sheriff I am just one of the security here in the airport. He may be upstairs in the waiting area. If you would like I will help you with your bags and take you upstairs."

"Would you please? There that black one is mine."

"Okay got it now follow me."

As they got off the escalator there was another older officer standing there with a very pretty young lady. And before either one cold speak they knew who they were looking at. Each running towards each other with tears and sobs of happiness they held each other for a long time. The older man said to them,

"We need to get out of these people's way and get started for home."

The girls backed up one step and looked into the eyes of the other one and still with big tears in their eyes and running down their cheeks could not speak to each other, the Cora took one arm from each other and with the sheriff with Gabbys luggage started for the car. At the exit they still did not say anything so after they were put into the car and the luggage in the trunk they started towards home. Still they were very quiet just the tears and sobs came from each of them. Down the road a way the sheriff finally spoke.

"Cora do you think that we should go to a clinic maybe they are in shock?"

"No I believe they are talking through telepathy and if we give them enough time they may come out of it where ever they are. Just before they got home Betty finally spoke up saying.

"Mom and dad this is my friend and sister her name is Gabby. Isn't she a lovely girl I am so excited to see her. Oh, by the way her name is Gabby because she talks so much."

They all had a very good laugh, this was going to be a fun time and it happened without any misfortunes on either of the girl's part. God had answered their prayers without either one of them knowing at the time.

They spent hours and into the night talking about school and what they both were going to do.  Gabby was going to school on scholarships and Betty was going with money that Thomas had and no one knew just where it had come from. It didn't matter they were both going to get an upper class education. They would do it in two different states and get out at the same time. They knew that they were going to spend all their summers together as much as they could. When they were planning their summer vacation time Betty said to Gabby.

"I don't think I can go back to Colorado where I used to live. Since I saw my mom and brother I do not feel drawn back there. I would like to see my dad but so far no one can tell me just where he is living. I was told that your sister and my brother were dating and had been for a long time. He did not seem to excited about it at the time I talked to him do you know if they are in love or just having someone to spend time with?"

"I do not believe that Al is serious about Jan as much as Jan thinks she is in love with him. I believe that if she stays much longer with him she will wind up getting into trouble. She lets him do about whatever he wants. I see them studying and I see his hands all over her in places I would not let a boy touch me. I told her to let him go and I was told. You are a stick in the mud and I am not. I get excited being with Al and I like the way he touches me and kisses me. I know if she is not careful she will be pregnant or having an abortion and my dad and mom will probably disown her. She has no respect for them and does just about whatever she wants to do.

"Do you think they are having sex so young?"

"I cannot prove it but I think so I saw her pill case more than once."

"Does your mom know?"

"If she does he does not let on that she knows."

"Al and my mom just seemed strange while they were here do you know if mom has another man in her life?"

"No one has seen her with anyone and your brother tell Jan when I cannot keep from hearing that he thinks she is like a prune all dried up. She never dresses very nice maybe they do not have the money even though she works all the time. I think she works one full job and one-part time job. Al never does anything but hang on to Jan sometimes they make me sick by the way they act. I do not want to talk about Jan she has been somewhat decent in the last eight months and she is still helping grandma Hedi each day so mom says."

"If I was to go and visit I would like to go and spend some time with grandma Hedi and grandpa Tom."

"I am sorry I should have told you before now that grandpa Tom passed away just after I started to college. Now grandma is all-alone except when my folks go to see her along with Jan. she is very frail taking care of grandpa for the last two years just about did her in, but mom says she is gaining back some weight and is feeling much better then she was when I left. Back to summer I have only about three weeks that I can take off I am helping grandma Hedi's son and his family. That is where I am staying while I am going to school."

"I do not know what time I can come because I have not started yet. So to catch up I may have to go into the summer months. They have not told me my schedule yet or the times I attend my classes. I know as soon as you leave I have to go to school. It is nice I can come home here any weekends I want. The sheriff said they would come and get me."

"You like them a lot don't you?"

"Yes they are the only ones I know that have been nice to me until you came."

"When summer gets closer we can discuss the time more I am sure Grandma Hedi would love to see you. She has prayed for you more then we have for so long. Seeing you would make her last days such a delight."

"I bet she will have some of her cookies and milk. When I was taken I missed our time the most, but soon it was all gone like a dream that turned bad, and never got any better until I was rescued by Karen's doctor who got the sheriff to come for me. You do not know but I tried to kill Thomas with a knife because he wanted to hurt me by raping me. I do not know if I will ever trust a man again. That is one reason I wanted to see my dad but that seems unlikely from what I have been told by my mom and brother."

"You do not hate the sheriff do you?"

"No but without Cora I do not know if I would or not."

"Oh Betty do not hate that will eat away your insides and leave you all alone. I believe that God was helping you to protect yourself from that man."

"I want to believe that but I also believe that like all things it will take a long time. I do know that since I have accepted Jesus I have been more at peace with what goes on around me. That is why I believe that the sheriff and Cora came into my life and now they are my family and will always be. At this time, I do not ever believe I will be close to my mom and brother, or ever see my dad again, but I have found love through these two people that I am going to hang onto no matter what. They care and love me for who I am not what I was or what I can become some time latter to them I am someone very special as you have noticed by now."

"Betty I am sorry for the bad times in your life but I do know that God has a plan for you and he has protected you even though here on earth we long to go and have peace in our lives. We still have to go through some differences before we can see just what Jesus wants us to be. I know he now has you on the right path and if you allow him to lead you, you will be filled to the top with his love and peace. When we were young he brought us together and has brought us together again after these last ten years. At this time, I believe he has great plans for us if we do what we believe he wants us to go and do. I want to go to the place and do what he has for me to do and in the process I want to glorify him in all things. I now know that you want the same things I do. Some day we will have our own families and we will know much better how to raise and keep that family together. Without you in my life I could have been lost but since then I have drawn closer to God and his Son Jesus. This I owe to you and my grandma Hedi and grandpa Tom. You three people have brought me more than any other people. Even my mom and dad tried to change me but it took you three to do that. I owe Jesus my life and the things and the people that he allowed to come into my life so far. I love you Betty Taylor and the time we had and the time we will have now and in the future again."

"I know it is late and you are going home early in the morning, but I will miss you terrible until we see each other again. I know that when I pray to God he sends it to you the same way I knew during my life when I knew that you were my sister and friend was praying for me. I feel that our lives are just starting now and only great things will come to us. And Jesus will watch over us until he comes back to take us with him. Until then we will always know the others thoughts. If people have angels watching over us, then I know that we have the same angel."

"I believe you and now it is good night for a new day is coming and that new day will propel us through this short time before we see each other face to face again."

Gabby I can tell you this I have lots of money I think but do not know what the judge is going to do or how much until the F B I and two more months is over. Then the judge will let me, and the sheriff know how much and when it will be in my control. I may be able to do as I wish with more than I could spend so I will be able to come and see you. Thomas's money will keep us together just like it kept us apart for so long. If you need anything you just let me know. Please do not say anything to my other family there is only us four knows about it. I want it to stay that way I may have suffered a lot but God is now paying me back for that suffering."

"Oh Betty that is so nice to hear I ask you now to keep your eyes focused on Jesus and God will bless you so much more. I need nothing at this time and all that money in this world cannot buy me what I already have."

"Okay, sis I will see you in the morning."

The next morning as they headed for the airport they just held hands and talked about the beauty of the dessert as they drove along. When Gabby was checked in and waiting they walked up and down the intercourse enjoying themselves nothing much was said, but they were talking all the time. When it was time they hugged each other and out a special small kiss on each cheek and then Gabby turned and waved and walked away but they never said goodbye.

As Gabby set on the plane her thoughts returned to the trip over one week ago. About the worrying and wondering about the reunion of her friend, and let out a small laugh then turning her thoughts to Jesus and praying silently to her God and his Son.

"Dear God thank you so much for your Son who came to die for me. Taking his life for my sins and wrongs to pave a way for me to come to Heaven someday. To be with the only true Father I will ever know. I want to thank you for your word that I may have to lean on when I am troubled. Thank you for your mercy and your Grace that you give so freely. Thank you Father for your strength that you let me draw from. Thank you for your patience when I am troubled and wrong. And with this and more I will never be able to thank you enough for what you have done for my friend Betty. Thank you, thank you over and over again that you never gave up on her. Now lead her to where you want her to be doing what you want her to be doing. Open her eyes so she can see through the last ten years of hard and beyond the life I cannot even imagine she went through. I pray that you can send the Holly Spirit into her so she can see and draw closer to you Jesus. Keep her and I there throughout the time we have left here before coming to Heaven. Let us grow in the family that you put down here in the beginning. Let us not forget the family we have that you gave us too. If it is your will for us to let us find the right partner you have for us to spend our life here together. Let us not forget what your son did for us. Let us always honor and respect you and your Son Jesus in all that we do. Thank you for the life you are going to give to us. I pray this to honor your son and for what he did for me. Let Betty and I always be caught in our wrongs by the Holly Spirit and to know when. This I left up in your precious name Jesus my Lord and Master and Savior of my soul. A-men."

At this time Betty is arriving back at her home with the thoughts of her last seven days with the friend sister that she thought she might never see again. She has at this time decide to tell her Jesus what she has on her mind and that it will be also let Gabby know of her thought also.

"Dear Jesus I want to be able to come to you like my friend Gabby does. I am trying to let you know how I feel and to thank you for this time you gave us after so much time apart. This is all new to me but Gabby says you hear before we ask any way I am asking you to be with us in our journey that she thinks we have and I want it too. I have this attraction towards her and I believe she has one towards me also. She is my best friend and my sister in love that we know it. Help us to stay in touch and protect us from the harms of this world. Keep her safe while we are apart and

I ask for your safety for me while I am away from the two people I love so much. Keep them save from harm at work and at home. Thank you Lord Jesus for what I now feel you did for me while I was trust up with Thomas and Karen. I do not want to go through my life hating them so help me to get them out of my mind and help me to forget. One more thing I ask you to look in on grandma Hedi up in Colorado help her to not be lonely since grandpa Tom has passed on to be with you in Heaven. I am praying to you Jesus so I hope you can hear me and except my prayer at this time. I am growing to love you and I want to keep reading your word so I can learn more about the person you were and what you are today. So in your name I ask this. A-men."

Gabby and Betty are now separated again but their hearts will always be together knowing that each one is constantly thinking of the other even so far apart.

# ENDING

# EPILOGUE

Early in Gabby's life, she found a true friend in Betty she also found out that true friendship was easily separated. Betty found that all things are not fun and games. There is a tuff side to life.

Even though this story started out with a great beginning it also ended with a great ending. All that happened in-between was and is a good example of what can happen in the life of any one person. This can happen at any time without that person even knowing it is going to be different soon. These two girls were taught a lot of wise things from their adopted grandparents. They also learned a lot from the family that God gave them in the first place. God is always watching but sometimes we are not.

Each girl went through a terrible thing in a short time frame. It was not easy for either one of them. Betty suffered a lot of facial stress and Gabby suffered a lot of menial stress. Un-de-nounced to either of them they still had their God watching over each of them to support them when they needed Him the most.

The drift of the story is that one girl knew how to pray and the other wished she could not be knowing that her friends God was the same one listening to her. In the end they were equal in what they believed. Jesus is real

These two girls survived because of Jesus and that they prayed for all things even when they did not know. When you have family praying for you God will be there and help. Your part is to listen and wait for God to respond to what you believe is wrong or the treatment you are going through. God's time and our time is two different things and it is hard for the human get up and go to set back and wait for Him to help in his way.

I pray as a writer that you have gotten something from this story. There was a quote I hope you got it. But just in case you did not get it or forgot by now it was. (In the human life you cannot push a rope.) The only one, who can do that is God, let him push your rope and grab a hold and hang on for the most enjoyable ride you will ever get. Let Him lead you to where he has planned for you to go long before you were born to this earth. It is okay to follow but beware of the leader if it is not God or Jesus then do not hang on to tight to the rope it may lead you into some things that you cannot get out of. A-men.

One last thing if you did not get it while reading is this. (STUPID IS FOREVER).

The end of this story and I pray that it is the beginning of a new one for you.

www.ingramcontent.com/pod-product-compliance
Lightning Source LLC
Chambersburg PA
CBHW071415200726

48294CB00002B/404